Setting Two Hearts Free

by

Janet Grunst

SMITTEN
HISTORICAL ROMANCE
LIGHTHOUSE PUBLISHING OF THE CAROLINAS

SETTING TWO HEARTS FREE BY JANET GRUNST
SMITTEN HISTORICAL ROMANCE is an imprint of LPCBooks
a division of Iron Stream Media
100 Missionary Ridge, Birmingham, AL 35242

ISBN: 978-1-64526-280-0
Copyright © 2020 by Janet Grunst
Cover design by Hannah Mae Linder
Interior design by Karthnick Srinivasan

Available in print from your local bookstore, online, or from the publisher at:
ShopLPC.com

For more information on this book and the author visit: janetgrunst.com

Brought to you by the creative team at LPCBooks:
Pegg Thomas, Karen Saari, Shonda Savage,

Library of Congress Cataloging-in-Publication Data
Author's Grunst, Janet.
Setting Two Hearts Free / Janet Grunst 1st ed.

Printed in the United States of America

PRAISE FOR *SETTING TWO HEARTS FREE*

A touching, timeless story of love and loyalty, hardship and hope. *Setting Two Hearts Free* honors our faith-filled forefathers, many of them Scottish like Mary Stewart and Donald Duncan, whose legacy is the lifeblood of our American heritage and must not be forgotten. Well done!

~**Laura Frantz**
Christy award-winning author of *An Uncommon Woman*

In *Setting Two Hearts Free*, Grunst shines at creating the engaging characters that populate the charming backcountry Virginia inn. Set in 1781, several years after the two previous books of the series, the story now centers on the Stewarts' older daughter, Mary, and Donald Duncan, the son of their friends in Alexandria.

Grunst vividly depicts the trauma of war from the front lines to the home front, where those left behind must maintain farms and businesses in the absence of husbands, sons, and brothers. A soldier in the Continental Army, Donald endures exhaustion, disillusionment, and the mental and emotional toll of battle. A future with Mary feels increasingly out of reach. With Donald's extended absences, Mary harbors doubts about their relationship as well, particularly when during a British invasion she suffers a shattering trauma.

Grunst realistically and compassionately portrays the harsh wounds of war that Donald and Mary individually endure. The healing process that gradually draws them into a deeper, more intimate relationship of mutual dependence and shared strength provides encouragement and spiritual insight for readers who may face struggles in their relationships.

~**J. M. Hochstetler**
Author of *The American Patriot Series*

It is often in the aftermath of tragedy's physical scars that we realize the deepest and most lasting wounds lie within. Author Janet Grunst brings us hope in this beautifully poignant tale of love torn apart by war's terrible secrets; and truth, the invitation to God's healing grace to make us whole. A beautifully heartrending story of love's triumph in truth amidst the atrocities of war.

~Kate Breslin
Bestselling author of *Far Side of the Sea*

Author Janet Grunst has again brought a crucial time in our nation's history to life through the continuing Stewart family saga. Separated by Donald Duncan's enlistment to fight for freedom during the Revolutionary War, he and Mary Stewart are no longer wide-eyed young teens filled with dreams, but they have become young adults facing difficult realities. Grunst weaves each of their stories with delicacy through the tragedies which befall them. Donald and Mary must decide whether they will allow these trials to determine their future. Readers of clean historical romance will be touched by this tender and positive story of what honesty, faith, and perseverance truly mean. Highly recommend!

~Kathleen Rouser
Award-winning author of *Rumors and Promises.*

In *Setting Two Hearts Set Free*, author Janet Grunst does a remarkable job tackling the subjects of PTSD and sexual abuse, without marginalizing the recovery processes. The author adds enough tension to keep readers turning the pages; she also adds enough doubt to keep them wondering how the story will end. Grunst tenderly relieves the characters' pain with poultices of faith, family, hope, and love. Though set in the American Revolutionary War era, this story transcends generations. Wonderful read.

~Clarice G. James
Award-winning author of *The Girl He Knew*

Acknowledgments

I'm grateful to Lighthouse Publishing of the Carolinas and now Iron Stream Media for their willingness to publish stories that deal with sensitive issues like post-traumatic stress disorder. Many thanks to Pegg Thomas, Managing Editor of LPC's Smitten imprint and General Editor Karen Saari for all their suggestions, wisdom, and guidance in making *Setting Two Hearts Free* a better story. The entire team of editors and designers at LPC may be working behind the scenes, but deserve credit for their work.

One of the greatest gifts on this publication journey is Linda Glaz, my agent with Hartline Literary Agency. Her wisdom, encouragement, and time are so appreciated by me as well as her other clients.

Kathy Rouser, my critique partner, has provided valuable feedback as well as friendship. I'm humbled and grateful for all my readers who take the time to write reviews. We authors would be lost without you.

Ken, my husband, is my first reader and one of God's greatest gifts. He eagerly reads and boldly bleeds red ink onto my manuscripts. His love and encouragement motivate me.

I had a dream … which later became a prayer to share stories that communicate the truths of the Christian faith, as well as entertain, bring inspiration, and encouragement to the reader. I'm indebted to the Lord Jesus Christ for His mercy and grace in my life. He plants the stories in my heart and guides me throughout the process.

> "Trust in the LORD with all your heart,
> and do not lean on your own understanding.
> In all your ways acknowledge him,
> and he will make straight your paths."
> Proverbs 3:5-6

Dedication

To all who suffer the invisible wounds of war and other trauma. And to their families and loved ones sometimes struggling to best know how to help and cope.

"Blessed be the God and Father of our Lord Jesus Christ, the Father of mercies and God of all comfort, who comforts us in all our affliction, so that we may be able to comfort those who are in any affliction, with the comfort with which we ourselves are comforted by God."
(2 Corinthians 1:3-4 ESV)

"Not only that, but we rejoice in our sufferings, knowing that suffering produces endurance, and endurance produces character, and character produces hope, and hope does not put us to shame, because God's love has been poured into our hearts through the Holy Spirit who has been given to us."
(Romans 5:3-5 ESV)

"To everything there is a season, and a time to every purpose under the heaven: A time to be born, and a time to die; a time to plant, and a time to pluck up that which is planted; A time to kill, and a time to heal; a time to break down, and a time to build up; A time to weep, and a time to laugh; a time to mourn, and a time to dance;"
Ecclesiastes 3:1–4

CHAPTER 1

March 1781

Donald Duncan's chest pounded as he gasped for air and struggled to carry Todd Gordon up the muddy road. The lad's wounds were severe, and he would surely die without help. Donald's back cramped under Todd's weight. *I hope I'm not making the injury worse.*

Another day filled with the unspeakable horror of the wounded and dying. Earlier, Donald thought he would certainly be numbered among them. *Put it behind you and focus on the camp ahead, or you will never make it up the hill, and Todd will die.* Breathing heavily, he passed several injured men limping, also aided by comrades. Together, they climbed to the Continentals' camp. There would be no rest until they cared for the wounded and buried the dead.

The sky threatened more rain. Donald shivered, and he laid Todd under the shelter of nearby trees and scanned the sea of soldiers. "Help! Somebody help!"

A medic stopped and eyed Todd. He bent over, opened Todd's jacket, and shook his head. "Too far gone."

Donald's stomach knotted as he grabbed the medic's sleeve.

"He needs aid. Please."

"You do it! I have others to help."

Trembling, Donald fell on his knees, searching for something to keep Todd from bleeding to death. Nothing. He tore off his kerchief. With his free hand, he pressed as hard as he could against the gaping wound in Todd's chest. "Stay with me, Todd."

Todd turned his head toward him, his breathing labored. Garbled words sputtered out. "Tell them ..." A pleading look filled his brown eyes. The vessels on his neck protruded before he relaxed.

He swallowed hard as he brushed a tear from Todd's dusty cheek. The lad's eyes dulled. *Please don't let him die, God.* Grabbing his canteen, he poured a little water on Todd's parted lips before again putting pressure on the wound. The kerchief was blood-soaked. Memories flooded of visits over the years to Stewarts' Green when he would hunt or fish with Todd and his brother. "Try, Todd, try. Think of home." He bent over Todd to listen. Shallow breathing, but still alive.

Todd grabbed his arm and tried to speak. His eyes opened, equally filled with desperation and resignation. "When this is over ..."

Donald leaned closer. "Don't try to talk." If only he could pour his strength into the lad.

Todd wheezed as he grasped his hand. "Tell folks I love them ... death ... not in vain."

Donald choked back tears and the acid taste rising in his throat. He gripped his friend's hand. "Todd, stay with me." Todd's death would devastate the Gordons and Stewarts.

Todd tightened his hold. His eyes flared for seconds. Blood oozed from his mouth. His hand relaxed. He was gone.

His head fell forward. Donald's tears fell on Todd's bloody chest. How would he ever face the Gordons with the news of their son's death? Would *he* even survive to deliver that message? *I have seen and experienced too much ... things I would sooner forget ... but I fear they will haunt me. How can I ever be free of this?*

He stood, legs shaking, and motioned to a group of soldiers assigned to pick up bodies for burial. His eyes fell again to his friend. "Go with God now, Todd." Did he still believe that God listened or even cared? Where had God been these past six years?

Rain and nightmares fell in torrents upon the land and his mind. Donald woke in a sweat before daybreak the next morning. His heart raced, like many other nights in the past year … with bitter memories of the bloody massacre at Waxhaws.

Colonel Abraham Buford had ordered the men to hold their fire until the British were within ten yards. Would he ever get that scene out of his mind? The butcher, Banastre Tarleton, had attacked the Patriots. Many Americans were cut down. Buford had escaped, and Donald, along with other stragglers, joined a new Virginia regiment with eighteen-month enlistments. Eight more months to go. He rubbed his aching head. If only he could forget all that he had seen, heard—and done.

Todd's death had left him drained. He had reconciled there was little or no control over life's circumstances. His tension increased each time he went into battle, but since the early years of the war, he'd learned to squelch his anger, frustration, and feelings. He had to function and not go crazy. Now he needed something for his growling belly.

He picked up his blanket and walked to the dwindling campfire. Men sat under a nearby tree, talking in low voices. He scooped beans onto his tin plate and poured a cup of tepid coffee, then sat and leaned against a fallen tree trunk.

How had they lost the battle yesterday when they outnumbered the British? He had overheard the major and captain. They said General Greene had prepared his defense in three lines. But the British army forced its way through the first two, before turning on the third. Tarleton, that devil. He and his Light Dragoons moved forward along the road and came out on open ground at Guilford Court House, attacking their large force of Continental Infantry. His lips trembled. "Tarleton's murderous green coats again."

He turned his thoughts to something more calming, toward home, Virginia. Four times he had been assigned as a courier to locations near Alexandria, making him more fortunate than most. But the last had been months ago.

Donald finished the beans and sipped the bitter brew, swill compared to the coffee at home. Home—the six years he had been absent seemed a lifetime. In another month, his sister was to be married. He should be at Jean and Peter's wedding, but years of war had robbed them all of a normal life. He still believed in the cause, he just had not anticipated the cost—in lives, time, and enthusiasm lost.

Life—so precious and fleeting. Donald wiped away the moisture from his eyes. *I'm sorry, Todd. Not even twenty and gone. I must write to the Gordon family and relay the circumstances of Todd's death and his final words. What to tell them—and how much?* There was no way he could make the death of their son palatable. But he had to do it, as hard as it would be, and soon so when the next post rider came through it would be ready.

Boyd Alexander approached. "You are up early, Duncan." The tall, lanky Scot poured himself some coffee and sat across from him. "Trouble sleepin'? The young fellow was your friend, I'm guessing."

"Todd was in the unit that joined ours last week. I knew him for near a decade, but not well. I told you about my family's best friends, the Stewarts, who have a farm and ordinary about twenty miles northwest of Alexandria. Todd's parents, Thomas and Polly Gordon, are tenant farmers at Stewarts' Green. He was their youngest son."

Boyd rubbed his stubbled chin. "I'm sorry. No matter how long we are in this fight, I never get used to all the dyin'. You going to write his folks?"

"Yes."

Another soldier joined them and spoke with Boyd. Leaning his head back against the tree trunk, Donald closed his eyes. He would go to Stewarts' Green to see Todd's family—and Mary.

His heart warmed just thinking about Mary Stewart. He could picture her walking along the path to the pond at the Green. Mary, with her chestnut hair and amber eyes, had owned his heart for more years than he could count. The stunning and spirited girl was a woman now. He had told her he planned to court her when he returned from the war. Was she still waiting for him?

He opened his eyes. Fog hid the stars, but the moon shown through the mist. A few hundred miles away, Mary might be observing the same moon. Was that Irish cabinetmaker from Philadelphia still pursuing her? Patrick O'Brian certainly had every opportunity, and he was sure to be there when his brother Peter married Jean. He shivered and wrapped the blanket around his shoulders. Jean and Mary were inseparable. The Stewarts would certainly be at the wedding.

A nearby scream jarred him. He tensed and covered his ears. Another injured, suffering soul whose life would be changed forever. He gripped his trembling leg to still it. *Will my life ever be the same?*

CHAPTER 2

Mary Stewart grabbed the side of the family's three-seated coach when it hit a rut in the road and held her bonnet steady with her other hand. Her nerves were already jostled, why not the rest of her body? The family's visit to Alexandria for Jean and Peter's wedding was supposed to be three delightful days away from the routine of their farm and ordinary. But since last night's vivid nightmare, she'd thought of little else on the twenty-mile trip to town. The image of Donald struggling uphill, covered with blood, and being shot at woke her with a jolt, sweating and heart racing. In all the years he had been gone at war, she'd never experienced such a frightening vision. Did the image in her dream really happen? Was Donald in more danger than usual?

Mama and Papa, in the coach's front seat, exchanged worried glances. Their mood had been somber since the family stopped at Brady's Mercantile on the outskirts of Alexandria. Douglas, seated between them, was examining the cribbage board just purchased.

When they turned onto Princess Street, she steadied Sara, seated beside her, and put her hand to her knotted stomach. *'Twas a dream. Put it out of your mind.* Her parents' unease only added to her own anxiety. She leaned forward. "Are you concerned we will have difficulties getting rooms at the inn?"

Mama shook her head while Papa steered the horses onto Cameron Street. "Nay. The Duncans reserved rooms for us over a fortnight ago when they established the wedding date and published the marriage banns."

Silence.

Six-year-old Sara squirmed, and Mary pulled her closer. "We

will be there soon, poppet."

Was there a problem at Brady's? News of the war?

Mama frowned at Papa then turned in her seat. "Nay, nothing to be concerned about."

There *was* more to what her parents were saying. She'd get it out of Mama later. "Will we have time this afternoon for a walk before attending the Lamonts' party?" Walks always calmed her nerves.

Douglas tugged at their father's sleeve. "I want to walk to the wharf to see the ships."

Mark, seated on Sara's other side, tapped his younger brother on the shoulder. "A fine idea."

Papa stared at Douglas and then at Mama. "No, we will stay at the Cameron Street Tavern until we leave for the Lamonts' party this evening. I know all of you are eager to wander around town … but not this trip."

"Why, Pa?" Mark's disappointment and curiosity seemed as piqued as hers.

"British brigs and tenders have been sighted on the Potomack River near Alexandria."

Mark's eyes bulged as he leaned forward in his seat, knocking Sara into Mary. "British ships? Did you bring our guns, Pa? We might need them if they attack."

"Calm down, son. I doubt they will raid Alexandria."

"But Pa, the British are not only fighting in the northeast, they are also in the Carolinas. They might strike us again in Virginia. I should be fighting with Donald, Todd, and the rest of them now I have turned fifteen."

Papa shook his head. "That last comment is a closed subject. As to the British, we have no way of knowing what they have in mind, but there is no need to put ourselves at risk. We are here for the festivities tonight at the Lamonts' and the wedding and dinner tomorrow. Sunday morning, we return home."

Mary chewed her lip. They were here for a joyous occasion.

Now the threat of a British invasion threatened that. Sara leaned into Mary. Her hat had fallen to her back, the ribbon still in a bow around her throat. Strands of light honey-colored curls escaped the child's linen cap. A frown now marred her sweet face. "The Lamonts? The family of the boy the British killed?"

Mark elbowed his little sister. "Owen Lamont died far from here, and that was three years ago."

Mama turned and caressed Sara's cheek until the fear in the child's eyes subsided. "We are safe, wee one. Do not fret, and you must not say anything about Owen at the party. 'Twould upset his family."

Mary cuddled her sister and glowered at Mark. He knew better than to say things that would frighten Sara. The child had been anxious since learning of Owen's death, and Tobias Whitcomb's return home from the war without one leg. *When will this wretched war be over, and our young men come home? Will life in Virginia ever return to normal?*

What would it be like to finally have Donald home? When he first declared his love for her and intention to court her, they had been so young. Warmth flooded her, recalling their few kisses. But it had grown more difficult to even remember his face. When she last saw him three years ago, Donald had been withdrawn and melancholy, probably because he had to return to the fighting. Would they still love each other when he returned home? She both longed for and dreaded the day when she would finally know. And now that horrible nightmare. Was it a premonition? Should she tell Mama? She wasn't superstitious, but best not to give voice to it. 'Twould only make it more real. *Please, God, protect Donald, and give me peace.*

As they traveled down Cameron Street toward the river, the rhythmic clip-clop of the horses' hooves on cobblestones competed with other noises on the city's bustling streets. Was it crowded because people were buying supplies in case the British attacked?

Two nights at the Cameron Street Tavern would be a novelty.

Staying at the Duncans' home for this visit was out of the question. Her family wouldn't dream of imposing on Jean's family with all the preparations underway for tomorrow's wedding.

Papa pulled back on the horses' reins. "Here we are. I will see to our accommodations and learn where to board the horses and coach."

Douglas stood. "Will we go to the Duncans'?"

Mama rose. "Nay. We will see them at the Lamonts' home later after we eat and get settled."

Papa stepped down from the wagon and handed Douglas a parcel. "Mark, please help me take the bags inside."

"Yes, Pa."

Mary followed Mama and Sara into the inn. Mama leaned close, raised her brows, and whispered. "I've no doubt Patrick O'Brian will be there tonight."

"I know."

Patrick was a dear friend to all of them. She was the one who had introduced Jean to his brother Peter. More importantly, Patrick played a vital role in recovering Papa after his imprisonment by the British. They were all deeply indebted to him. His attention to her had grown more obvious in recent years, even teasing about courting her when their visits to Alexandria coincided.

Would he raise that subject tonight or tomorrow? Discouraging his interest would be hard and may cost her his friendship. While fond of him, she must make it clear she was eager for Donald's return. Celebrating Jean and Peter's wedding should be a delightful holiday. But now with the British lurking about, frayed nerves over a senseless dream, and anticipating a difficult conversation, it was turning into something quite different.

CHAPTER 3

Mary shook out clothing from the portmanteau after dinner. Sara sat on the bed, playing with her doll. While Mary hung their gowns in the wardrobe, Mama stood at the window staring at the street below, her lips pressed together.

Mary approached her and whispered. "Are you worried about trouble with the British?"

Mama glanced at Sara, then responded in a hushed tone. "A wee bit. Papa wants us to avoid going anywhere there might be a potential problem."

She nodded. "Certainly." Papa's imprisonment at the onset of the war had made him overly cautious.

Sara's voice quivered as she handed Mama the pins and brush. "Is it safe to go out tonight? Will the British hurt us?"

Mama drew her youngest close in an embrace. "Nay, lass, we would not have come if we thought it unsafe." She looked over Sara's shoulder. "Mary, please go to the boys' room and make sure they have unpacked their bags. Tell them the carriage will be here at seven."

"Yes, ma'am, but I still need to freshen before we go."

"We should have plenty of time."

Papa walked through the door and approached Mama. "Don't worry, Heather, the innkeeper said he heard they are further downriver. I told the boys to unpack."

"I shall check on them and tell them you will join them soon to change." Mary left the door ajar as she walked out.

The room next door was empty. "Where are they?" She shook her head. They knew better than to thwart Papa's instructions. She hurried down the stairs, glancing into the tavern before running outside. She scanned the street in both directions, then headed toward the wharf. A block away, she spotted them approaching the quay. With brisk strides, she drew near. "Have you lost your minds to come out here after Papa forbade it?"

Douglas looked contrite while Mark kicked a rock and scowled. "We saw the three masts from our room and just wanted to see the ships up close. What's the harm in that?"

Douglas frowned. "Are you going to tell Pa?"

"Papa forbade it. 'Tis reason enough. You better hope you can get back to the room and change into your good clothes before he knows of your escapade. We leave at seven, so hurry." She shooed them off and scurried after.

When they reached the top of the stairs, she gave them a warning glare.

Outside her door, Papa's voice stopped her from going inside.

"Did Mary say anything to you about Patrick O'Brian? He is sure to be here for his brother's wedding."

"She knows."

Mary's heart pounded. Biting her lip, she scanned the narrow hall. No one was in sight. She remained plastered against the wall next to the door, straining to hear.

Papa's voice was barely audible. "Patrick has not yet asked to court Mary, but he's made no secret of his interest."

"Aye, she is fond of Patrick, and they enjoy teasing each other, but she loves Donald."

"As you are well aware, Donald wrote many months ago asking for my permission to court Mary when he returns. Is she still as serious about him?"

"Aye, she is. But the years of waiting and uncertainty have been difficult. We never imagined that the war would last so long."

"Is Patrick aware of Mary and Donald's attachment, because he has a right to know if she's spoken for. He is a good man and deserves a woman who can freely commit to him."

Mary wiped the perspiration from her brow. *Enough eavesdropping.* She entered the room. "I overheard you, Papa, and I agree, Patrick deserves a wife completely devoted to him."

Mama took her hand. "We are just concerned for your feelings as well as for Patrick's."

"I know that. I've been troubled thinking about the conversation I must have with Patrick. I don't want to hurt his feelings."

Papa hugged her. "Be honest with him. It may go better than you think. I'm off to make sure the boys are ready."

Mary lowered her eyes and sucked in a deep breath. *Those rascals better be dressed.*

Mama fastened her new hat and peered in the mirror. "When will you speak with Patrick?"

"As soon as possible." She arranged her lace cap. "I want it behind us so we can enjoy this evening and tomorrow."

Mama held out Mary's sheer apron and tied the bow in the back. "Might it not be best to wait until after the wedding to avoid any awkward situations tonight and tomorrow?"

"Hmm." Mary smiled at Mama's reflection in the mirror. "You're probably right. I'm sure it will all work out."

❧❀❀❀❀❧

The elegance of the Lamonts' large Georgian home was exactly as Mary remembered. She scanned the crowd in the center hall. No sight yet of Jean and Peter ... or Patrick. The fragrance of lilacs permeated the air as she and her family greeted Mr. and Mrs. Lamont.

When Sally Lamont approached, Mary curtsied. Why did Sally always make her feel a bit jealous? Did the beautiful, willowy blonde still hope to garner Donald's affection? "'Tis good to see you again, Sally."

Sally nodded. "Thank you. Peter and Jean are receiving everyone in the drawing room. I probably do not need to tell you that Patrick is here." Sally's eyebrows arched.

"Wonderful. I'm eager to learn if Jean has *more* recent news of Donald than I do." She curtsied, smiled, and entered the adjacent room. Would Sally's obvious efforts to pair her up with Patrick O'Brian never cease? *Humph! She must still have her cap set for Donald.*

Crystal sconces and large silver candelabra lit the ornate room. Mama and Papa stood with Maggie and Adam Duncan next to the walnut secretary desk. The men's expressions suggested they were in a serious conversation, but Mama and Maggie seemed in good spirits.

As Mary approached, Maggie opened her arms wide to embrace her. "You are more lovely than ever."

Mary returned the embrace. "Is everything ready for the wedding tomorrow?"

"As much as possible." Maggie laughed.

"I must go and congratulate Peter and Jean. I wondered, have you any news from Donald lately?"

"A letter came, and knowing you would be in town, he included a note for you, but I neglected to bring it tonight. I will give it to you tomorrow. He is in the Carolinas."

Finally. Letters from him had been few and far between. Each one a treasure. She curtsied. "Excuse me. I must give my best wishes to the happy couple."

Peter and Jean were greeting their guests. Jean looked radiant in a pale green gown. Her dove grey eyes sparkled, particularly when she looked at Peter. Her friends' joyful smiles after a long courtship warmed her heart.

Jean pulled her close. "I have never been as happy."

She hugged her friend. "That is obvious. Are you ready for tomorrow?"

"Yes." Jean frowned. "It shan't be the same without Donald around."

She squeezed Jean's hand. "He would have loved being here

and included some high jinks, no doubt. At least we need not anticipate his pranks."

Jean smiled. "We plan to go to Charlottesville in June. Peter has been commissioned to build several pieces of furniture that will need to be delivered. We plan to accompany the wagon for the delivery." Jean glanced at Peter and blushed. "After the wedding dinner, Peter and I will go right to his home. We have spent the past two days cleaning and organizing it."

She hugged Jean. "I'm delighted for you."

"As am I," a deep voice behind her announced. "I have never seen my brother so content."

A warm rush rose to her face as she turned and peered into Patrick's piercing blue eyes. "Good evening, Patrick." His black hair, ivory complexion, and engaging smile were as handsome as ever.

He nodded. "A pleasure to see you, Mary. 'Tis been six months, I believe."

"Yes, though we did correspond a couple of months back." She averted her eyes and fanned her warm face.

He smiled. "Yes, we did. Might we have that private conversation we addressed tomorrow?"

She kept her attention on the room full of people. "Certainly." *Disappointing him is regrettable, but must be done. Hopefully, it shan't end our friendship.*

CHAPTER 4

Out of breath and exhausted, Donald sat on his bedroll and drank from his canteen. He and a small group had finished carrying the wounded from Hobkirk's Hill. They brought them to the outside of Camden, where their unit encamped.

Pearson, an infantryman who had aided him in the recovery, sat cleaning his musket. "That hole in our line doomed our counterattack," he grumbled.

"Odd that Rowden's men did not pursue us, even though our forces were in retreat," Donald said.

Hours later, when Donald finished his day's ration of hard biscuits, beans, and pork, he leaned against a tree and half-listened to the men in his regiment. Few of them spoke of the battle or Rowden's victory and withdrawal. Two of the fellows griped about the duration of the war. His tentmate, Boyd, perched on a log nearby reading his Bible.

Donald rubbed his temples. *Confounded headache.* Where would the brigade go from here? When was the next skirmish? He cringed at the moaning of the wounded. Would he survive, or would he, too, meet the fate of those unfortunate souls?

"You're a fool if you think that book'll help you, Alexander," Pearson muttered. "It got any answers on how to get this war over?"

"This"—Boyd lifted his Bible, "helps me to keep goin' in spite of the war." He sounded restrained but confident.

Donald stared at Pearson. The man's habitual sarcasm annoyed him. *Leave Boyd be.*

Sergeant Carter stood and finished what remained of his cider.

"So, what does that book say that helps?"

Boyd shuffled through a few pages. "This is from the fourth chapter of Philippians … and there are many more like it. 'I know both how to be abased, and I know how to abound: every where and in all things I am instructed both to be full and to be hungry, both to abound and to suffer need. I can do all things through Christ which strengtheneth me.'"

Donald wiped his dishes with a rag. The circle of men were silent. Were they thinking about what Boyd said? It had been a while since a preacher had visited the troops and spoke the Scriptures. He stood and gathered his utensils, returning them to his haversack. Better to spend his time helping with the wounded than listening to Boyd. The Bible brought no answers for him.

The moonlight aided Donald in finding his way to the surgical tent. The flickering light shining inside the canvas shadowed the medics at work. Outside, wounded men lay on the ground.

Someone touched his leg. "Help me." A boy no more than seventeen moaned, his eyes pleading.

No need to go any further. Donald knelt by the wounded man. Blood-soaked bandages wrapped around his middle. "What is your name?"

"John."

"How can I help you, John?"

"Pray for me."

"Oh, no, I—" Was there time to go back and get Boyd? He groaned as he held John's cold hand. *I can do all things through Christ which strengtheneth me.* Boyd's words—no—the Bible's.

"Dear Heavenly Father, John is hurting. We don't know what Your plans are for him, to heal him or take him home. But we ask you to bring healing in whatever way You choose … to ease his pain … and to give him peace. Amen."

When was the last time he'd prayed other than calling out to God for help? Would God even listen to a backslider? But he prayed for the boy, not himself.

A slight smile appeared on John's lips. Panic left his eyes, and his hand relaxed. Within seconds, his eyes closed. Another young Patriot gone.

Donald bent his head, his shoulders shook, and tears flowed. *What if I had not stopped? Or prayed with him?* John was a stranger, but his heart broke for him and all the lost lives. He needed to control his emotions. *I'm no good to anyone like this.*

Donald made his way back to his tent some time later. Exhausted, he fell onto his blanket. He glanced beside him. Boyd slept. Maybe he would tell him about John and the prayer. But now, he longed to escape. The sights, putrid smells, and agonizing sounds of the wounded and dead were tortuous.

Oh, to be home and in his own bed, to smell and taste one of Ma's bannocks or beef pies and hear Jean, Cameron, and Will's voices. Even the chores Pa assigned would be welcome. His last visit home, Pa had expressed pride in him and all the others who fought for liberty. What had happened to the zeal he had for the cause these past six years? *I still believe we must be free of English oppression, but I'm not as naïve as I once was—and I'm war-weary.* Somehow, he must gather the grit needed to face the battles ahead. *Think about the future. When the war is over. Going home to Mary.* He needed a positive attitude to survive—or maybe something more?

I can do all things through Christ which strengtheneth me.

CHAPTER 5

Shutters creaking open and Mama's cheerful chatter put an end to a restless night. At least that nightmare had not returned. "The sun is shining. Such a bonny day for a wedding. Come, Mary, get out of bed."

Mary struggled to fully awaken. Sara's light-blue eyes and frolicsome smile were mere inches away. The child tugged at her coverlet.

She groaned. "'Tis early, poppet, and I'm tired."

"'Tis not early." Sara pulled back the coverlet and grabbed her hand. "Mama said we need to breakfast soon."

Mama leaned over her. All hope for sleep was gone.

"We do need to get started, lass. You asked me to dress your hair, and I have my own to do. The boys are already in the dining room. I can bring something upstairs for us to eat."

Mary rose and walked to the window, her shift swishing against her knees. "Yes, please, coffee and a scone or roll are all I want." The new spring leaves brightened the landscape. A few trees had already budded. The streets were busy but less crowded than yesterday. Perhaps fear of the British landing in Alexandria had subsided.

Mama took Sara by the hand. "Come with me. You can help me carry food upstairs while your sister dresses."

Mary washed her face and opened the wardrobe. She pulled out the amber gown. At last, an occasion to dress in elegant attire. The countryside offered few social events that required it. She bit her lip. She would quell Patrick's hope for a courtship. They had been friends for years, and it would be regrettable if that ended, particularly now that he would be Jean's brother-in-law. Had their mild flirting and fun-loving banter over the years given him false hopes? She had not meant to encourage him about a future together, and hurting him would grieve her. But she loved Donald, and he had expressed a desire to court her when he returned. She was all but promised to him. Her cheeks warmed, recalling the few kisses she and Donald had shared. She touched her fingertips to her lips. *I must be direct with Patrick without injuring him.*

❦

Papa turned the coach onto Pitt Street. "A grand day for a wedding."

"Aye." Mama smiled at him. "'Tis a bonny day."

Mary fidgeted and smoothed her skirt again. Getting the conversation with Patrick over with would be a relief. They would find a few private moments together, either before or after dinner.

Douglas repositioned his black three-corner hat. "Does it mean the British won't attack today since there are not as many people on the streets?"

"Douglas!" Mary placed her arm around the open-mouthed Sara. "Don't fret, Sara. He is just teasing us."

When the Stewarts' coach arrived at the Duncans' home on Oronoco Street, Patrick and Peter O'Brian, both smartly dressed, greeted them at the door of the modest brick residence. They were a year apart, but they could have been mistaken for twins with their pale skin, blue eyes, and almost-black hair.

Peter hailed a young man standing nearby before approaching Papa. "This fellow will see to your coach."

The others went to the parlor to greet the Duncans. Patrick drew her aside. He smiled and gave her a wink. "A splendid day for Peter and Jean's wedding."

"'Tis glorious—for them." *For goodness sake, don't give him false hope for a courtship.*

Patrick offered his arm and escorted her inside. He leaned close to whisper. "After the ceremony, we should have a few minutes before everyone gathers for the meal. I suggest we go to the garden."

"Agreed." Once their meeting settled any hopes of his, she could enjoy the dinner.

The small room filled with family and a few other friends. The sight of Maggie and Adam's infectious smiles warmed her heart. She stood alongside Jean. Patrick positioned himself next to Peter. Jean looked stunning, and the smile and the sparkle in her eyes filled Mary with joy.

Would she and Donald appear as happy on their wedding day? She took a deep breath. Best not get that cart before the horse. Donald needed to return first. Today was about Peter and Jean and their bliss. It had been a long courtship, first because of Jean's age and then due to Peter's protracted illness. With his health improved, there was no reason to believe the couple wouldn't have a long, happy marriage.

When the blessing and benediction were over, Patrick summoned her with a look. She followed him toward the kitchen. He held open the door to the service yard and garden, and she descended the brick steps. The fragrance of blooming flowers soothed her ruffled nerves.

Patrick's easy manner helped. She walked across the brick path and sat on the wrought-iron settee. "'Twas a beautiful wedding. I believe we were all a bit emotional."

"No doubt intensified by their long wait. I would not wish a long courtship." Patrick pointed to the seat beside her. "May I?"

"Of course." *Here it comes.*

He sat and placed his arm on the back of the settee. "I have wanted this opportunity to speak with you for a while. My hopes for us ... well, a letter did not seem to be the proper venue for such a personal discussion."

"I agree." The intimacy of their seating made her heart skip a beat. Hopefully, he would refrain from holding her hands, which were now quite clammy.

"We need to address our … friendship." Patrick wiped his brow. "As you well know, I have subtly pursued you off and on for years, even though you gave me little encouragement."

She let out a breath. Could he sense her agitation? *Assure him of your deep friendship and let him down easy.* "Yes, it probably is time."

Patrick rubbed a finger between his neck and his steenkirk. "About six months ago, I formed a special friendship with the sister of a good friend." For a moment, he studied the tree, a warm smile lit up his face. "Emily has filled an empty place in my heart. My hope is that we will be married before the year is out. I wanted to tell you before you heard anything about her from Peter or perhaps Jean when she learns of her."

CHAPTER 6

What?

Mary closed her mouth, placed one hand on the seat of the settee, and curled her fingers through the wrought-iron design. She stared into Patrick's penetrating blue eyes. Silence. He did not want to court her … but another. The lump in her throat and churning stomach provided an odd distraction.

Peter took her free hand. "I've obviously stunned you. Perhaps, I should have written."

She released her grip on the settee and raised that hand to the lace kerchief that framed her bodice. "'Tis a surprise." His declaration freed her from declining him and possibly hurting his feelings. *Perfect. So why am I perturbed?*

He studied her hand in his. "For years I suspected your interests were elsewhere … and lately … well, I needed to allow my heart to be open to other possibilities."

"I *am* pleased you have someone you care for." Such generous and not entirely honest words spilled from her mouth. Her tone and expression must not betray her fraudulent sentiments.

Patrick glanced toward the house. "We should return to the others. They may be wondering where we are."

"Yes, they probably have started the dinner by now." With any luck, her agitated state would not be evident.

In the kitchen, Maggie handed her a folded note. "The note I mentioned."

Forcing a smile, Mary put it in her pocket.

Mark handed her a plate. "Ma said ladies are to serve themselves first, so get in line. I'm hungry."

The small rooms made for a tight fit with this crowd, but the merry voices provided a needed distraction.

Mary smiled and nodded at the appropriate times, though Patrick's revelation made concentrating on the conversations around her impossible. The joyous scene around the tables, and later after they were cleared, lasted until five o'clock when Jean and Peter left the party for his home less than a mile away.

Jean's new life had started, while Mary's days were fixed and going nowhere. Each time Mama glanced her way over the course of the afternoon, she resisted acknowledgment. The inevitable questions could wait until later in the privacy of their room at the inn. *Forget about Patrick and his new sweetheart. This is Jean and Peter's day.*

Mary stared out the coach window during the ride back to the Cameron Street Tavern and paid little attention to the family's animated comments about the wedding festivities. She would have preferred a brisk walk to the tavern to settle her restlessness, but it would have raised questions, and certainly would have been denied. *Papa and Mama were more relaxed than yesterday, with no more conversation about the British disturbing their peace.*

Tomorrow, life would resume at Stewarts' Green, the routine she had followed for years—waiting for Donald's return and wondering about their future. A lump formed in her throat. Was he in danger on a battlefield or traipsing through the countryside? Was he healthy, lonely, frightened? He had been gone since the summer of '75. His enlistment would be up in seven months. When would he return home?

At the tavern, the family gathered for a few games of draughts and cribbage, followed by supper in the dining room. When Mama and Papa struck up a conversation with friends, she offered to take Sara upstairs to their room.

In the dim lantern light in their room, Mary removed Sara's dress. "What are you pouting about?"

The child placed her hands on her hips. "I don't like going to bed before everyone else. Why does Douglas get to stay up?"

"Douglas is ten, and he will retire shortly when the rest of them come upstairs." She smiled and shook her head as she helped her sister into her sleeping gown. Was there ever a younger sibling that did not resent going to bed before the rest of the family?

"Will Mama come upstairs to kiss me goodnight?"

"She kissed you goodnight downstairs. She and Papa are visiting with friends in the common room. She will be up soon, and I will be right over there." She pointed to a Windsor chair by the window. "Now, say your prayers and go to sleep." She leaned down and kissed Sara.

"'Tis not fair." Still scowling, Sara crossed her arms and furrowed her brow before finally resting her head on the pillow. She drew her blanket around her. "Jean told me someday you will marry her brother, Donald. Does he look like Cameron or Will?"

"Sometimes I forget you were born after Donald left for war. I hope … I think Donald and I will marry … one day." She tucked Sara's loose hairs back into her nightcap. "Donald is taller than his brothers, and his hair has more red in it, which lightens in the summer, and his freckles are more pronounced then, too. His eyes are the color of the Potomack." Sara's eyes began to droop. "Sweet dreams, poppet."

Cameron Street appeared quiet and nearly deserted. Mesmerized by the flickering lantern on the small mahogany pie table, she pondered the unexpected invitation Jean made to her after dinner. It had taken her mind off of Patrick's startling declaration. The trip with Jean and Peter to Charlottesville in June offered an appealing change of routine from the Green. She had never been to Charlottesville—or that far from home before. Peter declared it a pleasant and growing area with wonderful views of the Blue Ridge Mountains.

The door eased open. Mama carried two steaming cups emitting a chocolate fragrance. "I thought we might enjoy this," she whispered as she set the cups down and bent over Sara's still form. "Poor exhausted child. 'Tis no wonder she fell asleep quickly."

"Not without sulking on the injustice of having to go to bed earlier than everyone else. The chocolate is comforting."

Mama sat in the other Windsor chair. "You appeared pale and fatigued when you and Patrick came in from the Duncans' garden before dinner. Did your chat with Patrick not go well? He seemed at peace, but men can hide their feelings."

"Oh yes, we chatted, but his comments took me by surprise." A tear rolled down her cheek.

Mama took her hand. The comforting gesture broke down her reserve.

"What is it, dear?"

She wiped her cheek and laughed. "I don't know why I'm emotional. It truly worked out for the best. Patrick told me that he has formed an attachment with a girl in Philadelphia. Her name is Emily."

Mama's eyes widened.

"And it must be serious because Patrick hopes they will be married by the end of the year."

"No wonder you were so wan." Mama cocked her head. "I thought you only sought a friendship with Patrick. Yet you seem hurt or disappointed."

"Stunned. But I cannot blame Patrick. He grew tired of waiting for me to encourage him. And he no doubt knew from Jean and Peter that Donald intended to court me when he returns." She studied the rich concoction in her cup.

Mama began readying for bed. "So … why are you fretting?"

"'Tis the uncertainty. Not knowing when—or if—Donald will return, and will we still feel the same way about each other. At times I think my life is going nowhere. That sounds selfish and superficial. My days are easy compared to all the men fighting to secure our liberty and those friends who have lost loved ones in this war."

"Your questions are quite natural. But don't be too hard on yourself. Most of us are tempted to fret about the future when we should entrust it to the Lord, Who holds it all in His hands."

Mary smiled. "You know more than anyone how impatient I am. It has always been a failing of mine."

Mama hung her gown in the wardrobe and returned to the chair. "Aye, but acknowledging your impatient tendencies is a start. We all have shortcomings, dear, be it impatience, a short temper, self-centeredness, a critical spirit, or any other bad habit. I think God allows us to encounter situations that challenge our shortcomings or faulty attitudes in order to refine us. And I suspect similar situations continue until we have surrendered them." She rose from the chair.

"Hmm. That is an unpleasant proposition to consider." She drained the chocolate and caught Mama's hand as she walked by. "You have always encouraged me and given wise counsel. I have not told you in a long time I'm grateful Papa married you. You are more like a mother than a stepmother."

"What a sweet thing to say." Mama squeezed her hand before getting settled under the bed's coverlet and resting her head on the pillow.

"Will we still leave for home in the morning?"

"Aye, your father wants to get an early start. He and Thomas still have planting he's eager to complete."

"Jean and Peter invited me to accompany them to Charlottesville in late May or early June when he has furniture to deliver. Would you mind my absence for a week or so? 'Twould be an exciting opportunity."

"Aye, 'twill be fine, and the change will do you good. Now, we should both try to sleep. Perhaps you will hear from Donald soon. That would lift your spirits."

The letter! How could she have forgotten Donald's letter?

Patrick's revelation had pushed it completely from her mind. She searched in the clothes cupboard for her gown, found the small sealed parchment, and returned to the chair near the lantern. The letter was dated early March, over six weeks ago.

Dear Mary,

We are in the Carolinas, though I give no specifics for obvious reasons. I cannot say what the next weeks will bring, but I'm sure we will be seeing further action.

I'm sorry to miss Jean and Peter's wedding next month. 'Tis sure to be a joyful celebration, particularly since they have waited a long time to marry.

My eighteen-month reenlistment ends in November. I'm impatient to return home and court you and hope you are equally eager. I have special memories of all our times together. There will be challenges ahead as we plan a life together after being separated for such a long time. With the many changes these past six years, I also wonder what employment I will find.

Other concerns filter through my mind. I have seen and experienced things which I'd sooner forget but I know I'll remember them for some time to come. I wonder what kind of an adverse effect all of this will have on my character when I return. Please pardon my contemplative mood. I needed to share my thoughts with you.

Your Donald

Mama's breathing had fallen into a steady pattern. Mary let the letter drop to her lap. A tear fell on the parchment, blurring the ink. *Oh, Donald, I long for you to come home. Stay safe so we will be able to make that new life together.*

CHAPTER 7

Mary rolled over in bed and rubbed her eyes. The sun shone through at the edges of the curtains. *Overslept again.* It had been two days since their return from Alexandria, and already that seemed like a distant memory.

She rose, dressed, and hurried downstairs. There were chores, but she had promised to go to the Whitcombs' farm to see Martha and tell her all about the wedding.

The main hall and common room were empty. Eyeing the clock, she gulped. Nearly seven thirty. The guests must have already departed. She peered out the common room window. Mama was bent over, pulling weeds in the kitchen garden. Sara and Laura Gordon were close by, picking beans. Those two, born only months apart, were inseparable.

Mary tied her straw hat on over her cap and joined them. "I'm here. What would you like me to do?"

Mama's teasing eyes needed no explanation. "I almost sent Sara in to see if you were feeling ill."

"I know, I know. I'm late again. Have the guests left?"

"Aye, nearly an hour ago. How did you not awaken with the sound of their carriage below your window?"

"Exhaustion. Have the eggs been gathered yet?"

"Aye, Douglas saw to that, and the milking." Mama dumped the basket of weeds onto a pile outside the garden. "Your brothers are planting with Thomas and Papa. Philip should be bringing chickens in for dinner later. You might prepare those and get them roasting. Have you eaten?"

"Not yet. I planned to walk to Martha's later. She wants to hear all about the wedding."

Mama removed her garden gloves and joined her on the porch. "Sara, Laura, and I are going to the washhouse to help Polly. Breakfast, then perhaps you could clean the guest rooms and begin bread and pastry for pies. There will be time after dinner to go to the Whitcombs'."

"Yes, ma'am." She walked to the kitchen, started the bread, and then went upstairs to tend to the rooms. Shortly after ten, she returned to the kitchen to work on the bread and pies.

Philip, tall and lanky, sauntered through the door. His pail had two plucked and gutted chickens hanging over the side.

"Your ma wanted these, and I could find no one else around to kill 'em." His anguished grimace changed to a generous grin when she smiled at him. Philip always brought on a flood of mixed emotions. His obvious fondness for her had been both a blessing and a burden over the years.

She took the bucket. "I appreciate your taking care of the chickens for me. I hate killing and gutting them. There are still biscuits from this morning if you are hungry."

He took off his hat and ran his fingers through his dark amber curls. "I can always use a couple more." He pulled up a chair, turned, and straddled it in one smooth movement, never taking his eyes off her. "I sure miss Todd. It seems like forever instead of two years since he left. Do you think I should have joined the fight too, Mary?"

"No!" She shuddered. Philip could barely bring himself to kill a chicken, much less take up arms against the enemy. "Stewarts' Green could not do without you. We all miss Todd, but so grateful you agreed to help with the farm and the ordinary." She dug the heels of her palms into the soft dough.

His head bobbed. "Even if I'm a little … slow?"

She ached for him as he grimaced. Who had uttered those words to disparage him? Certainly not the families hereabouts. Everyone who knew Philip admired his sweet spirit. "You have common sense. You can fix almost anything. You are kind, generous, and loyal, so do not belittle yourself."

Philip's grin reappeared as he rose and returned the chair to the table. "I'm glad I killed and cleaned them for you."

"Not as much as I am."

⊚⊱⊰⊱⊰⊚

Mary made the ten-minute walk from the Green up the hill past their wheat field to the Whitcomb farm after dinner, her sewing basket tucked under her arm. A slight breeze felt good against her skin on what was turning into a hot day. Martha was picking flowers as she approached the Whitcombs' front porch.

"I thought you might come yesterday. I want to hear all about the wedding." A few of her friend's dark curls had escaped her linen cap, and her straw hat hung down her back. At five feet tall, she looked younger than her twenty-one years.

"I have plenty to tell." Mary followed Martha inside to the main room. "Are these new curtains?" Creamy linen draped the sides of the windows.

"Yes. You have not been here in a fortnight. The log walls make the room look dark. I thought the lighter fabric would brighten it."

"They do. 'Tis cheerful."

Over the next hour, they sat at the table working on their sewing projects and shared an account of the previous two week's activities.

Martha poured more coffee. "You must have been stunned by Patrick's plan to court ..."

"Emily." Mary set the chemise she sewed on her lap. "'Twas a shock. I had prepared to be candid about my feelings for Donald. Patrick's declaration astonished me and made that unnecessary. I'm ashamed to admit it, but it initially injured my pride."

"I never met Patrick, but you always made him sound charming."

"He is charming. We should have been more forthright with

❦ 30 ❧

each other years ago."

Martha passed her the cream. "We both wait for the end of the war and Donald and James to return."

Mary knotted the thread. Poor Martha. Communication from those serving in the Continental Navy was terrible. "Have you heard anything from James?"

"Nothing. I'm not sure whether to be fearful or hurt. Posts from men serving on ships are rare. Four letters in all these years. What am I to think?"

She set aside the chemise. What could she say to encourage Martha? "Perhaps the war will end before long, and all our young men will return."

Martha rose and placed the osnaburg shirt she sewed on the table and smoothed the coarse cotton fabric. "You have known the Macmillans for years. Does James seem at all fickle to you? Perhaps he has lost interest in me. In truth, we did not have any sort of understanding."

Mary sighed. "Those of us waiting at home cannot begin to imagine the world Donald, James, or any of these men face every day. No, James is not fickle."

Martha's brow furrowed as she glanced toward the back door. "Have you received any war news from travelers at the Green? We don't talk about it here since Tobias returned home ... injured."

"There was talk of British ships in the Potomack near Alexandria, but I have heard nothing since we came back. How is Tobias? Does he still prefer to be alone?"

"No different, still silent most of the time and keeps to himself. Other than when he is mired in self-pity and complaining about not being a whole man."

"I'm sure 'tis difficult to do farm chores with only one leg and needing the crutch. At least Teddy is here to help."

"Yes, but Teddy is resentful and berates Tobias about not doing his share of the work. He is more crippled by his attitude than the loss of his limb. There are things he can do seated, but no, he wanders off with never a word where. If he took on more responsibility, he might feel better, and it might keep Pa and Teddy from arguing all the time."

"I'm sorry. Your family has had much to contend with in recent years."

"After Ma died, it was hard, but in time we got used to it only being Pa, Teddy, and me. We hoped and prayed for the war to end and for Tobias to come home, and everything would be as before. But this place is as gloomy and tense as it was when Ma was … sick."

Mary returned to her sewing. How could she encourage Martha? "Do you think it would help if a person outside of the family, like my father, spoke with Tobias? He also suffered at the hands of the British. Perhaps he could make Tobias feel less defensive."

"Possibly. I better ask Pa first before we arrange anything. Forgive me for grumbling, but 'tis helpful to share my thoughts. Everyone here is on tenterhooks about Tobias."

The next hour passed with more details of the Lamonts' party and of Jean's gown. When the time came to leave, Mary gathered her things. "I almost forgot to mention, Peter has a furniture delivery to make in Charlottesville in early June, and they invited me to accompany them."

"Oh, Mary, what a treat. I have never been to Charlottesville. But that is so far away."

"Tis over one hundred fifteen miles. We will stay with a couple of their friends and at inns along the way." When they got to the porch, she hugged Martha. "We will be at services on Sunday. Let me know if you want me to mention to my father about talking to Tobias."

"I will. Meanwhile, please pray for him, Mary."

"Of course." She hugged Martha. "It will get better."

CHAPTER 8

Mary placed the last damp shirt on the boxwood. It wouldn't take long for laundry to dry in the May sunshine. Hoofbeats approaching the Green caught her attention. *The post rider.* Her heart skipped a beat. Too soon for news from Donald again.

The horse slowed to a stop, and the rider pulled several items from his pouch. He handed them to Papa, and they began a conversation.

She headed inside. Mama might need help before the Gordons and the family gathered for dinner.

The delicious aroma of Mama's cock-a-leekie soup, full of chicken, leeks, barley, and spices, wafted through the rooms. Sara and Laura had set the large table and placed a couple of vases of wildflowers on it. She shook her head and laughed at the two six-year-olds, miniatures of their mothers, Sara with her fair skin and blonde hair, and Laura with her creamy skin and brown hair.

Papa entered the room and set the post items on the hutch.

She moved toward it. "Was there anything of interest in the post?"

"After dinner, Mary."

When they were all gathered around the table, Papa offered the blessing, and Mama ladled the soup into bowls. She passed him a bowl.

Philip passed the bread to Thomas. "We going to finish cutting that timber after dinner, Pa?"

"S'pose so. That and the fence repairs need to get done."

Polly placed her hand on her husband's arm. "You may be quittin' early. Animals are restless, and the sky is overcast. My aches feel like a storm is headed our way."

Dinner was almost over when lightning lit up the sky followed shortly by a sharp crack of thunder. Everyone hurried, following an unspoken drill. The men saw to the horses, and the boys secured the barn. Sara and Laura herded the chickens to the pen, and the women closed windows and shutters at the Gordons' cottage and at the Green. It was pouring within minutes.

Mary examined the post items on the table. *Something from Donald.* Surprising to receive another letter so soon. She sat in the window seat and opened the parchment carefully. A smaller note dropped into her lap with *The Gordons* written on it. How odd for him to be writing to the Gordons. Reading Donald's note would not be put off any longer.

Dear Mary,

'Tis March and we recently came through a fight in Carolina with many losses, mostly British. I included a note for the Gordon family to tell them that Todd fought bravely but perished in my arms a short time ago. He understood that the liberty we are fighting to secure for our country comes at a cost. He was a fine man, willing to pay the price. It saddens me to have to share this news.

Mary covered her quivering mouth as her throat tightened. The sound of Mama and Polly's laughter flowed from the kitchen. Only Laura and Sara were in the room with her, playing with their dolls. Thomas and Philip were likely still in the barn with Papa. Her head dropped, and she returned to reading Donald's letter.

The Army will most certainly inform the Gordons. They may have already heard.

Who knows when you will receive this, but I wanted to let all of you know that I was with Todd. At times I wonder, Mary, how this war will change me. I've seen much I would like to forget. I know it has already affected me.

I miss you and the family and hope this will end before too long.

Yours affectionately,
Donald

Her eyes burned. She turned away when Polly returned to the room to clear dishes. The Gordons' lives were about to change forever. If only she could hold back the news. But they had to know—and begin to grieve. Nothing had come yet from the Army. Where was Todd now? Buried in a graveyard in the Carolinas?

Mama came back to the common room and stopped abruptly. "What is it? Bad news?"

She handed over Donald's letter.

Tears filled Mama's eyes as she scanned the missive, fist pressed to her chest. She took a deep breath and whispered. "I must find your father."

Mary followed. "Where is Philip? He should be here."

"Outside. One of the sheep got loose."

"I shall get him." Mary avoided Polly's eyes as she picked up her shawl. Philip came through the door, drenched.

"'Tis wet and windy out there. You cannot go outside yet."

"Let me get you a towel. Then go on in the common room."

"You sure? I should probably dry off out here."

She took a towel from the pantry shelf and handed it to him. "'Tis all right, go on. I will bring you coffee."

"You are sweet, Mary." He tilted his head, and adoration poured from his eyes.

Her shoulders dropped. "No, I'm not sweet."

Mama whispered. "I told the girls to take their dolls upstairs to play."

Mary nodded. Her pain mirrored in Mama's eyes.

Thomas and Papa came into the kitchen and dried off.

"Matthew, would you please help me get a jar off the high

pantry shelf? Thomas, Polly, go on in the common room. We will be there in a minute with coffee."

Mary's hands shook as she prepared the coffee. A quick glance caught Polly and Thomas staring at each other, confusion written on their faces. A lump formed in her throat that no amount of swallowing could dislodge.

⚜

Minutes later, Mama and Mary distributed the coffee in the common room.

Thomas, next to the window, scanned the sky. "I wonder how long this storm will last."

Papa and Mama's eyes met for a moment. He cleared his throat. "Mary received a letter from Donald today." His voiced cracked, a reaction she had not witnessed since her mother died.

Polly glanced first at Papa, then at her. "Something's wrong. Is Donald injured?"

Papa continued, his eyes on the Gordons. "No, Donald is fine. He wrote about a battle ... and he enclosed a letter for you." He handed the note to Thomas as he drew near, brows furrowed.

Polly tilted her head, squinting at her husband.

Thomas, his teeth clenched, slowly made his way to her. The anguish in his dark eyes made Mary's chest tighten. Polly placed a hand on his back while he unfolded, and they read the letter. When Polly gasped and swayed, Thomas put his arms around her.

"Ma, you sick?" Philip stopped drying his hair and came to her side.

"No, son. Read the letter out loud, Thomas."

He took a deep breath.

Dear Mr. and Mrs. Gordon,

Earlier today, Todd and I were in a battle in Carolina. I can give no specific details, but I believe the Army will furnish you with them. Todd fought bravely but was seriously injured. I remained with him and tried to give aid, but he perished in my arms a short time ago.

Thomas's voice cracked. He closed his eyes a moment, then continued.

He seemed at peace and wanted to assure you he had no regrets about his choice to serve the Patriot cause. His last words were that he loved you. He was a fine man, and like all of you, I grieve his loss.

When this is over, I hope to come and pay my respects and perhaps answer any questions you might have.

Respectfully,
Donald Duncan

Philip took a step back. "Perished, Ma?"

Thomas placed his arm around his oldest son. "Donald has written to tell us that your brother was wounded … and later died."

Philip's eyes grew wide. "Died?"

"Yes, son."

"No! Not Todd." He ran from the room.

Thomas took Polly in his arms, one hand caressing the back of her head. "Hold on to me, love. We *will* get through this."

The kitchen door slammed, and Mary took a step toward it. "I will go to Philip."

Mama stopped her. "See to the girls upstairs, dear. Papa will talk to him."

"Of course." The Gordons needed time to gather their thoughts before they told Laura. Wiping tears from her cheeks, she left as Papa went in pursuit of Philip.

Mary headed to the orchard with a basket. The blueberries were ripe, and the men and boys busy in the fields. She set the basket down and moved the ladder Papa had brought out earlier. An unspoken sadness hovered over the Green since learning last week of Todd's death. Escaping from it even briefly helped.

Her mouth watered at the fragrance of the ripened fruit. Uneven footsteps drew her attention when she placed the blue and purple berries in the basket. Tobias Whitcomb hobbled toward her with his crutch under one arm. He carried a fishing pole and bucket in his other hand. He rarely came to the Green. "Good day, Tobias. What brings you by today?"

"I'm on my way to the river, and the route is shorter through your place. Figured I could help the family by catching a few fish." His brows pulled together as he studied her.

She stepped off the ladder and emptied the ripe berries she had collected in her apron into the basket. "The fishing will do you good, and your family will be grateful for the catch."

"Pa and Teddy are busy planting and don't have time to fish. Sad news about Todd. The Gordons must be taking it hard."

She reached for a few ripe berries. "Yes, they grieve but say little about it to us. Except for Philip. He constantly mentions Todd."

Tobias set down his fishing gear and bucket. "People around here cannot understand what war is like. They don't know the fear of being ambushed. They have never been amid a battle raging around them. They know nothing of being wounded and watching the slaughter of your compatriots." His voice trembled.

She shuddered. "'Tis true. We have no way of understanding what all of you have been through. But we also hurt when we lose friends … or when they have been injured. When Papa disappeared for eleven months, our family suffered. Not knowing if he was alive or dead was horrible. Loved ones left at home struggle also." She placed some berries in his bucket. "Take these with you. Fishing can make one hungry."

Tobias had a strange look in his eyes and an odd smirk when he drew close and took her other hand.

Tobias hadn't been friendly to anyone since he returned home. Perhaps he was recovering.

He smiled, brought her hand to his lips, and kissed it.

Why did he do that? She drew it away and took a step back. He was obviously offended, so she placed more pears in his bucket. "Here, take some for your family."

He frowned, and his lips pressed together. "No. I don't s'pose you want the attention of the likes of me, half a man."

"You are not being fair to either of us, Tobias. I appreciate you and don't think any less of you because you lost your leg defending our freedom. Nor do others. We've been friends our whole lives. But I am …"

"Still got your cap set for that Alexandria fellow. What if he comes back without parts of his body … or does not come back at all?" He shuffled toward the river.

She stiffened, crushing the berries she held. Her jaw tightened when she noticed her stained hand. She stomped her foot. "You've become a bitter man, Tobias Whitcomb! Enjoy your fishing."

CHAPTER 9

Mary churned butter on the Green's front porch as Mark and Philip approached with strings of bluegills. Philip held up his catch, a grin spread across his face.

Philip placed a large plank on a couple of barrels and pulled two stools to the plank.

Mark said, "I will get the knives to fillet the fish."

"I can taste these already," Philip said. "Too bad supper is hours away."

In the weeks that followed news of Todd's death, Philip's gradual acceptance and his ability to still find joy in life had been a balm for his parents and her family.

Mark returned, handing Philip a knife. "When do Jean and Peter arrive?"

She took a deep breath and rubbed her shoulder. "Tomorrow, early. We hope to go as far as Newgate the first night." The trip to Charlottesville would be a welcome escape from the routine and talk of war for at least a week.

Philip frowned. "How long does it take to get to Charlottesville?"

"We will spend the second night at their friends' who have an ordinary near Culpeper. A couple days later, we arrive in Charlottesville."

"'Tis a long ways away, Mary. Why do you want to wander so far?"

"Seeing a new place and being with Jean and Peter will be exciting."

Mark put the cleaned fish on a trencher. "I'm surprised Pa and Ma are letting you go, with the possibility of the enemy being near

Richmond."

"Don't you dare suggest such a thing to them, Mark Stewart. Besides, there is no news of the British being anywhere near Charlottesville." She gathered the butter and poured the buttermilk into a jug. "I'm done here. I will leave you both to the business of filleting the fish for our supper."

"Tell Ma we have plenty for everyone," Mark said.

Mama was in the kitchen, cutting vegetables. "Just in time. I need the buttermilk for baking."

"The boys said there is plenty of fish for supper. I need to finish packing, but I will help with the cooking when you are ready."

Mama looked up. "You must be getting excited about the trip."

"I am. Neither Jean nor I have ever been so far from home, and Peter says the countryside is beautiful. Our time together in April was filled with people and wedding distractions, so this will be our real visit in ages."

She glanced out the window. "I can hardly believe it. Donald could be home within six months. That is even more exciting than visiting with his sister."

❧❀❧

Mary rose early to complete her chores the next morning. The trunk she'd packed the previous evening sat in the center hall. When she entered the kitchen, Sara and Douglas were eating at the table. Mama stirred porridge at the hearth.

"I will go for the eggs unless that has already been done." She picked up a basket.

Mama glanced her way. "That would be helpful. The others are already out in the fields."

She hummed as she gathered eggs in the henhouse. Jean and Peter were generous to include her on their trip. And to give them as much privacy as possible, she packed the novel, *The Vicar of Wakefield*.

When Mary's chores were completed and she had dressed in her traveling clothes, she joined Sara and Laura on the window seat in the common room. She listened and made corrections as they read. She glanced out the window often. Peter and Jean's coach should arrive at any time. The mild weather promised pleasant traveling.

Sara tugged at her sleeve. "Will Jean's brothers go to Charlottesville with you?"

"No. No one ever suggested that Cameron or Will would be going."

Laura grinned. "Mark told Philip that you might marry Jean's brother. Are you going to marry Cameron?"

She laughed and took a deep breath. "No, sweetie. Cameron is thirteen years old. We will not marry. Mark meant Donald, Jean's older brother, and he is still away from home." Only months until she would see him again. *Be safe, my love, and come home soon.*

Laura pulled at Mary's sleeve. "I see wagons coming up the lane."

Mary joined her mother outside on the front-drive as the couple waved from their coach. It had a small piece of furniture in the back of it. A loaded wagon covered with a tarpaulin followed close behind.

Mary approached the coach. "Welcome, we could not ask for better weather today. Was the trip easy?"

"For the most part," Jean said, smiling at Peter as he helped her down. "We stopped shortly after leaving Alexandria to adjust the padding around the pieces. Other than that, it went well."

Mary embraced Jean. "We have cool cider and water inside. You must tell me all the Alexandria news."

Philip saw to the horses while the O'Brians and the wagon driver went inside with the Stewarts to rest and refresh before they continued their first day's journey.

Donald cleaned his tin plate and fork and placed them back in his haversack. It had been two weeks since they had crossed the Saluda River at the Island Ford with the goal of securing British outpost Ninety-Six. He handed a jug of cider to Boyd and took a swig from his own. "I wonder how much longer till we lay siege to the fort?"

Boyd shook his head. "Asked myself the same thing." He picked up his Bible and began fingering the pages.

Donald rested on his blanket, studying the stars. "'Tis hot as an oven. July and August will be scorchers. I thought about taking a swim in the Spring Branch tonight, guard duty or not."

"Good thing you resisted that urge. You could have gotten shot."

Donald grunted. "I know." General Greene had riflemen posted there so the British wouldn't get access to it.

Boyd shrugged and leaned back. "We will lay siege to the fort one of these days." He took another swig before setting down the jug and returned to reading his Bible.

"What are you studying there? It won't give troop movements or redcoat strategies, will it?" *I'm beginning to sound like the others who harass him. Let the man be if it settles his fears.*

"It encourages me, and it reminds me to be thankful in all situations."

"Thankful? You *are* daft. What do we have to be thankful for?"

"We're alive, and except for the bug bites and occasional bouts of dysentery, we're in good health. And best of all, our enlistments are over in less than six months."

Donald laughed. "You have a strange way of looking at life." Boyd's optimism made him easy to be around—when it did not exasperate Donald. Boyd was friendly and not coarse like so many of the others.

Boyd rubbed his hand against the worn leather binding. "When I get to feelin' bad about the war or being away from home, I list things to thank God about. Makes me feel better. The circumstances don't change, but it sure changes how I get through-em."

"Hmm." Guileless Boyd had a way of saying things that made a body think. "We better get to sleep. More tunnel digging tomorrow."

Mary studied the Albemarle Inn sign in front of a story-and-a-half frame and clapboard structure as she stepped down from the coach. "Albemarle, how charming."

A man seated on a nearby bench stopped his whittling. "'Twas the Charlotte Arms, but that got changed a few years back. No longer needed a reference to her majesty."

"But the village is also named for her. Will it be changed?"

"Hard to say."

Jean walked up to her. "Peter is seeing to our rooms. You don't mind if Alex joins us for supper, do you?"

"Of course not." Alex worked in Peter's shop and drove the wagon with the furniture. He had dined with them the past two nights. And Alex had many entertaining stories. He unloaded their luggage from the back of the coach.

The room assigned to her upstairs was small but had a window that overlooked a lovely garden. They were tired from the trip, so there was little chance of seeing more of the village tonight, but tomorrow could be filled with new and exciting experiences. Touring the garden or exploring the shops while the men were about their business. She had a few coins in case she found something tempting. After washing, she made her way back downstairs for supper.

Peter poured their cider from the pitcher after the food arrived. "In the morning, Alex and I will deliver the furniture to the Woods' estate. You ladies can either stay here, or the innkeeper said there is a garden across the way you might enjoy."

Jean patted Peter's cuff. "Please don't worry. Mary and I can entertain ourselves."

Mary stifled a chuckle. Was it Jean's adoring look at her new husband that made Alex blush? She sipped her peanut soup, enjoying the nutty scent and flavor. "If the weather is nice, I would enjoy a walk. How far away is your delivery?"

"Not far. I suspect we will only be gone two to three hours." Peter placed his hand on Jean's. "There is the possibility that when the Woods learn you both are traveling with us, they may invite us to dine with them, so don't wander too far."

A serving woman brought rice pudding to the table. "Is there anything else you might need?"

Jean's eyes lit. "I cannot think of a thing. This will satisfy me."

The smell of cinnamon, nutmeg, raisins, and vanilla made Mary's mouth water as she served some into a bowl.

Alex took a large helping. "I heard the gent over there say the Governor's home is near here."

The server collected the empty dishes. "Aye, 'tis only a few miles away."

Jean grinned. "Perhaps we might pass by Governor Jefferson's home on the way to the Woods' estate."

The server shook her head. "Might not be the best time. The British have occupied Richmond. Heard the Governor and Legislature are rumored to be meeting in or around Charlotteville, possibly at the Governor's home."

"I had no idea." Peter and Alex exchanged nervous looks. "Interesting, but we won't be around here long enough to find out. We may leave Charlottesville tomorrow or the day after that."

Jean's brow furrowed. "But, Peter, I thought we would be here a few days."

"'Tis best, my dear."

Mary wiped her mouth and placed the napkin on the table. Alex and Peter's lighthearted demeanor had quickly grown serious. Mark's remark a few days earlier about the enemy being near Richmond came to mind. 'Twas disappointing they couldn't stay longer, but the men were probably just being cautious. "We can walk to the garden and have a lovely day while the men are about their work." If only the war would end soon.

Donald followed Boyd to their tent, brushing the worst of the day's diggings from his clothing. When they arrived, Donald grabbed his blanket and tossed it on the ground by a fallen tree trunk. "Still too hot for the tent. How many more trenches do we dig in this granite-like clay while the enemy is firing at us? And the tunnel …"

Boyd passed him some dried pork and biscuits. "Relax, we are makin' progress, slow as it seems."

Exhausted, Donald rested his head against the trunk. "One day, we will capture Star Fort. Best get to sleep. 'Tis back to digging in the morning." He chewed the tough meat and finished the dry biscuit while searching the night sky. The image of a dead Patriot boy shot the previous night haunted him. Those sights shocked him less than they once had. How the war had hardened him. His infernal headache had returned.

"Duncan, you still awake?" Sergeant Brown's voice pulled Donald from the brink of sleep.

"Yes, Sergeant." Donald pushed himself up and stood. *Sleep may have to wait.* "Can I help you?"

"Yes. You were a courier in Virginia. The major has a dispatch he wants you to take. Get some rest and come to his tent at first light."

"Yes, sir." *Wonder what that is about?* At least he would be in Virginia.

He awoke in a cold sweat, moaning. Boyd's even breathing beside him meant he still slumbered.

Getting back to sleep seemed doubtful with the visions of dead and dying soldiers terrorizing him. He couldn't forget the lives he had taken. It was war, and people got killed in wars. The cause of freedom and the fight necessary to maintain their liberty still mattered. Why did it continually besiege him?

"You awake?" Boyd's deep voice jolted him.

"Huh?"

"You have been tossin' and turnin' most of the night."

"Sorry." A shame his terrors disturbed Boyd.

"No need to apologize. We have been through many rough times. 'Tis bound to trouble a body."

"I cannot turn off the nightmares."

"They used to bother me more. Now, when my mind heads down that dark hole, I focus on all the good things God has done and is doin'. Seems to help."

Donald wiped the sweat from his face. Boyd's calm demeanor and confident attitude never seemed to falter. "You have no guilt … for the killing and maiming we do? That we lived when others died?"

"It grieves me somethin' fierce. Believin' in the cause we are fightin' for helps me put it in perspective. I keep goin' to God and ask forgiveness for my sins. I trust in His mercy and grace."

"You make it sound simple."

"God makes it simple. Easy enough for a child to understand. The hard part is to accept His forgiveness."

There were days when he debated between strangling or hugging Boyd. *First light is almost here. Best sleep fast and find out what the major's mission is all about.*

CHAPTER 10

Mourning doves cooed outside Mary's window. She drew back the curtain, and one flew off the brick ledge. Another studied her and continued his mournful sound. The sun shone, and the day promised adventure.

This would be the first time since the wedding she and Jean would spend time alone. She took the sheer wheat-colored lawn gown, her favorite summer frock, from the wardrobe. It would also be fine to wear it to the Woods' home if they were extended an invitation.

Thirty minutes later, she walked downstairs to the dining room. Peter and Alex were eating and deep in conversation.

"Where is Jean? Has she already breakfasted?"

Peter frowned. "She may be a bit late coming downstairs. She is feeling poorly."

"Oh, I'm sorry. Shall I take a food tray upstairs for her?"

Peter shook his head. "She declined when I offered, but I'm sure your company will cheer her. I'm afraid we must leave. Alex and I need to get to the coach barn."

"Of course. I will order and take a meal upstairs for us. I hope all goes well with your delivery, gentlemen."

Alex nodded and left.

A crease formed on Peter's forehead. "I hate leaving Jean when she is ill but—"

"Don't worry. I shall see to her."

"Breakfast might help, and you may still have time for your walk. Please don't venture far if you do go out. This is unfamiliar territory."

"You fret too much."

❦

Mary tapped on Jean's door. When Jean finally opened it, her pallor resembled the shade of her light green shawl. "Peter and Alex have left for their delivery to the Woods. He said you were feeling ill, so I thought I'd bring you breakfast."

"Um-hum."

"You *are* pale." She set the tray on a table and searched for the source of the acrid smell filling the room.

Jean pointed to a chamber pot. "'Tis over there." She climbed on the bed, rested her head on the pillow, and closed her eyes.

Mary pulled back the curtain and opened the window. "I'm sorry you are feeling ill. Fresh air will help you to feel better." She picked up the chamber pot. "I will take care of this." She searched the empty hallway. Where was the chambermaid? No matter, she could take it to the privy herself.

Jean's color appeared no better when Mary returned to the room. And Jean had so looked forward to seeing the village. "Surely something on the plate tempts you. We have chamomile tea, toast, and berries." She handed Jean a cup. "Perhaps this will ease your stomach."

Jean rolled her eyes but took a few sips of the tea and bites of the toast. Minutes later, she hugged and refilled chamber pot.

Poor dear. Mary dampened a cloth and wiped Jean's face. "Would you like me to locate a doctor?"

"No. I'm sure I will be better soon. Perhaps something I ate disagreed with me."

"Hmm." Peter, she, and Alex had all had the same food. Mary disposed of the pot's contents and stopped by her room to get her book. She could read while Jean convalesced.

She put a hand to Jean's head. "You don't seem feverish."

A half hour later, Jean seemed no better. "You don't need to stay with me," she moaned. "Go take a walk or find an activity."

"I want to be with you unless you would be left alone. I'm just sorry you're ailing. While downstairs, I asked the cook for ginger to make you tea. It can ease a sick belly and nausea. The cook had none but suggested an apothecary not far from here. I would be happy to get it for you."

"Please do. I don't want to disappoint Peter if he made plans for later today, though I cannot imagine going to the Woods' home for a meal."

Mary hesitated at the door. "I shall go for it and be back as soon as possible. We might yet get that walk in."

❦

With the cook's directions in hand, Mary headed down the lane. Other than the well-dressed gentleman who nodded as he passed her, no one else was about. She turned down a side street, narrower than the previous one. Why so little activity on such a nice day? Must not be that near to the Governor's home or where the Legislature intended to meet.

Had she misunderstood the directions? There were a few cottages set in among the shops. She peered up the dusty road. An apothecary's sign stood at the far end, not thirty feet beyond a haberdashery and a silversmith's shop. *Finally*. Jean and she might still enjoy some time alone if the ginger brought her relief.

Not fifty feet away, a large well-outfitted soldier lounged in a doorway with a smart green jacket and buff pants. *Finally, another person. Soldiers must be in town to protect the Legislature.* The man in the striking uniform, green jacket, leather helmet, and fancy plume sneered and stumbled a bit. Was he injured—or had he been drinking? She gulped and crossed the road.

"Lost, lass? I can help you." He stepped toward her.

"No, thank you. I've found where I'm going." Her heartbeat and gait increased, but the crunch of gravel suggested he was following. *Just get to the apothe…*

"You stinkin rebels think you're too good fer us."

She gasped. *British.*

His massive hand grasped her arm, pinching it.

"Sir! Let me go at once!" She tried pulling away, but his grip tightened. Anger quickly turned to fear at the acrid smell of alcohol and sweat as he towered over her. He slapped her face and then covered her mouth when she opened it to scream and dragged her through a nearby doorway. Twisting in his arms, her stomach knotted as she struggled to escape. He lifted her as if her struggles were nothing, keeping his hand over her mouth.

Was there no one on the street who noticed she desperately needed help? Surely someone had seen them and would come to her aid. *Please, God, send someone to help me.* Her heart raced, and a sour taste filled her mouth. Waves of fear washed over her. Drowning in helplessness, she began to shake.

In three drunken steps, he stopped and dropped her onto the floor. She gagged at the thought of what loomed in front of her, as she sucked in a deep breath to scream.

He pulled a wicked-looking knife from his boot and brandished it unsteadily in front of her face. "One peep, and I will slit your pretty little throat." The wild look in his eyes left her no doubt that he would kill her without a qualm.

No one could save her now. Years anticipating becoming Donald's bride, making a home with him, bearing his children flashed through her mind–now destroyed. Holding her head up in the community–now impossible. She sobbed silently as her hopes died, more with every second that passed while the filthy man plundered her body.

Her throat thick with grief, her eyes squeezed closed. *"Oh God, deliver me!"*

The soldier grunted and shoved her aside like a limp doll. "That will teach you, you witless wench." He laughed—a horrible, mocking sound—and staggered from the building.

She pulled herself into a ball, her knees to her chest and wailed. She had been afraid he was going to kill her … and now she wished he had.

Minutes later, Mary huddled in a corner of the musty room, trembling and sobbing. Could the monster still be nearby? Would he return and hurt her again? *I must get back to the inn.* Her body tensed, and her eyes darted about. Bile rose in her throat until she vomited her breakfast.

Grasping the wall behind her, she pushed herself up, but her body hurt and shook like jelly. She covered her quivering mouth to stifle her cries. The dirt and blood staining her torn dress brought fresh tears. A visible reminder of her despoiled body. Strands of hair covered her face. Her cap, where was her hat?

Her teeth clenched. *Get back to the inn.*

She retrieved her hairpins and coins that lay scattered on the ground. He had not taken those from her, but what he had taken could never be retrieved. *How dare he!*

Outside, she blinked to shield her eyes from the light. *Still deserted.* She looked a mess. Could she get back to the inn without being seen? *I'll order a tub and hot water sent to my room.* The road back to the inn was uninhabited as it had been earlier. Once inside, she spotted a chambermaid.

The girl's eyes grew wide, and her mouth dropped open. "What happened, miss?"

She fought back tears. "I … I was injured and tore my gown when I took a bad fall. Please send a tub and hot water to my room, 203, at the end of the hall."

"Your face …"

Mary put her hand to her sore cheek. "If you have any bandages, please bring them also." Her hands and nails were blood-stained.

"Certainly."

"And please, do not mention this to anyone. I do not want to distress my traveling companions."

"Yes, miss." Doubt colored the young woman's expression and voice.

In her room, her back to the door, the shaking increased. She placed her hands over her mouth and wept.

She had been raped. She was ruined. *Why Lord? How could You let this happen?*

She peeled off her clothes. The once-loved gown, now torn fabric with its grime and bloodstains, made her ill—an excruciating reminder of today's horror. She bundled it and stuffed it in the wardrobe. Standing in her shift, she caught her reflection in the mirror. She touched her bloodied lips. The red areas on her face would likely darken. Her fingers worked through the tangled hair to the nasty bloody lump on the back of her head. Her reddened arms would show bruises soon. She pulled a wrap from her portmanteau and put it on.

The knock at the door made her jump. A muffled voice said, "I have your tub and water, miss."

Opening the door, she lowered her eyes. The chambermaid carried buckets of water inside, and a heavier woman placed the tub near the empty hearth. The maid brought in more buckets that were outside the door and poured the water into the tub.

She handed the girl two coins as she left.

Pulling a kerchief and lavender soap from her portmanteau, she stepped into the tub. The warm water did not bring the relief she sought. Through muffled sobs and tears, she scrubbed furiously from the top of her head to her legs. If only she could wash away the memories and degradation. Her teeth ground together. Screaming her lungs out might relieve the rage, but it was certain to bring the inn's staff. Sobbing, she kept scrubbing until the water grew cold.

Wrapped in a blanket and huddled on the floor in a corner of the room, she shook. *I'm ruined. What am I to do?* Her lips clenched tight while tears streamed down her face. A knock on her door made her jump. "Who is there?"

"'Tis me ... Jean. I'm feeling much better and thought we

might go for a walk."

"No!" *What do I tell her?* "I'm not well. I need to rest."

"I'm sorry, Mary. 'Tis my fault, you must have gotten what ailed me. May I come in? We need not yell at each other through the door."

"No!"

Silence.

"I will check on you later." Jean sounded hurt. "We may be invited to the Woods', remember?"

Mary squeezed her eyes closed. She had not meant to be harsh with Jean. More guilt. "You and Peter go. I'm staying here and will see you tomorrow." *Calm yourself—and think.* She would need a believable story by morning.

"May I bring food for you?"

"No. I'm not hungry."

"Get a good rest." Jean's receding footsteps brought small relief.

Mary dressed in her sleeping gown, opened the wardrobe, and stared at the lawn dress and petticoat. *Disgusting.* She pulled the garments out and shredded them. She would dispose of them before leaving Charlottesville.

Sweat dripped from Donald's face. His arms ached from carrying Todd, bullets flying all around them. *Get him to safety.* The cannon blast hurt his ears. The smell of putrid flesh made him gag. "Somebody help us!" Who shook him?

"Wake up," Boyd's voice. "'Twas a bad dream."

He opened his eyes to darkness everywhere. He shook all over. "I cannot see. Was I hit? Am I blind?"

"No, chum. You are fine. You had another nightmare."

"Todd?"

"Come to, Duncan. Todd died months ago." Boyd put the canteen to Donald's mouth. "Water will make you feel better."

"I feel—" He rose and ran a distance and retched. A few minutes later, he returned to his blanket with a vile taste in his mouth. "I will take that water now."

"Here." Boyd handed him the canteen. You are soaked, and 'tis not that hot for June."

He took a drink between ragged breaths. "Sorry, I woke you."

"Glad I was here. 'Tis first light, and you have that mission ahead of you."

He sat back on his bedroll and wiped the sweat off his face and neck with a cloth. Riding to Virginia would take days. If the dispatch delivery took him anywhere near Alexandria, he would find a way to get to Stewarts' Green. Seeing Mary, holding her again, knowing she still waited for him, would help him get through the rest of his enlistment. Perhaps the past might not haunt him as much if he could focus on Mary and the future.

CHAPTER 11

Mary sat stone-still on the edge of her bed, arms crossed tight across her middle. She ached all over, mostly inside. The sunlight filtering into the room from the edges of the curtains could not lighten her spirits. Since her return to Stewarts' Green yesterday afternoon, she had stayed in her room with the pretext of a bad headache and still sore from her fall. Not a complete falsehood. She had told Jean she was ill and manufactured a tale of falling down a flight of stairs at the Charlottesville inn. The days since Charlottesville had been a blur. She spoke little to anyone traveling back to Stewarts' Green. The O'Brians had been solicitous and not pressed her. The evenings she had taken her meals in her room, though she had eaten little. Lying to the O'Brians and her family only increased her guilt, but it was the only way to explain her silence and desire to be left alone. But feigning sickness or discomfort would only work so long. Revealing her shame would accomplish nothing and only invite pity, worry, and talk. Keeping it from Mama would be her biggest challenge. That woman could pry food from a starving man.

If only she had not gone off by herself, it would never have happened. Her parents had warned her over the years not to take undue risks. Now, she would forever pay the price for her imprudence. Her trunk sat undisturbed, where Papa had set it near the wardrobe yesterday.

"Mary?" Mama called through the door.

She jumped. She must continue playing the role she had devised over the past few days. It had been successful with Jean and Peter. "Come in."

"Are you feeling any better?" Mama walked to the window. "May I open the curtain, or will that aggravate your headache?"

She stared at her hands, clasped in her lap.

Mama pulled back the drapes and turned toward her. "Your face, dear." She squinted and gently lifted her chin.

She kept her eyes averted.

"Aye, 'tis a bad bruise. Your arms are also discolored. 'Tis fortunate you did not break anything. Falls can be very dangerous."

My heart is broken.

"Are you well enough to come downstairs? Everyone else has breakfasted."

"I'm not hungry, but I will be down as soon as I dress."

Mama spotted the trunk and cocked her head. She sat beside Mary and took her hand. "Would you like me to unpack your trunk?"

"No."

"Jean said you ate almost nothing the last few days. Is your stomach still upset?"

"Please stop fretting over me. Jean was ill several days ago while we were in Charlottesville, and I probably caught whatever ailed her. She improved, and so will I." *Another lie.* She sighed. *If only people would stop asking questions, I wouldn't have to keep lying.*

Mama squinted when she touched the bump on the back of Mary's head. "An odd fall wounding your head in back as well as your face."

"You don't need to keep bringing it up," she snapped.

Mama's brows furrowed. She took a deep breath and rose. "I will see you downstairs then." She frowned, hesitated briefly when she reached the door, then left.

Mary pulled a pale-yellow calico gown from the wardrobe, then stuffed it back in and slammed the door. She could not wear it. Perhaps in a week or month, it would remind her less of the wheat lawn dress. Opening the trunk, she pulled the blue-and-white print frock out to wear. Who cared if it was wrinkled?

Downstairs in the common room, she picked up her sewing basket and the mending she had put off. Mama walked through with a broom and pail, headed toward the center hall.

"If you need the rooms swept, I can do that."

"Your mending is less taxing than cleaning floors, especially if you are still ailing." Mama's skeptical expression returned.

"No, I have been too idle." Mary set the petticoat aside, took the broom from Mama, and began sweeping. The physical activity helped. Visions of her attacker invaded her thoughts. Would that day always haunt her? She had only been at the task a few moments when she felt someone grasped her skirt from behind. "No!" In one fluid movement, she turned, swung, and hit Sara with the broom handle.

Sara lay on the floor, screaming, terror in her eyes. Mama rushed to her and held Sara close, but her angry, questioning eyes were focused on Mary.

Mary dropped the broom and fell panting on the floor by Sara. "I'm so sorry, poppet. I did not know 'twas you." When she extended her arms toward the child, Sara pulled back further into Mama's arms, sobbing.

"Please, please forgive me." Tears blurred her vision.

Mama continued to study her even after Sara calmed down.

Mary rose, picked up the broom and pail. "I will go clean upstairs. Perhaps I could read to you later, Sara."

Regret and guilt shadowed her for the rest of the day. Later, when they sat in the window seat reading, Sara stayed at a distance. Mary took Sara's hand. "I hit you because I was startled and thought someone was going to hurt me. I was trying to protect myself. Please believe me, I would never hit you on purpose, precious girl."

Sara nodded, her eyes downcast. "I missed you and wanted to … I should not have run up behind you and grabbed you."

"You are not at fault. You meant well. And I missed you, also."

Mama, seated at the garden window table sewing, frowned as she watched in silence.

Mama was angry, and justifiably so.

When the supper dishes were cleaned and put away, Mary walked to the pond and paced back and forth. Her stomach churned. How could she lash out like that at Sara? That behavior would only raise questions she could not address. Drained, she sat on the bench but jerked around at the sound of footsteps. "Mama."

"I hope you do not mind my following you." Mama came around to the front of the bench and sat beside her. "I'm concerned about you."

She stared at the pond. "I'm appalled I hit Sara, and I'm sorry."

"I know you are, but I'm more troubled about why you struck her. Your face displayed more rage than surprise. I have never seen you in such a temper. Please tell me what has made you this nervous and angry. You have been out of sorts since you returned from Charlottesville."

"Nothing." She hated lying but dared not relive the horror of that morning. "Please, I need to be alone."

"Not telling me your troubles is also unlike you." Mama sighed and rose. "I'm ready to listen when you are prepared to open up." Mama touched her shoulder, then returned to the Green.

I cannot speak of this shameful act. If only I could go away, a place where no one knows me or asks questions. But how and where? She covered her face with her hands. In truth, the thought of going anywhere or being around strangers was terrifying. *How do I run away from myself? Donald will be home in five months.* She sobbed. *I cannot tell Donald … and if I cannot be honest with him, I shan't marry him.*

Two days later, Mary churned cream on the back porch while Sara and Laura weeded the kitchen garden. The girls' laughter took her mind off her troubles and the hot, muggy weather.

Polly came out the door carrying two baskets. "'Tis good to see the girls at work. Your ma asked them to weed this morning before she left for the Turners'. They had every excuse imaginable to avoid it, but I promised them a pudding if they did not dally."

"They did dally, but I also bribed them." She let go of the kirn and stretched. "I told them I would take them for a swim at the pond to cool off when they finished."

"Well done, Mary. Give them another hour if they last that long. I will see to dinner."

"Mama said she was working on a quilt with Amelia Turner and a few other neighbors. Do you know when she planned to return?"

Polly put her gloves on. "Near two, she said. They wanted to finish it before the Martin wedding next week."

"Oh, that." Mr. Martin, the schoolmaster, was to marry a young Leesburg widow. She continued her churning while Polly joined the girls in the garden.

Martha Whitcomb's "Hello," came from around the side of the house. Mary rolled her eyes. More lies to tell.

"When I asked after you at church yesterday, your ma said you were feeling poorly." Martha's eyes widened. "What happened to your face?"

"I tripped and fell … a few days ago. I'm better today."

"I'm sorry. No wonder you chose not to come to services yesterday. I want to hear all about your Charlottesville adventure."

The last thing she wanted to do was fabricate another story. "I told the girls I would take them to the pond for a swim when they finished weeding."

"I will go with you. You look like you still feel ill."

"I'm not myself." She would need to be hospitable and manage to get through the time with Martha. "May I get you water?"

"Finish your churning. I can wait." Martha sat on a bench next to her. "Have you seen Tobias today? We wondered if he went off with Philip or Mark. He has not been around all morning and 'tis making Teddy and Pa cross."

"No. He has not been here." She hadn't spoken with Tobias

since he'd gotten cross with her, and she had hurt his feelings.

"How are the bride and groom? Was Charlottesville wonderful? Tell me everything."

She lowered her eyes and bit her lip. Tell her everything? That she would never do. "Jean and Peter are fine. They seem happy together. Unfortunately, Jean took ill shortly after we arrived in Charlotteville. We did not get out as we planned. Then I fell ill and fell. We returned home."

"What a shame. You must have been terribly disappointed."

"It was not the trip I anticipated. Now tell me about your family." For once, she would be content if Martha spent the rest of their time together focused on her own activities and concerns.

Thirty minutes later, the four of them headed to the pond. Sara and Laura peeled down to their undergarments and ran giggling into the pond while she and Martha sat on the bench.

Her mind wandered while Martha shared the past two weeks of neighborhood gossip.

"Where are you, Mary Stewart?"

"What do you mean?"

"I don't think you have you heard a word I said." Martha toyed with the stalks of Queen Anne's Lace she had gathered on the way.

"I was still thinking about everyone being cross with Tobias."

"Hmm. Do you remember when we were as lighthearted as these little ones?"

Sara and Laura, full of glee, splashed each other while four ducks scattered to the far side of the pond.

Mary crossed her arms. Would she ever feel gleeful again? "'Tis difficult to recall."

Martha set the wildflowers aside. "I agree. Timothy's death changed everything for our family. Then Tobias joined the militia, and Ma's confusion and mind troubles until she passed. Now, Tobias mopes, Teddy is resentful, and Pa is melancholy. I'm weary of the sadness and bickering. I want nothing more than to marry, establish my own home, and feel joy again."

Mary stared out at dragonflies skimming the surface of the pond near where the girls splashed. "That may not be easy given the shortage of marriageable men in the neighborhood, particularly now that Mr. Martin is taken."

"My hopes are still on James Macmillan, though that may seem far-fetched. 'Tis not like you and Donald. You two are promised to one another. James and I have no understanding … and far less communication in the past five years."

She turned toward Martha. "The war has changed everything for all of us. There are no certainties. People change, and what may have seemed probable or possible years ago now seems little more than a fantasy."

A crease formed on Martha's brow. "You are in a sour mood. Do you have news of James that I have not heard?"

She shuddered. "No, I spoke for all of us. None of our lives will be what we hoped."

"Why are you so sullen today?"

She stood and smoothed her skirt. "I should get back to the Green. Forgive me for sounding gloomy. James may be the answer to your prayers. I have no news of him." She walked to the edge of the pond. "Come, girls, 'tis time to go home."

Sara and Laura reluctantly got out of the water and dried off. She and Martha helped them to dress.

As they all headed up the path leading home, Laura turned to Sara. "Race you back to the Green." The little girls took off giggling.

Martha leaned down and picked more wildflowers. "Your bruises will fade in time, if that is what has you in such a dour mood. At any rate, I welcome your company if you are inclined to visit."

The internal bruises would never fade, no matter how hard she tried to make them. "Soon, I promise." A rider approached the Green as Papa waved from the barn. "'Tis Aaron Turner."

Martha pointed to the path that led to the Whitcomb farm.

"I will head home. If you see Tobias, tell him his family has been searching for him."

She nodded. "I will." She went through the side door that led to the kitchen where Polly ladled stew into bowls. "How can I help you?"

Polly glanced out the window. "Aaron Turner is walking in with your pa. He must have wanted to get away from all the quilting ladies. Go ahead and take these to the table. Your ma should be back soon."

Papa and Mr. Turner entered the common room right as Mary set the last of the dishes on the large table.

Papa took his hat off and motioned for Mr. Turner to take a seat. "Stay for dinner. We have plenty of stew."

Mr. Turner removed his hat. "Appreciate it, but no, Amelia expects me back. The ladies were finishing their quilt. Heather is on her way. I wanted to fill you in on what happened. My brother passed through this morning on his way to Alexandria with the news of Tarleton's raid on Charlottesville."

Papa shook his head. "Tarleton and his green-jacket legionnaires have a ruthless reputation since the massacre at Waxhaws."

"One wonders how he learned the government retreated to Charlottesville to conduct business." Mr. Turner wiped his damp brow. "'Twas a daring plan to capture Jefferson and the Legislature."

Green jacket? A bitter taste came up her throat. She gripped the edge of the table to keep her balance. Heat flooded her face. Had her attacker been one of Tarleton's men?

Mr. Turner smacked his hand on the table, and she flinched. "It had to have been divine Providence that alerted them in time to escape. Taking them would have been a disaster. Harrison, Nelson, Lee, and Jefferson would have been executed for signing the Declaration of Independence, and that firebrand Henry would have been hung along with them."

Where was divine Providence when I needed it? She took her handkerchief from her pocket and wiped her brow.

Papa's voice grew louder. "Mary? I asked if you knew anything about the raid?"

She shook her head in silence.

Papa crossed his arms. "Peter O'Brian said nothing about any enemy activity when you were there. But, I suppose it may not have been known by all in the area at the time." He faced Mr. Turner. "Mary and her friends were in Charlottesville during that period. I thank God their party came to no harm."

Mary put her hand to her mouth. "Excuse me." She darted out the side door to the privy and emptied her stomach.

CHAPTER 12

Donald arrived in Hicksford in southeastern Virginia after ten days of travel. The major's orders designated he was to wear a hunting shirt instead of a uniform to avoid drawing attention. About seventy more miles to James City County to deliver his dispatches to General Anthony Wayne.

The major had chosen each place he overnighted, including Isaac Hunter's tavern near Raleigh. They were safe places where Patriots met to avoid discovery and obtain a fresh horse.

Hicksford 'twas hardly a village, but at least he'd arrived in Virginia. Once he located the ordinary, he arranged for the care of his horse with the proprietress. He wanted only a good night's sleep.

"You can get a meal in there." The portly woman pointed to the adjoining room.

"My thanks."

An appetizing smell coming from the almost empty common room set his belly to growling. Food before sleep. Two men sat at a table at the far end of the small room. The smell of the moss in the daubing between the log walls competed with the savory scent of venison.

The cook brought stew and ale, then hovered. "Never seen you here before. Mind if I sit?"

"Not at all." He nodded at the burly cook.

"Name's Micah Lamb. You travelin' through?"

Donald studied the man. He had a striking resemblance to the proprietress "Yes. I had work in the Carolinas but need to get home. Victuals sure smell fine." He savored the meal while listening to the man's chitchat.

"Where is home?"

Donald took another bite. "Richmond." Lying was not his nature, but mentioning Richmond might provide a needed decoy. He could not be sure whom to trust.

"My sister Millie and I were born in Chesterfield County." The cook pointed to the woman who had served him upon his arrival.

"Ahh." That explained their resemblance. Donald sipped the ale.

"Whereabouts in Richmond?"

Donald took a deep breath. Fine time to recall his geography lessons. *State the code and see what happens.*

"North of there. I'm trying to get to the family farm."

The man searched his face and gave an understanding nod. "Be careful. British troops have occupied it. Even tried to capture the Legislature while they met in secret near the Governor's home."

Donald sat back in the booth. "Really?" Jefferson's home was further west than Richmond, near Charlottesville. "I had not heard. Were they successful?"

"Caught a few of them, but no matter, the Redcoats are all over the place. Last May, Tarleton's cavalry came through here headed north. "Twas his troops and the cavalry that made the raid."

The cook rose when another patron entered the room. "Enjoy the meal and safe travels."

A foul taste filled his mouth, and beads of sweat broke out on his forehead. Even hearing the name Banastre Tarleton turned his stomach. The horror of Waxhaws, Guilford Courthouse, and Todd's death flooded his thoughts. He pushed the bowl of the stew away.

Upstairs in his room, Donald sat on the mattress and pulled out his map. The place he should shelter in Surry would inform him about recent troop movements giving him the best information available. He would also need to know where the ferries were to cross the James River either near James Island or into Charles City

County. The James River narrowed near Charles City County, but that meant he would also require conveyance across the Chickahominy River. He could deal with that tomorrow, tonight he needed sleep.

A knock at the door woke Donald. He rose, grabbed his gun, and eased the door open. Micah Lamb stood with a candle.

"Is there a problem?" *Please don't let there be something wrong with the horse.*

"Wanted to let you know some Loyalists arrived. You might want to take your leave."

Mary finished setting the laundry to dry on the privet and boxwood hedges. It should dry before the potluck at church. Odd for a Wednesday, but this day they gathered to celebrate the fifth anniversary of the signing of the Declaration of Independence. *There will be far more to celebrate when the war ends and the English are far from our shores.*

She glanced about. The barnyard was empty, and no one in sight. She headed back inside the washhouse and latched the door. Peeling off her clothes, she grabbed a rag and eased into the large washtub still full of water. She scrubbed until her skin hurt, then she pressed her face against her upright knees. Mama was standing by the tub when she raised her head. A pained expression marred her face.

"I saw you come back inside, lass. We can speak of it here, or you can dress, and we will take a walk, but this has gone on long enough."

She shook her head. "I cannot."

Mama held a towel. "Come now. You have kept your own counsel, and I have not pressed you, but no more. A walk to the pond, no one will bother us there."

Mama's pale-blue eyes searched hers. For the past eleven years,

Mama had been her closest confidant. *Will telling her ease this agony?*

She got out of the tub, dried off, and dressed in silence. *Please don't think less of me.*

They walked without a word until they approached the pond. Mama led her to the bench where they both sat in silence for a time under the shade of the tall oak. The melodious honking of geese on the pond provided a convenient distraction.

The pond was a mossy green today, as murky as her mood, her life. She clenched her hands on her lap. How to tell Mama? Shame, her constant intruder, returned. She had been foolish to walk alone in an unfamiliar area. She already berated herself daily for that.

Mama pried Mary's hands apart, took one, and held it firmly. "You have not been the same since your trip with the O'Brians. You are withdrawn, unusually sharp, and you have bathed more in the last month than you would in a year. Tell me what was said or what happened to cause you such turmoil. Your father and I love you and are deeply concerned about you."

◎&⚛%◎

An hour later, the two women sat silent. Mama cradled her in her arms. The ducks and geese under a nearby tree, the sunlight on the water, and the tranquil setting belied the anguish they shared.

"As embarrassed or humiliated as you feel, you should have told us … or me. We cannot alter what happened, but we can comfort and love you. We can pray for you."

Mary wiped her cheeks. "When I'm not feeling sorry for myself, I'm angry. I thought if I said nothing, I could put it behind me, make it less real. But I have been fooling myself. It will always be with me."

"I'm truly sorry, precious girl. 'Tis an open wound right now, but in time you will heal and be able to put it behind you. Sharing what happened may help in the process."

"How does anyone heal from such a savage act?" Her voice

cracked. "I'm soiled, ruined, without hope for the future I wanted."

"Nay, lass. You are not ruined and not at fault." Mama turned her chin so she could not avoid her eyes. "Are you concerned there will be a child?"

"No … not anymore. But *this* has spoiled any chance of marriage. Donald deserves someone pure. I cannot offer him that."

"You can give him love and loyalty. The attack does not change that."

"It has changed"—she pulled away far enough to thump her fist against her chest—"me."

"Aye, it has, but it does not define who you are. Dearest, none of us are unscarred by life. Please try not to anticipate how you might feel or think in four or five months."

"Donald's enlistment is over in November. I cannot foresee changing my mind by then."

"No decisions have to be made now." Mama rose and stared at the pond. "We need to tell your father about this."

"No!" Mary grabbed her hand. "He does not need to know. 'Twill make him angry, and there is nothing he can do about it."

"Aye, he will be angry." She faced Mary. "But not at you. He is worried about the change in you, and we do not keep things from each other. He is your father. It need not go any further. I can tell him for you if you wish."

"Please, no. I will try to calm myself." Her pleading only made Mama more unhappy. "Not yet. Perhaps in time." *Would that satisfy Mama?*

"We will let it rest for now. We need to get back and get ready for the church social."

"Must I go? I would rather stay here." She crossed her arms.

"This is exactly what I mean. You are not yourself, and it raises questions. Your father, as well as Martha, will wonder why you are not there. You are a source of encouragement for Martha. She is worried about Tobias and his disappearances. He usually is gone a day or two, but it has been several days this time. Yesterday, Aaron

Turner and your father searched the woods and near the river with George to no avail."

"I'm sorry. I have been too focused on my own misery to think about anyone else's. Martha mentioned his moodiness and how his not helping with the chores aggravated the family." Had her earlier rebuff to Tobias' taking her hand provoked his extended disappearance? She hoped not. While she'd wanted to discourage his behavior, she'd never want to hurt him. "Perhaps he just wanted some time alone. I will pray for him and go to the picnic to encourage Martha."

As they walked back to the Green, Mama picked wildflowers growing along the path. "I feel bad for George, Martha, and Teddy. I know they are disappointed and, at times, impatient with Tobias because of his difficulty adjusting to his limitations. 'Tis a quandary to know how to help them other than to keep praying for them."

Maybe she and Tobias weren't so different. Her family was baffled by her actions since Charlottesville. She cringed imagining Papa's reaction should he learn of what had happened to her there. Beyond being angry, he would pity her, and that would be unbearable. Was that what Tobias couldn't stand? People's pity?

The best way to avoid that was to focus on someone other than herself. Going to the picnic was a start.

❦

The Gordons' wagon followed the Stewarts' to the grassy area near the church. Mary searched for Martha while she and the others carried baskets to the tables brought out from the schoolhouse for the food. Blue, white, and red braided fabric hung from branches on the dogwood trees.

Many attended the social, and much of the attention focused on Mr. Martin and his new bride. Mary made her way to Teddy and Mr. Whitcomb, who were carrying benches from the schoolhouse. "Where is Martha?"

"Over there." Teddy pointed to the graveyard beyond the church. "She brought flowers for Ma's grave."

She walked uphill toward where Martha stood with Betsy Edwards. "Good day, Mrs. Edwards, Martha." Had she interrupted a private conversation?

Mrs. Edwards smiled and approached her. "I thought I would keep Martha company. Now that you are here, I will go and help serve the meal."

Martha pulled some grass away from the headstone. "I'm done. We can go now."

They left the gravesite to join the other ladies. "I did not see Doctor Edwards anywhere near the tables," Mary said. "I know how he is usually first in line for Mama's cock-a-leekie soup. Is he off tending to a patient?"

Mrs. Edwards' wrinkles grew more exaggerated when she smiled. "He will be disappointed to miss it, but I suspect he is having a great day fishing with Philip."

Mary smiled. "I knew Philip had gone fishing, but I did not know he went with your husband."

Mrs. Edwards' expression grew wistful. "Thomas wanted to spend time with Philip since Todd's passing. We remember how sad we were when we lost our son near thirty years ago."

"Mama had mentioned you lost a son. What a thoughtful gesture for him to come alongside Philip."

"Yes." She laughed. "But he also likes to go fishing and hiking around the river, and Philip is good company."

"Philip will appreciate your husband's kindness," Martha said. "When Timothy died, even though the Gordons had only lived in the area about six months, Philip went out of his way to be nice to us."

Mrs. Edwards walked toward the tables while Mary and Martha stopped.

"I had forgotten Philip did that. 'Twas shortly after the Gordons helped us build the Green."

"I'm embarrassed to admit it." Martha squinted. "I was a bit wary of Philip in the beginning. I had never met anyone … well … like him. But Philip is a friend to everyone."

"I have come to appreciate Philip as I have gotten older." They continued down the hill. Mary pointed to the grassy area where Doctor Edwards was parking his wagon next to the others. "Twould seem the doctor and Philip made it back in time for the food. From the looks on their faces, they had an unsuccessful fishing trip. I'm glad they decided to join us."

"Something is wrong," Martha said. "It appears more serious than not catching fish,"

The doctor spoke first to his wife and then strode over to Martha's father. Dr. Edwards put his arm around George Whitcomb, and they walked back to the wagon. Philip scanned the crowd, and when he spotted Martha and her, he came their way.

Mary stiffened. The look on his face did not bode well. "What is it, Philip?" Mary asked.

He did not take his eyes off of Martha. "Is Teddy here?"

Martha took a deep, unsteady breath. "He is probably with Mark at the creek. What happened?"

Philip took Martha by the arm. "I will walk you over to your pa."

Mary swallowed hard while staying close to Martha. Mr. Whitcomb was bent over beside the doctor's wagon. A canvas covered the back.

Philip's face was lined with sorrow. "The doc and I were hiking along the river, went quite a distance, all the way to the falls. Walking those paths can be dangerous."

Mary reached for Martha's hand and squeezed it. The shock in her friend's eyes tore at her heart. Mary pulled her into a hug. How would her friend get through yet another tragic death?

Had it been the loss of his leg or not being able to cope with the horrors of war that made Tobias continually wander off and withdraw from his family and friends? Leaving them filled with worry and frustration. So wrapped up in his own grief that he couldn't see theirs.

Had retreating from life also become a refuge for her? Mary shuddered.

CHAPTER 13

The schoolhouse filled with neighbors after Tobias Whitcomb's service and burial in the church graveyard beside his mother and brother. Mary set the basket of bread she carried with the other food. "Mama, I know you need help serving, but I think I should go to Martha."

Mama's eyes grew moist. "Aye, she is fragile and needs your friendship now more than ever."

Martha's pale countenance was a stark contrast to her black gown as she grasped the chair back.

Mary placed her arm on Martha's back and guided her to a bench placed against the wall. "Come and sit with me a while." What could she say to comfort her? "Tobias is at peace now."

Martha sighed. "'Twill be the first peace he has known since he returned from the war. I never understood why he took all the walks, wandered off for hours or days at a time. What made him think he could traverse such a treacherous area of the Potomack with only one leg and a crutch?"

She sighed. "Walking relieves tension. But I have no answers for why he disappeared for hours … or more." Her head hung. "The boys always loved walking the trails along the river. Papa suggested that Tobias may not have gone as far as the cliffs. He may have fallen in the river much closer to us. The spring rains always make the current stronger."

"Pa said that, too." Martha wiped a tear from her eye. "We should be grateful that his body got caught up in the brush along the bank, or it may never have been found once it got to the falls. And we would never know."

"True." She stood. "I'm going to get us something to eat. You need your strength for the days ahead."

Mary glanced back at Martha after preparing two plates of food. Philip had joined her on the bench, completely attentive to her. *Sensitive Philip.* She headed their way. "I brought you both food. I'm off to herd some of the little ones who are beginning to run wild. See you later."

The comfort Philip could provide was more meaningful than anything more Mary could say since he had so recently lost his brother.

⊚❧⊚

Donald entered Norrell's Tavern with Major Cooper, General Wayne's aide. His empty stomach growled. The major, in his mid-thirties, took the dispatch. "You made good time getting here."

"Long days in the saddle." The sight and smell of food made his mouth water.

The major ushered him into a small whitewashed room where four officers were eating at a rough-hewn table. He pointed them each out. "This is Porter, Donaldson, White, and McGuire." He waved his hand at Donald. "Duncan is a courier from General Greene at Ninety-Six, near the Saluda River in South Carolina."

Donald stood at attention. The men eyed him. They looked as weary as he felt. The large pot in the center of the table nearest him smelled like stew. He could almost taste it.

"Sit down." Major Cooper waved to a cook to serve him and sat beside him. "I will show you where you can bunk later. The General may have a dispatch for you to take back to General Greene. Have much trouble getting here?"

"'Twas a challenge, particularly crossing the James and Chickahominy Rivers. British troops were nearby. Saw smoke from burning vessels on the Chickahominy."

"Those would be ours." One of them—Donald couldn't recall

❧ 75 ❧

his name—shook his head. "They sank our naval force on the Chickahominy River."

"Oh." Donald smiled and nodded at the cook, who set a pewter mug and bowl of stew in front of him.

The major moved a pitcher of water toward him. "The British have been in Virginia since January. They routed a force of our militia at Petersburg, burned and occupied Richmond, and nearly captured the Legislature around Charlottesville. Now Cornwallis is here and looking toward the James and the bay for resupply and reinforcements. But we are going to stop him."

Donald poured some water. *Good luck.*

A lieutenant passed him the bread. "I had a cousin who served in the Carolinas under Greene. Heard he got killed at Guilford Courthouse."

Donald put his spoon down and leaned back. "Sorry to hear that. Many good men were lost there."

Major Cooper stood. "If you are finished, fill your canteen and come with me."

Donald filled his wooden canteen from the pitcher on the table, took a couple of pieces of the warm crusty bread, picked up his gear, and followed the major out of the tavern. They walked to a church where the troops had made encampment.

Donald studied the mass of troops. "Where exactly are we?"

"About six or eight miles from James Island. You can sleep inside the church. 'Tis quieter, and I need to know where to find you if the general has a dispatch for you." The major grinned. "He may have you join us tomorrow."

"My orders are to return once I deliver the packet."

"Sleep like a log then, while you can." The major left.

Judging from the meals being passed around in the camp, it was about seven o'clock. He opened the door and wandered into the small church. A soldier kneeling in a pew turned and nodded at him before refocusing on the altar.

Weary, he found a dark corner and spread his bedroll. How

long would he get to rest before the major returned? Could the man be serious when he suggested he might be pulled into action here? Which general's orders took precedence? He closed his eyes. How long had it been since he was in a church? What would Ma say if she knew he planned to sleep in one? Too much to think about.

He woke well before dawn the next morning. Rays of moonlight beamed through a window onto the altar in the dark church. He took a drink from his canteen and went outside. The camp was still. He saw to his needs then returned inside. For a moment, he paused, an odd feeling traveled through his body, not heat, not cold. He sank onto a pew.

I have not spoken to You in a while, Lord, other than to call for help. Or ask why. And I have asked a lot of whys. Do you listen to backsliders? He rubbed the back of his neck. *I imagine You do. This place will be a beehive of activity soon. Please watch over and protect these men against the opposing forces. Do I stay and fight or head back to the Carolinas?* His prayer was interrupted by the door opening.

A low voice called out. "Duncan?"

"Yes, sir. I'm here," he whispered.

Major Cooper handed him a packet. "This for you to take to General Greene. General Wayne wants you to join his troops for the battle. That way, additional intelligence can also be provided later in another dispatch. Your horse is stabled here until you return to your unit."

"Yes, sir." He had one question answered. "Where do I—"

"Get your gear. Victuals are available outside. No telling when there will be time to eat again. You will serve under Captain Tyler. We are heading out now."

Donald marched with Captain Tyler's unit through swampy terrain for hours before finally arriving at the fields surrounding an estate. "Who lives here?" he asked the captain.

"Green Spring Plantation was the home of Governor Berkeley a century ago."

Someone mentioned the Marquis de Lafayette and his men had joined General Wayne marshaling their forces before engaging the enemy. The attack began.

Donald joined with Wayne's riflemen and dragoons in the surrounding marshlands. The smell and deafening sound of gunpowder exploding made his heart race. The gut-wrenching cries of the wounded and dying rekindled his fear and anguish. Panic and rage filled him when he saw the green-coated regiment advance.

Banastre Tarleton again.

Major Cooper rode by shouting, "We are severely outnumbered. They set a trap for us."

They charged the advancing British forces, exchanging fire throughout the afternoon. General Wayne repeatedly ordered the line to charge, but the close order made it difficult to advance and preserve their order. The woodsy area complicated making any headway.

The major yelled. "Fall back! Fall back!"

Donald gaped behind him several times during their retreat. The opposing forces were far greater. Why again were the Brtish not pursuing them? Could it be Providence?

CHAPTER 14

Mary dropped into a chair at the kitchen table. "The common room and back porch have been swept, tables and chairs all wiped down. Shall I help Polly upstairs with the girls, or have you something else you need to be done?"

"Rest a bit," Mama said. "We are having cold ham, bread, and corn pudding for supper."

She poured herself water from the pitcher. "'Tis warm even for the end of July."

Mama handed her a rag, which she promptly dampened and used to wipe her face and neck. "'Tis good to have all the guests gone," she said. "But then, there is always the tidying up."

"We *do* run an ordinary, lass." Mama raised an eyebrow and poured another cup of water. "I'm hoping we shall have no other guests when Andrew and Susan Macmillan come so we can get in a good visit."

"'Twill be good to see them again. Perhaps, they will have news of James that I can give Martha. I cannot understand why he has not written to her since he has not been at sea."

Mama wiped her brow. "Andrew's letter said James would be in Philadelphia until early summer, waiting for his ship's repairs to be completed. Do you think he and Martha have an understanding?"

"No. She has said there was none, but I do hope Mr. Macmillan has information about James for her. She could use cheering." Mary tapped her fingers on the table. "Would you be offended if I asked you a personal question?"

"What kind of question?"

"'Tis not about me. I was wondering … well, I have been

curious for years ..."

"What is it, lass?"

"Papa was gone nearly a year, and we were informed he had ... died. More than once, I wondered toward the end of Papa's absence, whether Mr. Macmillan was sweet on you. I found no fault in that. He had been a widower and such a good friend of our family."

Mama picked up the fan and began fanning herself. "My, 'tis warm in here." She cleared her throat. "I believe Andrew still grieved Rebecca's passing. He recognized and understood my grief. As you well know, he wanted to help us in any way he could. And he did by discovering what happened to your father. He brought him home to us."

Mama clearly understood the meaning of her query. "Yes," Mary paused. "He is a wonderful man to whom we are all indebted. But I was fifteen, old enough to recognize the way he looked at you. We all believed Papa had died months before."

Mama closed her fan and placed it on the table. "And the good Lord brought Susan into Andrew's life to fill his lonely heart. Now, I shall get the dinner served. Would you be kind enough to go upstairs and rescue Polly from the girls?"

She did nothing to hide her grin. "Yes, Mama." Mr. Macmillan had been sweet on Mama, of that she had no doubt.

⊙⋐⋛⋑⊙

When Andrew and Susan Macmillan arrived around five thirty the following evening, Mary showed them upstairs to their room. After getting settled, the Macmillans joined the Gordons and Stewarts in the common room. Polly and Mama brought serving dishes, and Mary poured water into cups. Surely Mr. Macmillan would comment on James soon.

Papa took the initiative not ten minutes after their meal began. "Have you heard anything from James? Is he still in Philadelphia?"

Mr. Macmillan smiled at his wife before turning to Papa. "We received a letter from him a couple of weeks ago. He has been reassigned to Philadelphia until the *Trumbull* refitting is complete. He expects it will be seaworthy by later this summer, at which time he will rejoin the crew. Apparently, his time in Philadelphia has not been wasted. He has been enjoying the company of the local residents, and even met a few of the Delegates of the Congress of the Confederation."

Papa lifted his cup. "Good for him. A good respite after all the action he has seen."

Mr. Macmillan continued, "And, we understand James has formed an attachment to a Philadelphia lass and anticipates an engagement." Mr. Macmillan appeared pleased as he glanced around the table. When his eyes met hers, his expression changed to concern. Did he notice the dismay that must have been evident on her face? Poor Martha, another heartbreak.

After supper, Mr. Macmillan approached her as she cleared the dishes. "I have a note James gave me for Martha. Please extend our sympathy to her and her family for the loss of Tobias. I know they are heartbroken."

She smiled at him as he handed it to her. "I will tell them and give this to her. Martha is fond of James. I'm sure she will be happy for him, as we all are."

"I hope so." Mr. Macmillan rejoined her parents and his wife.

A heaviness filled her chest as she studied the small, folded, sealed parchment. First Patrick and now James. What was it about those *Philadelphia lasses* that captured their hearts?

Tomorrow—she would take it to Martha tomorrow. What could she say to soften this blow?

Later, sitting on her milking stool on the back porch, Mary watched Laura, Sara, and Douglas playing a game of quoits. Oh, to have lives like theirs, uncomplicated. She jolted and nearly toppled from the stool when Philip appeared beside her.

"Why are you so jumpy?" Philip picked up another stool and

sat.

"You startled me. Nothing more."

"You seemed sad when Mr. Macmillan said James planned to marry. Did that upset you?"

"No, of course not." Philip did not miss much.

"Well, I think it will upset Martha." His arms rested on his legs, and his hands folded as if in prayer.

"I believe you're right." She sniffled. Martha did not need any additional sorrow.

Philip silently studied her a moment then gave her a sympathetic smile. "We will need to be extra kind to Martha. When are you going to tell her?"

She would try to take the sting out of this disappointing news. "Tomorrow."

Philip stood and walked away.

Her eyes followed him. This world needed more Philips.

The Macmillans left the next afternoon after dinner, and Mary headed for the Whitcomb home with the note and her sewing, in case Martha wanted her to stay. As she walked the well-worn path, Philip, his father, and Papa worked in the adjacent field. She returned Philip's wave as she passed by.

Mary wandered to the back of the Whitcomb cottage when no one answered her knock at the front door. Martha was bent over picking tomatoes and placing them in a white oak basket.

She opened the gate and went inside. "Want an excuse to stop for a bit?" She waved her sewing basket.

"Absolutely. Come inside."

"I thought you could use a visit." A knot formed in her stomach as she followed Martha through the back door.

"I'm thirsty. Care for some water?" Martha set the basket of tomatoes and peppers down. She washed her hands and poured them each a cup. "I need to get these preserved soon. The larder is getting full."

Mary set her sewing basket on the table. "I could bring our vegetables and pots. We could work on it together. 'Twill be more enjoyable, and Mama would appreciate help with that chore."

Martha smiled and gave her a hearty hug.

Mary flinched and stepped back. She groaned at the hurt on Martha's face. "Pardon me. I did not expect …"

Martha shook her head. "Put off by a hug? Why are you so edgy lately?" She looked more puzzled than hurt.

"Nothing. How is your family since … Tobias."

"Sad. If only we could have eased his melancholy and been able to convince him to help with the farm. Perhaps, he would not have taken to wandering off, and he might still be here."

Mary stroked Martha's hand. *If only*. How many times over the past weeks had she assailed herself with *if only* for the choice she made to go out on her own in Charlottesville? Regret had a way of festering. *Martha, I need to help Martha.* "You look tired, my friend. I know you are hurting and frustrated, but you and your family are not responsible for what happened to Tobias. He chose to take those long walks."

"'Tis difficult to sleep some nights. I tend to dwell on it. To answer your question, Pa and Teddy never mention Tobias. Perhaps they feel bad about complaining when he would not even try to help with the chores. The two of them work all day in the fields. It has been lonely for me. As sour as Tobias could be at times, he usually remained inside and provided company."

Mary gave Martha's hand a squeeze.

"I'm feeling sorry for myself." Martha pointed to the chair. "Sit down. You can show me what you are working on."

She sat at the table and fingered the partially embroidered apron resting on the top of her basket. *Lord, please help me share this news about James and have the right words to comfort Martha.* "Mr. and Mrs. Macmillan arrived yesterday for a visit."

Martha's eyes widened as she took a seat beside her. "Have they heard from James? Is he still in Connecticut while his ship is in repairs? If he is not at sea, why has he not written?"

"Actually, he has been reassigned to Philadelphia until the *Trumbull* is seaworthy again. He's well." She took a sip from the cup and cleared her throat. "Mr. Macmillan told us he has formed an attachment with a young lady there."

Martha's jaw dropped, and she grew pale.

Mary took her hand. "I know this unexpected news must be a shock and a disappointment." What could she say to help? "This war has changed countless lives in many different ways. No one is untouched by it."

Martha's slumped shoulders and the dark circles under her eyes made her appear older than her twenty-one years. "I'm not entirely surprised. I wondered if James had lost interest when I heard nothing from him. He is an attractive, friendly, and kind fellow. Were he in town for any prolonged period, I'm certain any number of ladies would enjoy his company." Martha shrugged. "We had no understanding. 'Twas my hope that when the war ended, he would come here and—."

Mary placed an arm around Martha's shoulder. "I know you are hurt, but I cannot help but believe in the future there will be someone else who will fill your heart."

"You and I live in a rural area, with most of the young men away at war. We have little chance of finding suitable partners." Martha's brow furrowed as she took a sip from her cup. "I shall probably remain a spinster and care for Pa and Teddy until he marries."

"The men will come home when the war ends. You have much to offer any man."

"Be thankful that Donald will return in a few months, and you will not have to face life alone."

Mary stared out the window, Martha's voice fading into the background. Long years stretched before her, endless years of remaining at home without Donald or the family she so desired.

"There are no certainties for any of us." She could not tell Martha that she also anticipated a solitary life because she would ask why. And she never wanted to speak of the reason again.

CHAPTER 15

Donald trudged through the mud back toward his tent. The meager meal had hardly been worth going to the mess line. His trip back to South Carolina had been uneventful, and now August was half over. With the summer rains and flooded creeks, Greene had moved his troops to the high hills of the Santee, south of Camden, and above the swampy lowlands. They had gone into a stand-down as had the British forces. Fine with him. The Americans were weary and suffering from injuries, disease, and malnutrition. What army could function like that?

When he reached the tent, Boyd came out carrying his Bible. "How were the victuals, Duncan?"

"About as paltry as usual. Where are you headed?"

"Tryin to see if I can be of any use to the sick and wounded," Boyd held up his worn Bible. "'Tis better than sittin around feelin sorry for myself and listenin to the troop's complaints."

Donald groaned. A few raindrops fell, good weather for a nap if he could tame his growling belly. Boyd could be annoying, but he was an engaging and generous man.

Boyd smiled and sauntered off in the direction of the field hospital.

He rummaged through his haversack and pulled out his last letter from Mary.

Dear Donald,

Your letter regarding Todd's death was appreciated, but of course, was devastating news. Thomas and Polly courageously get through each day. Philip was inconsolable for a time but is better now and a great comfort to his parents. We have lost other friends, but Todd's death has made the war too close to home again. Tobias Whitcomb continues in his melancholy coping with the loss of his leg.

I hope you got my letter detailing Jean and Peter's wedding and their invitation for me to join them on their trip to Charlottesville. 'Tis coming up soon, and I'm looking forward to it. Any interesting diversion helps the time pass quicker until you return. 'Twould be so much more entertaining though if you were part of the party.

You are always in my prayers, my family's also. Please be careful. We will all be rejoicing when your enlistment ends in six months.

Affectionately,
Mary

He tucked the letter away. If Mary had written since late May, he hadn't received it. Perhaps something would come soon. She was sure to regale him with anecdotes about her trip to Charlottesville.

Might as well join Boyd and be of use to someone else.

After spending a couple of hours at the field hospital, Donald returned to his tent by way of the mess carrying two biscuits, salt pork, and two pears. The rain finally passed and cooled the air.

Outside the tent, Boyd leaned against a log, peering at the sky. "Beautiful evenin."

"See what my foray to the mess brought us." He tossed Boyd a pear. "Plunder from a local orchard." He handed Boyd a hard biscuit and a piece of pork.

"Now that is a find, and 'twas good of you to save some for me." Boyd pointed to the sky. "First clear night in a while. I'm constantly amazed at the stars. 'Tis the same night sky that directed our parents' or grandparents' journey from the motherland to America in search of a new life." He took a bite of the fruit and grinned.

"You are philosophical tonight." Donald sat beside him and poured cold coffee into each of their cups. "So now we kill the people who resist that change and want us tied to the past." He savored his pear.

"Now who is philosophical? When this is over, and I return to Rockbridge County, I'm goin to build a cabin near my folks' place on the North River, find myself a good woman, and plant an apple orchard." Boyd studied the fruit in his hand. "Maybe pears, too."

"Spoken like a starving man. What's it like? Is there much work to be found there, where you come from?"

"Rockbridge County is growin. Must be a few thousand residents, mostly farmers. The village of Lexington has all a man needs." Boyd tossed the pear core into the woods. "It has the most amazing natural bridge over a ravine. Nothing like the beauty of the Blue Ridge Mountains and the Shenandoah Valley. Many Scotch-Irish settled in the valley. My folks came over from Scotland in '48. You should come for a visit when our enlistment is up."

Donald leaned his head back and closed his eyes. "Less than three months if all goes well. Though I expect we will see more action before that."

"Probably so. Our job is to survive and put all this behind us. I have no doubt we Americans will prevail and sustain our independence."

Boyd's optimism never faltered. How could any of these men put all they had witnessed and done behind them? He glanced at Boyd. "I never asked you, do you have a girl back home?" The affable man was sure to have attracted more than one.

"There was a lass, but she married the blacksmith. God will supply the right one at the right time."

Donald rolled his eyes. "Does anything ever get you down, Boyd?"

"Absolutely! We are in a war with people with whom we share a common faith, culture, language, and history. They are often friends and neighbors. Some of our troops are English deserters, and others have crossed sides to the English. They have families, hopes, and ambitions like we do. I'm sure many of them would be grateful to go back to Britain and pursue the same things we want. That frustrates me every day." Boyd stretched. "It grieves me thinkin about it."

Donald finished the pork and biscuit. "Well, I hope you find that lady and make a good life in the valley."

"So you plan to court Mary when you get home. Will you settle in Alexandria or move west, where she lives?"

"Not sure. My pa has connections in town, but I'm not certain I want to stay there. I've been giving thought to apprenticing for a printer. Folks are always eager for news, and there will be much to write about as our country takes shape."

Boyd sat up and wrapped his arms around his knees. "Tell me about your Mary. You said your families have been friends forever."

Donald shifted to his side. "Mary is beautiful, twenty, with brown hair and golden-brown eyes, and a smile that can draw a fellow right in. She is sweet but a bit too independent at times."

"Must be a comfort to know she is waitin for you."

He nodded. "The future seems so unsure right now. I need to find a job and get established. I hope she is still waiting for me. In six years, people change. We have been separated from each other for a very long time. Perhaps our feelings have changed. Agh! Thinking about it does no good. Too much is out of my control."

"Give it to God, Duncan. He's the only One who knows the future. Trust Him."

"You make it sound easy."

"He means it to be easy to trust in Him and feel secure in His love and provision. Children understand. 'Tis adults who make it complicated and dependent on their waverin notions."

He stared at Boyd in the flickering light from a nearby fire. "Hard to believe in a loving God with so much killing around us, and men so bent on evil." A vision of green-jacketed men flashed through his mind and gnawed at his gut.

"'Tis an imperfect world filled with flawed people. We need to be a light in the darkness."

"Forget the farming, Boyd. You should be a preacher. We best get to sleep. No telling what tomorrow will bring." *Would it bring more fighting? I hope not.*

Donald turned on his other side. *I have lost friends and so much time away from family and people I care about. I had a tranquil life. Can I get it back when this is over?* Boyd was already asleep and snoring. *Knowing Boyd has been the best part of these years, even when he gets under my skin.*

Mary stuck another pin in the hem of Sara's new blue muslin dress. "Turn a bit, poppet." She pressed the hemline with her fingers as she placed the pins every inch and a half.

Laura held out the skirt of her new dress, waiting her turn for a fitting. "You really like sewing, don't you, Mary?"

"Yes. 'Tis relaxing and gives me a sense of accomplishment to see a garment take shape from what started as a piece of cloth."

Laura twirled in a circle, laughing. "Ma says you could make clothes for the gentry."

"That is sweet of her. Please try to stand still, Laura. I don't want you to trip on the skirt before we can get the hem pinned." Kind of Polly to acclaim her handiwork. She glanced up at her little sister. "Turn more, now."

Sara complied. "Are we almost done?"

"Yes, dear. I will help you take it off before I start pinning Laura's."

Sara patted the white cap covering her hair. "Douglas said he would take us to the pond to swim when they are finished sowing the wheat."

"That will be after supper. I suspect Mark and Philip will want to cool off too after such a hot day in the fields. Teddy Whitcomb might even show up." She rose to her knees and helped Sara off with the gown.

Sara grabbed her day dress. "Your turn, Laura."

Fifteen minutes later, Mary settled on a chair in the common room while Sara and Laura went outside to gather the dry laundry. She knotted and pulled threads through the hem of Sara's dress. Tonight she would start embroidering the floral designs around the bodice on each of the dresses.

Mama came into the room carrying two vases of white and blue wildflowers. "You are making great progress with the girls' dresses. Did you work into the night again? There is no rush to finish. The girls do have other garments to wear."

Her sleep had been scant, so sewing seemed a useful remedy. "The flowers smell wonderful."

Mama sat the vases on the table before putting her hands on her hips, with a sigh.

"Yes, I worked late, but I was not up all night." She kept her eyes on her work. "Laura told me that Polly thought my work was professional enough to sew for the gentry. 'Twas a kind thing to say."

"Polly is right. You are proficient."

"I owe it all to you for patiently teaching me to sew, embroider, applique, and even do a bit of lacework."

"I'm delighted you have a useful enterprise that brings you joy and peace, but I am concerned you may be using it as an escape." Mama cupped Mary's cheeks between her palms. "Please look at me."

She swallowed and lifted her head, fighting back tears. "Mama, I'm fine. This is a good thing to pour my energy into."

"You have withdrawn from us and others. Martha thinks you are avoiding her, and when the ladies gathered to make and roll bandages, the Turner twins were disappointed you did not join us."

How could she make Mama understand that she found socializing difficult? "I don't mean to be rude. I'm happier alone.

91

Martha and others keep asking questions about Charlottesville. I'm sorry I've neglected Martha, particularly now." She put down the dress. "What am I to do, Mama? I cannot seem to get beyond … it. I still wake with nightmares, and memories of the attack follow me throughout the day."

"You bear no fault in what happened, and you must put it behind you and move ahead with your life. Do not let the evil done to you rule you. Allow God to heal the hurt so you can have the full life He wants for you."

"How? And what am I to do about Donald? 'Tis almost September. He is expected home within the next two months. How can I face him with what has happened? What if I never want to be touched—in that way—again? Do I keep it from him and live a lie? 'Twould always be a barrier between us."

Mama took her hand. "It need not be. I have honored your request not to tell your father, but I think it might help. He has a man's perspective. He is concerned about the change in you, and he may be able to advise you."

"No. Please do not tell Papa. He will only say something to make me feel better. Stop suggesting I tell him."

Mama stared out the window a moment. "Donald loves you. He has witnessed much and would surely understand that you bear no responsibility for being attacked. Give him credit for some compassion."

Mary wiped the perspiration on her brow. "I'm ashamed and feel guilty. More than once, you warned me not to go off on walks by myself. But I never heeded your advice. I wandered wherever I wanted, never thinking I might be exposing myself to danger. I enjoyed the exercise and time alone to think and plan—"

"Stop! You are punishing yourself needlessly." Mama rubbed the back of her neck. "You went out that morning to find a curative for Jean. You were trying to aid your friend, and no one could ever fault you for that."

"So why, in helping Jean, did this heinous act happen?"

"Why evil happens is a question as old as mankind." Mama's shoulders slumped. "We live in a fallen world, and though we may not be responsible for the evil that comes our way, we are accountable in how we respond to it." Mama sighed. "Keep working on the dresses. Polly is helping me with the meal." She went into the kitchen.

Mary returned to hemming. Was Mama right, that Donald would not be repulsed, that he would understand and have compassion? She put the dress down. "But how do I tell him?" She groaned and closed her eyes. *I can't bear to think about how he'll look at me and respond.*

She opened her eyes and gazed down at the dress, rubbing her fingers against the soft fabric. *It might be better if I went someplace and made a different life for myself. I could be a seamstress. But where?* 'Twould need to be a substantial town that could support a dressmaker. But not Alexandria. She shuddered. Where once the thought of living in town seemed exciting, now it terrified her. There was no assurance of safety—and that was a priority. She felt safe here at the Green. Could she make a different life for herself without leaving home?

CHAPTER 16

Donald lifted Boyd's head to give him water. "You were lucky today." The open tent flap brought in humid but fresh air. "The surgeon removed the bullets from your arm and said if no infection sets in, you have a good chance of recovering."

"Not luck … God's providence."

Donald rolled his eyes. "I should have known you would say something like that. I saved your Bible for you."

Boyd's smile turned into a grimace. "What a fellow has to do to get you to open the Good Book. Did we win today?"

"Hard to say. I overheard an officer say that General Greene placed the militia in the front line, and General Sumner led three brigades of North Carolina Continentals. A group of us veterans of Guilford Court House and Hobkirk's Hill drove them back. The men said the camp was fully supplied. They broke off and began looting it. The Army was in total disarray. I suspect we will be back at the fight tomorrow. You hungry?"

"Always."

Donald laughed. "I will bring you back something." He took their tin plates and walked by the wounded on one side of the path and bodies set in rows on the other. The sight of torn flesh, blood, and entrails turned his stomach. In the distance, prisoners were being processed. After getting food and listening to men argue about who won Eutaw Springs, he was approached by two officers.

Moments later, Donald walked back to the tent with a spring in his step. He could not remember being this happy in years.

Boyd looked at the plate of stew. "Wonder what kind of meat this is."

"Best not to think about it."

"From the look on your face, I'm guessing we did, in fact, win the battle."

Wait till I tell you what your wound has given us. "Sounds like both sides suffered many losses." He grinned. "The good news is, your badly shot up arm just got us our release from the Army a fortnight early."

Boyd looked up, his brow furrowed. "What?"

"You heard me. The major stopped me. He knows we are both Virginians. Since you can't use your arm, and we both have so few days left on our enlistments, I'm tasked with ministering to your arm and getting you home. Unless we run into opposition, this war is over for us. Do you hear me? We are going home—to our families and the future." *The war is over for us. Those words meant life, home, and Mary.*

⚜

Mary sat sewing in the common room. *If I tell Donald of the rape, I must suffer his reaction, be it disappointment, disgust, or despair. If he still wanted to marry, 'twould always be between us. If I don't tell him, our marriage would be based on a lie, and 'twould still be between us. And what if I cannot love him the way he should be loved?*

A knock at the door startled her. Polly and Mama were at the Turners,' and she was to aid any of the Green's guests in their absence. She put her work aside and headed to the central hall. She reached for the handle and froze. Was it safe to open it? From the kitchen stairs, she could see who was at the front door.

She peered over the boxwood to the front of the Green and sighed. Just Martha holding her sewing basket. She walked around to the front. "Martha, how nice to see you. Come in."

"I decided I would pay you a visit since you have not been by our place in weeks."

Another prick to her conscience. "I'm glad you came. I will

heat some coffee." She ushered Martha into the kitchen and went to the hearth.

"How have I offended you? You have kept your distance at fellowships after church … when you attended." Martha tugged at Mary's sleeve. "Why are you avoiding me?"

Martha's hurt expression and warranted comments deserved more than evasive remarks. "No, you have not offended me, and I never intended to hurt you. I've not been in a social mood lately. Truly, it has nothing to do with you."

"Hmm. Philip and Mark said you have been out of sorts all summer."

"Surely, you all must have better things to discuss than my disposition."

"Why has our lighthearted lass became moody Mary?"

"Clever."

"What is bothering you? Does it have anything to do with Donald?" Martha set her bag on the table and took a seat. "I would expect you to be excited about his return in the next few weeks."

She stiffened, turned her back, and poured them each coffee. "I may be a bit anxious about his return." Best to steer the conversation to more palatable topics. "Let me see what you are working on."

"Shirts for Pa and Teddy."

Mary put the cups on a tray. "There is more room and light in the common room."

They sat at the garden window table. A few minutes later, Martha set her sewing in her lap. "We have been friends forever, and I have shared my heartaches and frustrations over the years with you. Are you going to tell me what troubles you?"

Beads of perspiration formed on her face and neck. "I treasure our friendship, and I'm sorry I have been distant lately. I will try to do better."

Martha picked up the osnaburg shirt again. "Why are you anxious about Donald's return? Have you changed your mind about a courtship?"

"I'm not sure I want to marry." There, she had said it.

Martha's eyes grew wide. "What woman seeks spinsterhood?"

"I did not say I would not marry. I'm only trying to figure out what I want." Would that satisfy Martha? How could she explain her confusion without venturing into matters she wanted to avoid?

"I'm surprised. You have loved Donald for years and been impatient for his return. You have that far away look again. When Donald returns, I wonder how he will take your uncertainty?"

"As do I."

⊙⅔⊛⊚

Donald turned to Boyd, riding beside him. They had been traveling to Virginia for days. "How is your arm?"

"Better than yesterday. Can't complain."

Donald rubbed the ache, starting in his temples. "How much further to Rockbridge County?"

Boyd winced. "My guess is less than one hundred miles."

Donald looked all around. "Where are we?"

"On the Carolina Road, part of the Great Wagon Road. This is the Maggodee Gap. Nothing like fall in the Blue Ridge and Shenandoah Valley."

The sunlight disappeared, and dark clouds formed overhead. "Time to make camp for the night. A good night's sleep and food would do us both good."

"It looks like rain. I see a sheltered area up ahead near the creek. We should reach the main part of the Wagon Road not long after we get started in the mornin." When Boyd picked up speed, he followed.

Minutes later, the rains came, and a strong wind blew more leaves off the trees. Boyd yelled to be heard over the wind. "You take care of the horses, and I'll look for kindling."

After the horses were taken care of, Donald started a small fire in a rock shelter. "Go sit under the tree and rest that arm. The wind has died down. I will fill the canteens when the rain lets up. We need to rest as much as the horses do. I still cannot believe the deal we got on them and the saddles." The damp chill penetrated his body as well as his mood. Excitement and anticipation were tempered by so many unknowns. Finding work and determining where things stood with Mary. Her letters the last few months had been rare and somewhat perfunctory.

Boyd rubbed his wounded arm. "I appreciate Greene lettin us go a fortnight early. He is a good man, a strategic thinker, and one who cares for his people. They were right, this arm has rendered me useless."

Donald leaned against his saddle and wrapped his blanket around his shoulders. "Don't say that, Boyd. You've helped more than you know by talking to the wounded and keeping their spirits up. Let me check that bandage."

Boyd shrugged his shoulders. "Keepin hope alive in others benefits me too."

When they left camp, the medics had given him clean bandages for Boyd's arm, and now he pulled one from his haversack. The wound was bloody, but it didn't look angry. "You have used your arm too much." He wrapped the clean cloth around Boyd's arm and tied it.

He handed Boyd bread and a bit of the dried pork they had gotten in the same village where they purchased the horses. Hopefully, the victuals would relieve his throbbing head. Minutes later, after eating and listening to Boyd drone on about Rockbridge County and his sister, Jenny, and their family, he leaned back and relaxed. His headache was gone. "Looks like the rain is letting up."

"I find a gentle rain soothin, and 'tis good for the crops. Can you believe the mass of color all around on the ground and trees?"

Donald laughed. "Leave it to you to see the fall colors and not fret about the rain while we try to sleep. Is it usually this chilly here in mid-October?"

"Night in the Blue Ridge Mountains can be cold. Given any

more thought of stayin with my family a couple of days? They will extend the welcome. Jenny will be glad to meet you."

"That is generous of them. I will stay a day but then head north. I need to get home." He would miss Boyd. As annoying as he could be at times, overall he was a tonic to those with whom he came in contact. But getting home to his family—and Mary—became a mental drumbeat. Pa might have ideas about work prospects in town for him. Couldn't recall a printshop thereabouts, and the idea of apprenticing in one kept invading his thoughts. A day with Boyd's family, then it would be on to Charlottesville, Culpeper, and home. And Mary. He closed his eyes. The gentle rain was calming. Boyd was right again.

CHAPTER 17

Donald followed Boyd back to the Alexanders' stone cottage after a morning of fishing along the rocky banks of the North River. He held up the bucket of fish he had dressed out by the river. "I'm glad you talked me into staying an extra day."

"Ma will be pleased with our catch. I have been dreamin of fresh fish for weeks." Boyd carried the poles with his good arm. "Thought a day of rest would do you good. 'Tis a perfect break with all the days of travel behind us and those ahead for you."

Donald looked downhill toward the river. "Sure is a pretty spot. Tomorrow I will get an early start. If all goes well, I should be home in five or six days." He had enjoyed the days with Boyd and his family. Now, he wanted to get home and see what the future held. After a few days in Alexandria, he would head out to Stewarts' Green to pay his respects to Todd's family and the Stewarts.

"You countin the days till you see your Mary?"

"She is not my Mary yet. It used to be only months between times we saw each other, but we always picked up where we left off. Now, years have gone by since we were together. What if we are strangers?"

"That could make a fellow a bit anxious. I bet it will be easier than you think."

Mrs. Alexander came to the front door as they arrived at the top of the rocky hill. "Yer back, and did ye bring us any fish?"

"Aye, Ma. Fry them up, and I will be in heaven. Pa and Jenny back yet?"

"Nay. But I expect them soon." She took the buckets of fish. "Go pick squash for the meal." She handed Boyd an empty basket.

Boyd pointed to a fenced-off kitchen garden beside the barn. "Come with me. I told you Jenny was helpin a cousin who had a babe this past week. Pa went to get her for the rest of the day."

"Won't she mind?"

"She will be grateful for the break. My cousin has five children, and they called her in to corral them. Their pa can manage for a while."

When Boyd had spoken of his sister, he had nothing but praises for her. "Is she like you?"

"She is bonnier."

"I hope so."

An hour later, Donald sat at the Alexander table as the family continued bringing Boyd up to date on years of events as well as neighborhood news. Jenny was pretty, a redhead with nothing but adoring eyes for her older brother. Surprisingly, at twenty-three, she had not married. The Alexanders' cheer and laughter raised his own spirits.

Jenny refilled their tankards with hot cider. "Have ye brothers and sisters, Mr. Duncan?" Her smile was as engaging as Boyd's.

"I have a younger sister who married this last spring and two younger brothers."

"They will be over the moon to have you home." She smiled at her brother. "Boyd's absence left such a hole in our hearts. He has missed much, but now 'tis a blessin for all of us he is back."

Donald cupped the hot tankard in his hands and stared out the window. Would his arrival at home be the same? Impossible for all the returning soldiers to recover their missed years.

When Boyd suggested they take a walk after dinner, Donald put his hands up. "You do not need to entertain me. Spend time with your family. 'Tis obvious how much they have missed you."

"My family will still be here tomorrow. You are leavin. Come with me."

They walked for about ten minutes on a path leading to an overlook that provided a breathtaking vista of mountains and a river meandering through the valley below. Several large boulders provided places to sit. Boyd pointed to the river. "'Tis the North River, upstream from where we fished today. Those mountains to the west are the Appalachians, to the east the Blue Ridge, where we came through. I wanted you to see this."

Donald breathed in the crisp fall air. The lowering sun highlighted yellow, orange, and red leaves on the sea of trees. The moving water shimmered below. "'Tis grand. I see why you love your valley. A special place and peaceful."

"Exactly. It reminds me of the vastness of God's creation, and at the same time, the detail of each individual formation, plant, or animal that inhabits it. There is a feeling of continuity and serenity." Boyd looked at him. "You seem to be searchin for peace."

Donald swallowed, fighting back the lump in his throat. "I suspect that is the plight of mankind. I'm glad you have found it here."

"Aye, but 'tis more than the landscape before us. The peace I found does not come from the valley, river, or mountains. It comes from inside." Boyd leaned forward from where he sat on the rock. He folded his hands. "The peace you are seekin for will not be found in a place, or people, or the job you secure. It comes with a surrendered heart to the One who created all this ... and you."

He gave a low laugh. "You really should become a preacher. Should have figured you would send me off with more religion."

"Not religion. You have that in your head, and 'tis a good start. I want you to find the peace that comes when you open your heart to all the ways God has been workin in your life."

He met Boyd's steady gaze. The man said things that stung, yet he would miss his friend's discerning comments—and his kindness. "Your friendship has meant a great deal to me."

"'Tis mutual. Perhaps that eighteen-month reenlistment had more of a purpose than fightin in the war. I know you are figurin out what is ahead for you. We all are. But in your plannin and buildin a life, know that you are always welcome here. The valley has opportunities, be it farmin or other enterprises you can pursue."

"I will keep that in mind." Boyd was right. Something about this place, including the Alexander family, made it particularly inviting.

Mary pulled the laundry from the hedges. The clothes were stiff from the early November chill. An approaching rider caught her attention. Despite the cold, heat rose to her neck and face. The post rider. Could there be news yet of Donald's return? His enlistment would end soon, and he may have returned home if he was uninjured ... or ... *Do not even think about that. Please, God, bring him safely home.*

A few days ago, a patron had brought news of the victory at Yorktown, which caused more celebration than she had expected. Perhaps it would mean the end of the war, though Papa had cautioned that fighting was sure to continue elsewhere. Had Donald been at Yorktown, or was he still in the Carolinas? Would he come here or go directly home? Too many unknowns.

She met the rider, pulled a coin from her pocket, and took the packet. "Our thanks." He turned and continued on his route. A couple of items for Papa, and a note from Jean. Surely, with encouraging news of Donald's expected return and not—*Why do I do that? My mind wanders to the worst thing possible.* She broke the wax seal and opened the parchment.

Dear Mary,

We have not communicated in a long time, and there is much to share. I am thrilled to tell you that Peter and I will become parents this coming winter. Our other happy news is that Donald arrived a few days ago. We are all thankful that he is uninjured and home.

She closed her eyes, put a hand to her lips, and sighed. *Thank You, Lord.* She held the letter to her chest while tears ran down her cheeks. Then she continued reading.

> *I know you and your family rejoice with us. There is such a mood of excitement in Alexandria since the surrender at Yorktown. We hold such hope that hostilities with England will soon cease everywhere.*
>
> *My parents and brothers plan to visit the Green soon as well as travel on to my aunt and uncle in Leesburg. We were hoping that you would return to Alexandria with them and stay at our home for a fortnight or more. It has been too long since we have been together. Charlottesville turned out to be a bit disappointing since I took ill and infected you.*

Mary shuddered. Disappointing hardly, devastating was more like it. She resumed reading.

> *'Twill be such a blessing to have you here to help me prepare a nursery, not to mention provide plenty of opportunities for you and Donald to renew your affections. There may even be a few social events, which I'm sure you are starved for. Though it may mean you will have to miss hog-killing time. Can you stand the loss? I hear you laughing now.*
>
> *Peter is due back from the shop soon. I will close. I'm eager for your visit, dear friend.*
>
> *Jean*

Mary folded the letter. The Duncans were coming. The letter was dated five days prior. They could arrive at any time. She picked up the laundry basket and scampered through the front door into the center hall, setting it down near the stairs before heading through the common room to the kitchen.

Mama kneaded bread at the worktable while the aroma of

stew wafted through the Green. "I could use your help getting dinner served. Douglas has gone for Mark, and your father and the Gordons will join us."

"Smells heavenly. I hope you made plenty in case boarders come later." She waved Jean's letter.

Mama grinned. "A post?"

"A letter from Jean. Donald is home."

"Oh, Mary." She set a round of bread dough down, came around the table, and embraced her. "Praise God!" She stepped back. "He is well? I thought it might be a few more weeks before we heard anything."

Mary nodded and bit her lips for a moment. She must keep her emotions at bay. "Yes, he seems to be fine. Perhaps he came home earlier because of Yorktown. Jean did not say. She and Peter are expecting a child this winter, and she mentioned her parents and brothers would visit soon. The letter is dated five days ago."

Mama returned to the table beaming. "Oh my! Maggie must be pleased to become a grandmother. All is well, and our prayers answered. The Duncans could come at any time."

"Would you care to read Jean's letter? She hopes I will return with her family."

"Aye, let me see it." Mama scanned the page. "Spending time at the O'Brians' sounds grand. 'Twill give you and Donald time together. Exactly what you need." Mama's expression hid nothing. "I will be praying for you, lass, for the right time and opportunity to talk about the things on your hearts. You know that."

Mary peered out the window a moment then sliced the bread. "I'm still of a mixed mind as to what and how to tell him about … it."

"I have been praying about that also. Keeping it from your father has been difficult."

"I'm grateful you honored my request." She picked up the trencher with bread as Papa and the boys came through the back door. The weeks ahead could be life-changing. *Why am I so indecisive? One minute I'm thrilled about Donald's return and the prospect of a future together, and the next minute I'm terrified and want to run away.*

CHAPTER 18

Mary examined the new stays as she slipped the maple busks into the narrow pockets she had stitched. "I would much prefer to be embroidering a pocket or stomacher."

"But the stomacher needs the stays." Martha laid her sewing in her lap. "Do you care for more coffee?"

"No. I should leave. 'Tis late, and I must return home."

"I'm grateful you came. And I'm thrilled about your news of Donald."

"We all are." As she placed the stays in her bag, there was a knock at the door.

Martha put her hemming aside and opened it. "Good day, Philip. Come inside out of the cold."

Mary fought back a smile. At twenty-one, Philip was still as attentive as ever. He did not need to accompany her home.

"I brought these for you, Martha. Wish it could be flowers."

Mary sat up straight and bit her lip. He handed Martha a bunch of holly leaves covered with red berries, and Martha's face appeared only a few shades lighter than the berries.

Surprise etched his face. "I did not know you were here, Mary."

He clearly had not come to escort her home. There would be a better time to ask Martha what this was all about. "Actually, I was getting ready to go home. I'm sure Mama can use my help."

"Yes, she could." Philip gazed at Martha like there was no one else in the room. "The Duncans are there."

"They are?" Mary grabbed her bag with all her sewing and strode toward the door, passing Philip. "I will see you later, Martha. I must go. Good day."

"Wait." Martha brought her cape and placed it over her shoulders. "'Tis cold out there. You need your wrap."

Philip gave her a quick glance. "Be careful. I will be there soon."

Chuckling, she briskly made her way home. Martha did not seem piqued to be the object of Philip's attention—and that might be a good thing. Her heart leapt as she hastened down the path to the Green.

Donald and she together, after so many years. Would they be awkward around each other, or pick up right where they'd left off? Unlikely. She was no longer the lighthearted young lass he had loved. The war—and Charlottesville—had altered everything. How had the time apart changed Donald?

The Green's common room filled Donald with happy memories and wondering if more would be made here. The Stewarts had welcomed him with open arms. Mary would return soon from the Whitcombs' home. He rubbed the back of his neck and wiped his brow. *I'm as nervous as an adolescent anticipating his first kiss.* Would their reunion be as sweet as he hoped? Or awkward? Mary had been in Alexandria the last time he had a courier assignment there, three years ago. No longer the girl he remembered, but a woman. When he'd reminded her he intended to court her, she had encouraged him with words, looks, and a few kisses. *More of that would be nice.*

Mrs. Stewart approached with coffee. He put his hand up. "No, not now. If you don't mind, I would like to speak with the Gordons before supper. I assume they are next door."

"Aye, and they know you arrived with your family." Her pale-blue eyes filled with tears. "They will be glad to see you. Take whatever time you need."

He and his parents exchanged glances before he left the group. They knew he desired to talk to the Gordons about his time with

Todd at the end. He would try to answer any questions they might have.

The door of the Gordon cottage opened when he knocked. Mr. Gordon smiled. "Come inside, Donald. We thought you might come by when we saw your folks' coach."

Mrs. Gordon stood by a settee, older and thinner but with the warm smile he remembered. "Do sit down." She sat on the settee, and Mr. Gordon stood beside her.

Donald sat in the Windsor chair across from her. "I wanted to pay my respects." He leaned forward. "I was with Todd at the end. I'm proud to have known such a fine man and a good soldier."

Mrs. Gordon's lips pressed tightly together. Her arm went around the small girl who approached and snuggled in close to her. "This is our Laura."

"Good day, Laura. 'Tis nice to meet you." She looked much like her mother.

Mr. Gordon walked behind the settee and placed a hand on his wife's shoulder. "Your letter meant so much to us. We also received a note from his commanding officer. He said you carried Todd off the battlefield to a safe place, and you tried to stop his bleeding. We are grateful for your aid, and that he did not have to die alone."

Mrs. Gordon sniffled. "Did he … linger, suffer?"

"No, ma'am. He was lucid until the end and passed peacefully. As I said in the letter, he wanted me to tell you how much he loved his family and that he did not die in vain. Todd sincerely believed the pursuit of liberty was worth … whatever the cost."

Mr. Gordon nodded. "We are proud of Todd. We understand that he is buried with others near Guilford's Courthouse."

"Yes, sir." His eyes darted around the room. "May I ask how Philip has dealt with the loss of his brother? I know they were close."

Mr. Gordon rubbed his chin. "'Tis been rough on him. Even though he was younger, Todd always encouraged Philip. When he left to fight, Philip became more independent. Knowing Todd will not return has made him take on more challenges. He should be back soon, I know he will be as glad for your visit as we are."

"I look forward to seeing him. I should get back to the Green." He picked up his hat.

When he rose to leave, Mrs. Gordon rose and gave him a warm hug. She whispered, "God bless you, Donald."

"I'm privileged to have been there with him."

Mr. Gordon gripped his shoulder briefly. "Godspeed."

The Gordons were outwardly temperate in their grief, but it was obvious their pain was raw. *Will this war cause us all to erect walls around ourselves?* Donald cleared his throat and left the family to grieve in peace. The weight of Todd's death followed him out the door.

Mary entered the kitchen and hung her cape on a nearby hook. *They must all be in the common room.* She could not get upstairs to freshen herself without going through that room. She grabbed the silver plate on the hutch. Peering in it, she smoothed her hair and pinched her cheeks and lips before casually entering the common room. Her heart sank after a quick scan of the area. Where was Donald? Mr. Duncan and Papa sat at the far end of the room talking, and Cameron and Will played a game with Douglas. Donald must be with Mark, or had she misunderstood Jean's letter? She opened her arms as Maggie approached. "'Tis good to see you all again. Jean wrote that you were coming for a visit."

Maggie drew her into an embrace. "Aye, and 'tis been too long. Jean said she told you about the babe."

"Yes, yes she did. You must be thrilled to be a grandmama next year."

"Aye. 'Tis a joyful time for the family, anticipating a new babe and also that Donald is finally home."

Mama came alongside her. "Maggie mentioned Jean and Peter

are eager to have you for a visit."

Mary scanned the room and stiffened. Where was Donald?

"Donald is at the Gordons," Mama added. "He wanted to call on them right away."

She let out a deep breath. He had come. "Of course, he wanted to see them. 'Twill be a bittersweet reminder for the Gordons."

Mama placed a pitcher of water on the table. "How are Martha and her family?"

"They are doing well. Martha and I spent the afternoon sewing and sharing news. I only learned the Duncans had arrived when Philip came."

Mary nodded at Maggie. "And yes, I'm looking forward to a visit with Jean and Peter. I understand you are going to Leesburg to visit your sister."

Maggie smiled. "Aye, Stewarts' Green has been the perfect midpoint to get in a visit here and with my family in Leesburg. We thought you could join us on the return trip Sunday."

"If my parents can spare me, I would be delighted."

"Oh, we can spare you for a fortnight." Mama gave her a knowing grin. "You will be home by hog-killing time."

Mary looked away. "My thoughts exactly. Shall I help you get supper ready?" She must keep busy while she waited for Donald's return. She could fetch water or slice the bread.

They had not been in the kitchen five minutes when the front door creaking made her chest throb. Donald. Would he come through the door from the common room?

Mama watched her. "Go on in there. I can finish."

She took a deep breath and walked toward the door.

"You won't need that knife to greet him," Mama said with a chuckle.

"Right." She shuddered and put the large bread knife down on the table before going to the common room. He stood next to the hearth and turned toward her, grinning as soon as she entered. Those eyes that searched her face and that smile that showed his dimple set her heart fluttering.

'Twas good to be around so many others while they eased into each other's company. How long would it take for them—or perhaps just her—to relax? What if he kissed her? *How will I react if he does?*

CHAPTER 19

Donald's shoulders had filled out, and he was taller and leaner, but as handsome as ever. She approached him with her hands extended. "Welcome home, Donald. We've missed you."

He took her hands and drew her close, planting a kiss on her cheek. "'Tis good to be home and to see you and your family again." He held on to one hand when she stepped back. "I went to see the Gordons, or I would have been here when you got home."

"Well, I was at the Whitcombs' when you arrived, so we're even." His chuckle made her smile, but he appeared as nervous as she felt. "I know it must have been difficult, but I hope your time with the Gordons went well."

He gave a wistful nod.

"Please, sit down. I should get back to the kitchen but—"

"Come here." He sat on the settee and tugged her hand, drawing her closer.

She moved to his side, even though part of her wanted to move farther away. It must have shown in her eyes.

"Don't run away," he said. "The Gordons were very gracious, but Philip was absent."

"He is at the Whitcombs', but I'm sure he will be back soon," she said.

Maggie came alongside her. "You stay here, Mary. I can help Heather."

When Maggie left, she sat next to Donald. A trace of freckles covered his nose and cheeks, and his rusty brown hair was tied back in a queue. "I hardly know what to ask you first."

He glanced at Douglas reading to Sara on the other side of

the room. "When I see the youngsters, I realize how much has changed in the six years I have been gone. Sara had not even been born."

"I know. Everything is different. I mean, one sees the passage of time in young children … even your brothers." How long would this awkwardness between them continue?

He gave her a quizzical nod. "True. I need to get to know them again."

"There will be time now that you are back in Alexandria." Still the same kind-hearted Donald, but older. A distant look flashed in his sea-green eyes. If she asked him what his plans were, he might think she meant in terms of their relationship. "I imagine you will be looking for employment soon."

"Yes, I—"

"Everyone, please gather, supper is ready," Mama called. She and Maggie set platters and bowls on the table. An inviting aroma filled the common room.

Papa gave thanks for the meal and for Donald's safe return before they gathered around the two tables that had been pushed together.

Donald's hand warmed her back as he guided her to the table. He held out a chair and took the seat beside her. She should have been eager for the meal since she had eaten little at dinner. The smoked ham, roasted squash, and freshly baked bread smelled delicious, but her appetite had waned. With eleven at the tables, and everyone talking, a private conversation with Donald would need to wait.

Just as well. She was at a loss as to what she wanted to say.

His answers to all the questions were brief and judicious, but his glances at her were warm. The once spirited boy had matured to a contemplative man. There was an unfamiliar seriousness etched into his face.

When he reached for her hand under the table, her heart beat faster, but she forced herself to take his hand. Had he noticed the change in her? How would he respond when she told him? Pity, anger, disappointment, a wish to escape his earlier declarations? How could she stand it?

Upstairs at Stewarts' Green, Donald lay awake on a pallet in the room with Cameron and Will. He let them take the bed since he was used to far more meager places to rest. They obviously had no trouble getting to sleep. Ma and Pa were in the room next door, and from the sound of Pa's snoring, at least he slept. Hopefully, the racket did not carry to the other end of the hall where the Stewarts' bedrooms were located.

No other guests were staying at the ordinary, which had allowed for their festive meal and sharing of recollections of earlier times. Other than briefly addressing the victory at Yorktown, they had abstained from any talk of war. 'Twas obvious the younger boys had been admonished to avoid any such discussion. They had not brought it up since he returned home.

Thoughts and impressions flooded his mind. Stewarts' Green remained the same, but the younger children had truly changed. Mary also seemed different. *Take it slow with her.* They each needed some time together to determine if they still wanted a courtship.

He rose from the pallet and went to the window. The large, clear moon lit the front yard of the Green. No enemy soldiers in sight. Would he always study his surroundings this scrupulously?

The Gordons' cottage was dark. At least the meeting with them had gone as well as he could hope. The pain in Todd's parents' eyes wrenched his gut. Such a fine young man, but there were many good men lost, others severely wounded. Would they survive or ever have a normal life? *Must not think of those things.*

Mary had grown even lovelier. Seeing her, touching her, and hearing her low voice had brought on more emotions than he could put words to. He desired her as much as ever. She had changed, grown more reserved, not the vivacious lass he remembered.

Was her reserved demeanor because she was hesitant about their future together?

He had to believe that the awkwardness would vanish, and the feelings they had for each other would strengthen as they spent more time together. Mary's presence in Alexandria for the next fortnight would give them each a better sense of how to proceed.

He must tread carefully if they were to have a chance to recapture what they'd once had.

Meet me at the fence behind the barn when you get up. Donald

Mary's heart raced as she fumbled trying to get her stays tied. She glanced again at the parchment on her washstand. Donald must have shoved it under her bedroom door either during the night or early this morning. Overslept—again. Falling asleep the night before had taken forever. Would he still be waiting for her?

He wanted to be alone with her. She pressed her hands to her waist. Hopefully, it would be less awkward than last night. She nearly tripped, trying to reach the door without having her pigskin shoe fully on. *Slow down before you kill yourself. If he is not there, well—*

She all but ran down the center hall stairs and waved at Maggie and Mama as she scooted through the common room.

Polly greeted her in the kitchen. "You need not gather the eggs this morning. Douglas did that and fed the chickens. There are biscuits and bacon left."

She offered a sheepish smile for not being up earlier to help. "There is an errand I—"

"Donald breakfasted and said he is waiting." Polly muffled a laugh. "For mercy's sake, lass, put your cloak on. 'Tis November."

She grabbed it as she opened the door. Throwing it over her shoulders, she suddenly stopped. *Why am I so eager? I love him, but—he doesn't know what happened. Stop being so fearful. Take it one step at a time.* She slowed as she walked around the barn. Donald leaned on the fence, his back to her with one foot perched on a lower rail.

He turned as she approached. "So, the lady has finally arisen. Good to see certain things have not changed over the years."

"Oh hush!" She drew near the fence. "Are we going to study the cattle, or do you enjoy frosty November mornings?"

"I invited you here for a reason. Can you guess why?" He had that engagingly twisted smile that accented the dimple on his left cheek.

"Too early for a test, or are we playing a game?"

"You obviously have forgotten the last morning we stood here. Many years ago … and much earlier in the morning."

Her face warmed, but she did not turn away. "How could I ever forget. We stood here when you told me you were planning to join the militia." She placed her hands on the top rail and gave him a sly smile. She could mention he first kissed her that morning.

"You do remember." His hand slid over the top rail to where her left hand rested.

Her eyes met his. "I recall everything, Donald. 'Tis all I had to hold onto these long years."

He searched her face with a depth she had never seen before and squeezed her hand. "Shall we go for a walk to the pond?"

How do I tell him? "I would like that." The musty smell and crunch of dry leaves were a reminder of the end of a season. Did it also foretell the end of a season for them? They walked silently. Was he also trying to figure out how to move forward in their relationship?

He placed her hand in the crook of his arm and led her toward the bench by the pond. "Jean is already planning activities for your stay." He brushed leaves off the bench. "I'm eager for us to have time to talk and get reacquainted after being apart this long."

"I agree." Perhaps she should wait to say anything about

Charlottesville. It might be easier to figure a way to tell him after they had spent more time together in Alexandria—or might it be wiser to end it? *Caution or cowardice?* Could he hear her stomach churn?

He motioned for her to sit, settled beside her. They stared at the pond. "I need to find employment soon. If the war is truly ending, there will be many other men in my situation seeking work."

She sighed. "I keep thinking about the men who will not return … like Todd, and Owen Lamont."

"And Tobias. I had no knowledge of the Whitcombs' tragedy." His head bowed. "Too many men will not return. Others will come home injured and struggle to find work they can do. I know how fortunate I am."

Why had she brought up the losses? She needed to encourage him. "What will you do?" She pulled the cloak tight and wrapped her hands in it. She should have worn gloves.

"I'm not certain. Pa wants me to work for the city administration like he has these many years. He wasted no time introducing me to a few of the town aldermen."

"That sounds hopeful. And your father's connections should be to your advantage." He stared at the pond without a hint of enthusiasm for the opportunity.

"I'm not sure I'm best suited for that." He turned toward her. "I want to know more about what you have been doing in my absence, besides helping with the ordinary and farm. Jean tells me that you came for visits to Alexandria and that you accompanied Peter and her to Charlottesville." He took her other hand in his. "How did you like that part of Virginia?"

Her mouth went dry. Despite the chilly air, a warm sensation rose in her. She pulled her clammy hands away. "We saw little of it, and 'tis a place I don't care to revisit." *Tell him the truth about the attack or release him from our previous promises. He deserves that.*

"Oh." He rubbed his hands together. "Jean said she became ill and that you did also. That might color your impression." He put his arm across the back of the bench and faced her. "I traveled through many beautiful areas on my way north. I might want to settle someplace other than Alexandria." He studied her response.

That was it, an attempt to let her down easy, tell her that he wanted a different life. "'Tis understandable that you might want to explore new places. People's interests change over time."

He sat back, and his brows furrowed. "During that last eighteenth-month enlistment, I made a friend who lives in the Shenandoah Valley, Boyd Alexander. He was injured but not too badly. Since he still had little use of one arm, we traveled back to Virginia together. Boyd lives in the valley near Lexington with his parents and sister. He wants to get his own land and farm. Seems there might be interesting opportunities around there." His expression seemed hopeful. "I've given thought about learning the printing trade."

"That is commendable, but I'm sure your family would be sad to see you leave." She would grieve his departure, but perhaps having him far away would make parting easier for both of them. "'Tis cold. We should get back. I promised to help with the cleaning."

His shoulders sagged when he stood. "How thoughtless of me to keep you out and with no gloves. I wanted time alone with you to share our thoughts. We will be able to talk later in Alexandria."

"Of course." They retraced their steps to the Green.

He wanted to leave the area. If he was still intent on a courtship, surely he would want to remain nearby. Did his tender gestures signal his continued affection, or was he trying to minimize the hurt in releasing her? Her stomach churned. They needed to be forthright with one another. Alexandria would settle it.

It must.

Donald braced himself against the side of the rocking coach on the way to Leesburg the next day. Pa and Ma chatted with the boys seated in front of him. 'Twas good to be with the family again even though occasionally the conversation grew stilted. Cameron and William were young men, not the little boys he'd left behind. He would need to engage them more to get to know them. Ma and Pa never changed.

In a couple of days, they would return to Stewarts' Green for Mary. What was Mary thinking? *I tried to break through her reserve, but her manner and remarks yesterday were confusing. I suspected it might be difficult to pick up right where we left off. But I thought…*

Mary had been cordial, even lighthearted at times, but her comments about people's interests changing unnerved him. Did she mean her interest in him had changed? One minute her eyes were full of love. The next, she seemed distant. Time together in Alexandria should ease his anxiety and answer his questions.

"We should be there in another hour," Pa said.

"I hope we do not have to sleep with Donald again tonight." Cameron glowered over his shoulder. "He near scared Will and me to death when he woke us up screaming."

Ma turned in her seat. "Enough of that, lad. You should be grateful he is home." She glanced his way, then back at Pa.

He groaned. The nightmares that destroyed his peace left him sweating and, at times, sick to his stomach. They were beyond his control. If they annoyed his brothers, they would upset Mary. Did he want to terrify a bride? Easygoing Boyd did not seem to suffer from night terrors, but he understood. If he intended to ask for Mary's hand, he must first tell her of his struggles. He had to be honest with her and hope she would be patient and accepting.

CHAPTER 20

Mary lingered over last evening's moments alone with Donald as the coach rolled on. Some guests had arrived at five, an hour before the Duncans returned from Leesburg. With the added work, it was past nine when Donald urged her to slip away to the barn. Once inside, he'd taken her in his arms and was about to tell her something when Papa entered. Was Donald going to renew his desire to court her? *Agh!* The coach bumped over a rut. Well, once they reached Alexandria, they would have more time together.

She breathed in the autumn scents of many wood-burning fires and the city sounds of coaches, horses, and people. The twenty-mile trip from Stewarts' Green had been pleasant and full of chatter. She and Donald had exchanged pleasantries in the back seat, but he seemed satisfied to let Cameron and Will carry most of the conversation. Donald mentioned a couple of meetings he needed to attend that week with prospective employers, so perhaps he was planning on staying in Alexandria after all. But he acted indifferently. Perhaps he was tired. Maggie had whispered to her that his sleep had been fitful.

As they entered Alexandria, Donald stared ahead deep in thought. Was he worried about finding work? *Perhaps he wants to secure employment before approaching Papa.* While she looked forward to more time together in the next few days, the lump in her throat was a reminder she needed to find the courage and the words to tell him about Charlottesville.

The coach came to a stop in front of a brick row house on Fairfax Street.

"Here we are," Mr. Duncan said.

She studied the O'Brians' home while leaning closer to Donald. "I recognize this street. 'Tis not far from your home."

Jean came out of the front door grinning, her disappearing waist a reminder of her approaching motherhood. "'Tis so good to see you." Jean extended her arms from where she stood at the edge of the coach.

Donald exited first and extended his arms to Mary. "Allow me to help you down."

Her heart fluttered when she lingered a moment in his arms before stepping back. His moods had been changeable and, at times, hard to understand.

Now, his teasing smile tugged at her heart. "I will get your case."

What did Donald want from her? Finding that out would be her goal during her time in Alexandria. They needed to be able to settle where they stood with each other to face their futures. Together or apart.

She hugged Jean. "'Tis good to see you. Your condition has given you a lovely glow."

Jean called to the others. "Come inside, out of the chilly air." She ushered them into a warm gathering room filled with interesting pieces of furniture. "Peter will be back as soon as he is finished meeting with a client. I made hot chocolate for us."

Adam and Donald carried her portmanteau upstairs.

Mary followed Jean to the kitchen while Maggie and the younger boys warmed themselves by the hearth. "Your home is lovely. Did Peter make the furniture?"

"Most of it." Jean's eyes lit up as she filled the cups on a tray with steaming chocolate. "He's trying some new styles and filling our house with them."

They are lovely." She picked up the tray. "I can carry this." Jean and she returned to the gathering as Peter came through the door.

"Welcome to our home, Mary. I see Jean has already put you to work." He grinned as he took the tray from her and placed it on the table. "Please help yourselves."

Mary curtsied. "I'm delighted and will gladly help Jean in any way I can while I'm here."

"Good. I believe she has a list. And the more you do, the less I must."

The laughter calmed her unsettled emotions. Donald and his father returned, and the gathering took on a festive atmosphere.

Donald approached her, grinning. "Your laughter is a sound I truly missed. While you are here, we must put the frustrations of the past years behind us and enjoy the present."

Welcome words and his sea-green eyes wrinkled at the outer edges, endeared him, and made him as appealing as ever. Was it foolish to hold out hope?

❦

A bell attached to the door rang as Donald entered Brady's Mercantile. It looked the same after so many years. Iron hardware, tools, leather goods, and horse harnesses lined the far wall. Brooms were in the corners. Lanterns, ropes, and buckets hung from the ceiling. Shelves contained clothing, nuts, soaps, spices, crockery, iron pots, jars of preserved food, and much more. There were barrels of grain, and who knew what else. Two chairs sat next to a barrel with a game of draughts perched on top. Brady's was a place to meet and palaver as much as purchase needed wares.

He had only been back from Stewarts' Green and Leesburg a week, and already he had met with one of the aldermen. As expected, that held no interest. Pa said Mr. Brady also wanted to speak with him about a job. Initially, he had been reluctant to go. What did he know about working in a shop? Mr. Brady spoke with a customer in the corner, so Donald walked over to a bin of cartridges and shells. Muskets booming, the acrid scent of gunpowder, and soldiers crumpling to the ground invaded his thoughts.

"Donald, ya haven trouble hearing me, lad?" Mr. Brady stood next to him, grimacing.

How long had he been staring at the ammunition? "What?"

"I called ya, and ya seemed to be elsewhere."

"No, sir, I'm right here. Pa said you wanted to talk with me about possible employment."

"Come and sit over here with me. The store is empty." Mr. Brady pulled out a chair by the draught board and motioned for him to do the same. "My boy was killed at a place called Eutaw Springs." Mr. Brady's lips tightened, and he rocked back and forth in his chair.

"I'm sorry. I did not know Edward well. He was a couple of years younger than me."

"Been two months since he passed, but we only heard about it a month ago. The wife has taken ill and cannot assist me here. With my boy never coming home, I need help, a man who wants to learn the trade. Business should get better with more river trade when the war ends." He nodded in the direction of the wharf. "Does it interest ya?"

"I have been thinking of learning a trade, and I appreciate your consideration."

"You served our cause, our country. You came home." The proprietor rubbed his forehead and stood. "I will show you around, and you can let me know in the next day or so."

A man Donald didn't know entered the shop and put a scrap of paper on the counter.

Donald nodded. "Go help him. I can wait." He wandered over to a shelf and examined a blue-and-cream-colored bowl. 'Twould make a nice gift for Peter and Jean since he had not been there for their wedding. Two matching candle stands stood beside it.

"Sorry to hear about your boy, Brady." The man's deep voice carried. "My boy was lost at Waxhaws. I hope that somebody hangs that cold-blooded murderer, Tarleton."

Donald choked. *Tarleton*. His neck tightened. Memories

returned of Tarleton's Dragoons, their green-coated officers ordering the attack on surrendering Patriots—men not resisting. So many died, even more wounded. His head throbbed. Clenching his hand, he flung his arm across the shelf, sending pottery flying. The shattering crockery obliterated the shop's peace. His mouth went dry at the shocked stares of the men. He bent over, hands on his knees, struggling for breath. When he stood, the disappointed look in Brady's eyes turned his stomach. He had to get out of there. "I'm sorry. I will pay for the damage."

He stormed out the door and ran toward a grove of trees at the edge of town. When he finally stopped, he leaned against a tree, breathing heavily. What was he thinking? Why had he struck out? He had never been a hot-tempered or violent person. Why did he run instead of cleaning up the mess? *What a coward*. That would be the end of any job at Brady's.

Mary sewed pieces on the quilt for Jean and Peter's baby at the table. "Whatever is cooking smells wonderful. May I help? I can put this aside."

Jean called from the kitchen. "Keep working on the quilt. You know I'm not adept at sewing. I always relied on Ma to do that. 'Tis a meat pie for dinner."

She returned to her handwork, eager to see it in the beautiful cradle Peter had made for the baby. "Did you think Donald seemed withdrawn when we were at your parents' last night?"

Jean appeared in the kitchen doorway. "I don't know what has gotten into him. He hardly said a word at supper or the rest of the evening. When Peter asked him about his meeting with Mr. Brady, he snapped at him and walked out of the room. So unlike him." She retreated to the kitchen.

Mary put down the piece she was working on and closed her eyes. The meeting with Mr. Brady had not gone well. She'd overheard Donald tell his father he lost his temper at the shop, even breaking pottery. "He must feel driven to find employment." She had been at Jean's a week. Donald's demeanor had been pleasant, even at times mischievous. But he had also been uncharacteristically withdrawn on occasion.

Jean reappeared in the doorway with a tray. "I have hot cider." She ambled in and set the tray down on the table and frowned. "Donald was not very enthusiastic about his meetings with the aldermen Pa introduced him to. Has he mentioned some other interest he wants to pursue?"

Mary pushed the footstool nearer to Jean's chair. "Put your feet up. You look weary." She took one of the steaming cups and smiled. "He has spoken of apprenticing as a printer. I hope to learn more about it tomorrow after church when we go for dinner."

"Ah yes, Donald mentioned he had special plans for the two of you tomorrow, and that you would be gone most of the day."

She fanned her face with a scrap of cloth. "We are to dine at the Cameron Street Tavern and walk along the river."

Jean rubbed her belly. "We shall be at my parents' for dinner after services but should return by four. I doubt you will be home before that. Nevertheless, we keep a key to the house underneath the pot on the gravel path by the garden."

Mary sipped the warm brew. "Good to know in case the weather shortens our walk." She rubbed the back of her neck. Tomorrow, she would tell him about Charlottesville. Otherwise, she would spend the rest of her life wondering. *I don't want to live a life of what-ifs. I need to know if he can live with what happened.*

CHAPTER 21

Donald and his family lingered in a field outside Christ Church chatting with other members of the congregation after the service. He approached Mary as she left Jean and the group of women. "Are you ready for our outing?"

"By all means." She took his extended arm, and they said their goodbyes to the others and headed down Cameron Street toward the wharf.

The brisk but sunny day held great promise. Excitement pulsed through him. Asking for her hand at the tavern would be too public. *Wait until later on our walk.* Proposing prior to securing a job was audacious, but he wanted her assured of his commitment. Hopefully, she felt likewise. "I'm glad you remembered your gloves. I thought we might enjoy a meal and then walk along the quay and river for a bit? Are you cold?"

"I'm comfortable." She squeezed his arm. "What did you think of this morning's sermon?"

An opening to share his concerns. "No surprise, he spoke about peace. 'Tis all people talk about these days after the victory at Yorktown." He shook his head. "Peace is more than the absence of conflict on the battlefield. People search for peace within themselves, which may be more elusive … especially if one struggles to forget the evil they have experienced or lives with guilt."

Mary stopped, removed her arm, and stared at him. She paled, and her eyes grew wide.

Had he offended her? He meant to address his difficulties, not to encourage that barrier she too easily erected. "Come, the Cameron Street Tavern is only a block away."

Her smile was tentative. "'Tis the ordinary where we stayed when we came to town for Peter and Jean's wedding. Their food is quite good."

"Ah, yes, the wedding." He chuckled. "I regret missing that, but I was otherwise occupied in the Carolinas."

"'Twas a beautiful wedding and a festive dinner, but we all felt your absence."

"I confess to jealousy at the time since I assumed Peter's brother would be in attendance." He grinned. "How could an absent beau compete for your affections with the charming Patrick O'Brian?" Teasing her always brought out her spunky nature.

She laughed. "Well, the 'charming Patrick O'Brian' did not wait for me to extinguish his ardor. At the wedding, he privately announced his intentions to court another."

"Humph! Is that right? And all that fretting I did for nothing."

She punched his arm with her elbow.

"Well, I'm pleased for him … for many reasons." His eyes met hers, and for a moment, they stared at each other. In front of the closed tailor's shop, he drew her close, peered up and down the vacant street. He leaned in, kissed her, and lingered. Her sweet lips and soft moan invited another deeper kiss, but she pulled away, and caution filled her eyes. Still holding her arms, he backed off. "Forgive my boldness, my lack of discretion in public. I have been wanting to do that, and there have been few opportunities these last ten days."

She shook her head. "Don't apologize. I meant—" she sighed and turned her head. "There is the tavern. Shall we go inside?"

"Certainly." He opened the heavy oak door and followed her inside. The smell of roasting meat wafted from the dining area on the right. The only other patrons were a family seated by the hearth. The heat from the stone hearth made the atmosphere inviting.

A server approached. "I can give you a large table if there will be more joining you. Otherwise, may I offer you a smaller table by the window?"

Donald removed his hat. "There are only two of us." He searched Mary's face. "The window table?"

"Yes. The light is cheerful and makes it easier to read the bill of fare."

He helped her remove her cloak and take a seat at the square table.

Looking into her beautiful eyes took his breath away. Anticipating more kisses by the end of the day was enticing. *Stop leering at her.* He took the bill of fare the server gave him. "Since you have eaten here more recently, do you have any recommendations?"

"We enjoyed the shepherd's pie, but I'm tempted by the smell of the roast turkey." She surveyed the room as other people entered and were seated. "Do you suppose they are travelers staying at the ordinary or people from town?"

"Local taverns are a favorite place for people to go after church, particularly after sitting in a cold, drafty sanctuary." He took a deep breath when their server brought roast turkey, sweet potatoes, cornbread, and beans. "I hope this tastes as good as it smells."

The server grinned. "Enjoy your meal. Next week we will have venison. Cook tells me several large bucks were spotted on the edge of town."

He sobered as he took a bite of turkey. How many hungry soldiers wished for fare like this today? *Focus on the future, not the past.* "Your days here have gone by too quickly. I'm grateful for the meetings Pa set up, but they hold no interest. And, I have been distracted by thoughts of you ... we need more time together."

Mary's eyes lit up as she leaned forward. "I agree. You have been on my mind also. Tell me more about the printing business. People always seem to want to know what is happening locally and even elsewhere."

"Exactly what I thought, and there are not many towns with periodicals." He sat back in his chair. Mary looked enthused, every reason to believe she would want to join him in his venture into printing. Hopefully, he could find a position soon, and they could be married. Within the hour, he hoped to know her answer.

Mary pushed the vegetables around her plate, while Donald did most of the talking. He was excited about seeking a position apprenticing in the printing business. He had grown more serious as well as older, but then so had she. They had each experienced a great deal apart from each other. Yet, when he kissed her, it ignited something within her, and it felt like no time had passed at all. Perhaps intimacy would not prove difficult.

She took a bite of turkey, but his comments about forgetting the evil they had experienced, and living with guilt, made it hard to swallow. Only Mama knew about Charlottesville. If they ever hoped to have a life together, she had to tell him about the attack. Today, on their walk.

He squinted. "Mary, where are you? I have been gibbering on, and you seem far away."

"Forgive me. I *was* listening to you, but my mind wandered."

"The printer in Alexandria told me about the business, but his son is his apprentice, so he has no position to offer."

Donald did not appear upset. "How disappointing. Does that mean you will be leaving Alexandria?" What would his departure mean for them?

He leaned forward. "There are other villages and towns that may have better opportunities."

She sighed. "I'm sure you are right."

"I have some thoughts I want to share with you when we are finished here."

She folded her napkin and forced a smile. "'Twas delicious but 'tis enough."

He paid for their meal, and they went outside. She took his arm. The sun shone as they walked toward the quay. "I must find a master printer to work under. Then, in time, perhaps I could start my own printshop."

The way his eyes lit when he spoke of his plans warmed her. "Are there any master printers in any towns around here?"

"Not sure. I want to publish a news journal but would need other printing jobs, as well. The troops craved information from home and other places. They were curious about how the other assemblies or state bodies reacted to the events of the day."

He had given this plan much thought. "Visitors to the Green always want the Gazette, even if certain information in it seemed rather trivial. How many readers throughout the region need to know about Farmer Brown's missing cows in Williamsburg?"

"Right, but the advertising of goods and land to sell is also important to people. As Virginia villages grow, I suspect more news periodicals will spring up."

Her hands grew warm, and her heart began to race. *Direct the discussion to Charlottesville.*

"In a few days, you return to Stewarts' Green. Are you eager to get back to the country and your family, or are you still partial to city life?"

That question begged more than mere polite conversation. She peeled her gloves off her perspiring hands. "I enjoy city life, but I realize while I'm here, I'm a guest. Were I to live in Alexandria all the time, I would have responsibilities like everyone else." She glanced sideways. "I also love being at Stewarts' Green with my family and the wide-open spaces of rural Virginia."

They stopped near two benches, and she moved close to him on the quay as they observed the Potomack's teal waves. He turned to her. His expectant gaze was full of love. *Tell him before this goes any further.*

He took her arm. "You are shaking. Are you warm enough?"

"Yes, I'm fine." Plenty warm, in fact, she was perspiring.

The wind blew the waves toward the tree-lined river. *Courage, Mary.* "You asked me a while back what I thought about Charlottesville, and I must tell you about our time there."

He put his hand over hers. "I know you were ill while there, but 'tis a charming place."

"Yes, I know."

He wiped his brow. "There is something I wanted to discuss with you."

⊙⚜⊙

Donald's heart raced. He motioned to one of the benches. "Would you care to sit a while?"

She nodded. "Yes, by all means."

He settled her on the bench and then sat beside, close enough that their shoulders brushed. Had they had walked too long? Mary was breathless.

He took her hand. "These last few years have been hard, and it means everything to me that you waited. I …"

"Wait. I must tell you something first." The anguish in her eyes and expression was heartbreaking. Was she going to turn him down before he even asked? But she seemed so…

A musket fired. *The enemy was here in town and no warning.* Terror surged through him. *Protect Mary.* But he had no gun. The pounding in his chest, neck, and ears returned, making her words inaudible. He grabbed her arms and threw her to the ground, then flung himself on top of her. Her piercing scream, like a trapped red fox, stunned him. The confusing look in her eyes as she struggled to free herself penetrated his soul.

"Mary, I only …" Her fist hit his cheek hard, knocking his head against the side of the bench. Lights flashed with the pain.

She pulled away and stood. "Never, never do that again!" she screamed. Her shrill voice and the rage in her eyes stunned him.

His heart still racing, he staggered to his feet, looking around. Were they still threatened? His shoulders sagged. She was running back toward town. "Mary! Stop. Mary, come back." *What have I done?* He grasped the back of the bench. She grew smaller, the faster and farther away she ran. *Impulsive again. But who fires shots in town, scaring the wits out of folks?*

His head throbbed as he followed her back toward the center of town, and his chest pounded. Mary's anger, disgust, and words cut to the quick. He had frightened her, and she wanted no part of him. Any hope of marriage seemed over, but what did he have to offer her anyway, a man who could not control his emotions and actions? He had lost control at Brady's, and now he had terrified Mary. *I don't deserve her. She needs the freedom to find the life and partner she deserves. Put this all behind you.*

His future demanded a fresh start someplace else.

CHAPTER 22

Mary ran all the way back to the O'Brians' home, tears rolling down her cheeks. She had hit him—and screamed at him. When the gun fired, Donald had thrown himself on her to protect her. *I was about to tell him—but my nerves got the best of me again. What must he be thinking?* Tired and still shaking, she gasped for air as she slowed her pace.

When she knocked at the O'Brians' door, no one answered. *They must still be at the Duncans'.* The key. Jean had said she placed a key under a pot in the garden. She headed through the gate to the back.

Once inside, Mary left the key on the hall table. She lit a lantern, took her cloak to the kitchen, and dampened a rag. Would the muddy stain on the cloak come out or be a perpetual reminder of this disastrous day? After rubbing the stain out as best she could, she returned to the front room with the lantern. The clock on the mantel struck five. Too late to walk to the Duncans'. When Jean arrived, she could find out if Donald had returned home. Early tomorrow morning, she would go there, ask his forgiveness, and explain why she overreacted. *Tell him about Charlottesville.*

Restless, she walked to the kitchen and heated some coffee. The sound of the front door opening jolted her. Jean entered the kitchen, smiling.

"I saw the key on the front table. I'm surprised you are back so soon." Jean tilted her head. "You look pale. Are you unwell?"

"I'm fine. Did Donald arrive home before you left?"

Jean tilted her head. "No. What has upset you? Is it because you are returning home in a few days?"

"No. I ... oh 'tis not important." She couldn't tell Jean, it would only bring on questions she wasn't prepared to answer.

"The time has gone by too quickly. Would you mind helping me with a few alterations tomorrow? Your sewing skills far surpass mine."

"We could do that now if you like." *Anything to put aside today's calamity.*

"If you are not too tired. Let me take this to Peter, and I will be right back. Then, I want to hear about your afternoon. I thought you might have some exciting news to share." Jean winked and left with Peter's coffee.

Exciting news? Today's disaster was more a tragedy—one she would need to rectify tomorrow. If she could.

❦

Donald left the barn and entered the house through the back door. No need to disturb the family—yet. He headed upstairs, avoiding the planks where the stairs creaked.

Ma came around the corner, her eyes wide. "Home already? We did not expect you back yet."

"Is Pa home?"

"Aye, in the front room. Cameron and Will are next door but should be back soon." She frowned. "Is something wrong?"

"No, Ma. I will be down in a few minutes." He smiled, but that crease on her brow suggested she saw through his feigned composure. They would not be pleased with his news, but in time would understand. They loved him.

When he came downstairs carrying his haversack, he took a deep breath before heading to the front room.

Pa sat in his chair, his greying brows drew together. "Where are you going?"

Ma, sitting near the hearth, put her mending aside. Her pinched lips tore at his heart.

"I'm leaving Alexandria. There are things I need to do to move forward. Pa, I appreciate all you have done to try to aid me in securing employment, but these prospects are not a good fit for me. As I told you, I want to pursue the printing business. You both have been wonderful parents, but 'tis time for me to make a life for myself."

Ma stood. Her jaw hung open for a moment before she went to him. "What happened today?" She took his arm. "Where is Mary?"

"There is no future for me here. I have been thinking for a while of going west."

"What about Mary and your plans with her?" Ma's grip tightened, and her eyes bore a hole in him.

No time to go soft. "Over the years, Mary and I have grown apart, and our plans have changed. She deserves someone she genuinely cares for, a man who can give her far more than I can offer."

The front door opened, and Will came into the room. "We were in the barn and saw your mare saddled." Cameron followed behind him and stared at the haversack hanging on his shoulder. "Are you leaving?"

"Yes, and I expect you two to be good and not give the folks any trouble."

Pa stood and approached him. The concern on his face pained him. "Where are you going?"

"West. Not sure yet where I will settle. Depends where I find work."

Pa nodded. "You may be right about the printing business. Our nation is changing, and I suspect there is a hunger for information."

"Wait till the morning, son." Ma's lip quivered. "You might feel differently."

He swallowed hard. "No, Ma, I need to get away."

Tears formed in her eyes. "You will let us know where you settle."

"Of course, I will." He rubbed his aching forehead. He had hurt her, but when he got established, she would see the wisdom in his choice. "It may take time to find the right situation."

He hugged her then shook Pa's hand. "I'm grateful for all you have done for me." He roughed up each of his brothers' hair. "And you two take care of yourselves. Give Jean my best wishes." He turned and walked toward the back door.

"Wait," Ma called after him. "Take victuals with you." She grabbed a loaf of bread and dried meat, stuffing them in a canvas sack before giving him another hug. "We love you and will be praying for you, son."

"I know. I love you all."

He did. He loved Mary too, but he couldn't ask her to live with him … not the way the war had left him.

The mirror over the dresser reflected the telltale signs of another sleepless night on Mary's face. She rubbed the circles under her eyes. Her appearance was of no consequence. Seeking Donald's forgiveness—and explaining the reason for her reaction was all that mattered.

When she entered the kitchen, Peter stood. "You are up early. There is coffee and bread if you would like. I must leave for the shop, but Jean will be down soon."

She offered him as cheerful a smile as she could manage. "Thank you. I will enjoy a few minutes of quiet before the day starts."

After Peter left, she took a stoneware tankard of coffee into the front room and sat on the chair by the window. Outside, the wind blew leaves across the road. How would Donald respond to her revelation? Would he forgive her? She searched the desk for paper, ink, and a quill. A note to Jean would suffice, so she would not be concerned about her absence. The clock on the mantel showed nearly seven, Maggie would be up. 'Twas time.

The cold air felt good against her skin as she strode toward the Duncan home.

Maggie's startled expression greeted her when the older woman opened their front door.

"Miss Maggie, I …"

"Come in out of the cold, lass." She ushered her into the front room and took her cloak. "Sit down. Let me pour you a cup of beef tea to warm you after that walk."

"I know 'tis early, but I need to speak with Donald."

Maggie's eyebrows lifted. "Did you two quarrel?" She handed her the steaming mug.

"Not exactly. More a misunderstanding … and 'twas all my fault."

Maggie came alongside and hugged her. "I wish I could help you, lass."

Mary sniffled, she brought her fingers to her lips. "Please, I need to talk with Donald."

"I'm sure you do, but he is not here. He left last night, and I cannot even tell you where he went."

"What?" Her stomach knotted. "No! No." *Gone? How can I tell him I was wrong to run away—and why?*

CHAPTER 23

Three days after leaving Alexandria, Donald neared Charlottesville. Tonight, he needed to be more selective after spending last night at a dingy, rat-infested tavern. He could make camp, but the cold necessitated he find a cleaner ordinary. Spending as little as possible would make his resources last longer. Another two-day ride would get him to Boyd's place near Lexington.

With any luck, he'd find a job there, before his money ran out.

An occupation and seeing Boyd again would help get his mind off Mary. Long hours in the saddle had given him too much time to think—mostly about disappointing her and his family. The nightmares plagued him most nights, but at least he no longer woke Cameron and Will. He wrapped the scarf Ma made him tighter around his head to get warm. His ears and throat ached.

The wooden signboard hanging outside a lit establishment provided all the welcome he needed. He dismounted and tied his mare to a post before going inside. The aroma of roasting meat coming from the direction of the dining room distracted him from the woman asking questions.

"I said, did you want a room?" She raised her voice. "You want to eat, too?"

"Yes, yes, ma'am." Donald removed his scarf. "Is there a place to board my mare?"

"Around back in the barn. Husband's out there and will provide feed and water. You can have room four upstairs." She pointed to the dining area. "When you get back, go on in and take a seat. I will bring you a plate."

"Much obliged."

Thirty minutes later, his stomach satisfied, Donald stared at the empty plate and downed the last of the hot cider, soothing his raw throat. Mary was likely back at the Green by now and glad to be rid of him. She baffled him, wavering between warm and encouraging to being aloof. Had she erected a wall between them, or had she simply lost interest? How could he have been so wrong about her feelings for him? When he had panicked and frightened her … her fury would be etched in his mind forever. Any hope of a future with her was dead.

He shivered even though the fire blazed from the dining room hearth. *Probably coming down with a cold.* Would the room upstairs be warm? Mattered little, exhaustion demanded sleep.

He held on to one last hope that Boyd Alexander might have some contacts in Lexington or thereabouts where he could find employment. The man was sure to offer wisdom and encouragement. Donald wasn't too proud to admit to himself that he could use some of both.

He had been impetuous again, departing Alexandria in haste. Running away from trouble was a recent failing, one he needed to conquer. It probably wouldn't take Mary long to realize she was better off without him.

But how long would it take him to get over loving her?

After finally getting Sara settled, Mary unpacked her trunk and returned her clothes to the wardrobe. She sat on the edge of her bed and sighed. As much as she enjoyed the city, 'twas good to be home and away from the anguish of the last few days. When the Duncans' neighbors mentioned they were traveling to Leesburg and offered to take her to Stewarts' Green, she'd gratefully accepted. Leaving early saved Papa a trip.

She removed her gown and readied for bed. Mama had been busy with their guests, and Papa and Mark were making some stall repairs in the barn. Free from the conversation with family and alone, she let her mind drift.

Donald's unexpected departure and Maggie's words had haunted her ever since. Donald said he was going west, and that their plans had changed. "She deserves someone she genuinely cares for and a man who can give her far more than I can."

Oh, Donald, if you only knew how much I care. She wiped her face with a handkerchief. *How can I tell you how sorry I am for running away and for not being honest with you?* She crawled under her quilt. *God, please protect and guide him as he seeks the future he wants.*

Mama entered the henhouse in the morning as Mary gathered eggs. "I was looking for you. I wanted to hear about your time in Alexandria, but you were sleeping when I checked on you last night." She tilted her head. "You seemed troubled yesterday when you got home. What happened, lass?"

Mama would understand. She picked up the remaining eggs. "Have the guests gone?"

"Aye. Sara is with Laura and Polly. The boys and men are butchering the hogs, so I will be busy later. Can we talk now?"

Mary nodded. "I will watch the girls if Polly wants to help you with the hogs."

Mama's brows lifted. "Aye, we thought you might prefer that to salting the meat. Come, we can have some privacy in my room."

She followed Mama inside and set the basket on the kitchen table. Talking with Mama might quell the despair she felt.

Seated beside Mama on the bed, she poured out the events of her visit. "I ruined everything." She sniffled. "'Twas obvious Donald wanted to speak about our future. I was about to tell him what happened in Charlottesville." Her throat thickened. "To be honest with him before he declared himself."

Mama took her hand. "I'm proud of you. That took courage."

She shook her head. "I was already nervous when the gunfire interrupted our conversation. I never had the chance to tell him. Now, all is lost." Her last word came out more of a sob.

Mama sighed. "Not necessarily, though it may seem so right now."

Mary rose and paced. "How can you say that? Donald is gone, and we have no assurance that he will ever return."

Mama drew near with a reassuring smile. "My dear, he will write to his family and let them know how and where he found employment. He is a thoughtful son and will keep in contact with his parents. When we learn where he is, you can write to him and explain your feelings."

She walked to the window. "If Donald's feelings for me have changed, I do not want him to be under any sense of obligation."

"He loves you. Anyone can see that. We can pray that this misunderstanding will be resolved."

"I hurt him. Please pray he can forgive me and will write to his family soon."

"Of course. Donald's not the sort to hold a grudge. But you must be patient, dear. This may take time."

She bit her lip. "You know patience is not a virtue of mine."

"Perhaps you are being given an opportunity to refine that virtue." Mama wiped her hands on her apron. "I need to go. Polly is waiting for me."

She nodded. "I know. I will see to the girls and make supper."

"Good. Martha came by two days ago, wondering when you might be back. She misses you."

"I will go see her once the meat is packed."

"We should be finished tomorrow." Mama walked to the door. "Don't lose hope. None of us know what the future holds."

Mama was right. Donald would write home. Maggie surely would inform her when they received news from him. She would pray—for his well-being and that he would communicate with his family soon.

Donald swallowed, his throat still raw. How many days had he been at the Alexanders'? He recalled Boyd helping him off his horse and guiding him inside their home. He scanned the small room from the pallet he occupied. The empty pallet next to his had folded blankets and clothing on it. His miserable cold and high fever had left him incoherent and sleeping most of the time. Boyd must already be out tending to farm chores. Morning light shone through the window, and the smell of meat cooking made his mouth water. Boyd, his ma, and sister had all ministered to his needs. What a dolt! Nothing like showing up at their door uninvited and requiring care.

He threw back the quilt and eased himself up. Still dizzy. It was tempting to lay down again, but he needed to wash after days of fever. He pulled a clean shirt from his haversack. A pitcher and basin rested on a washstand at the far side of the room. A small oval mirror hung on the wall above it. Steadying himself as he rose, he ambled across the room and poured water into the basin. The water chilled his warm skin but refreshed him. The sight in the mirror made him flinch. Between his sickly pallor and a weeks' growth on his face, he looked as rough as the mountain men he had run across during the war. He rubbed his jaw. The red whiskers could be shaved off later. Washing was the more immediate need.

A soft knock on the door made him grab the washstand. "Just a minute." He pulled the clean shirt on over his head. "Come in."

The door eased open, and Boyd's sister peeked around the corner. Her bright smile, deep blue eyes, and the red curls edging her cap were as invigorating as the cold water.

"I'm glad to see you up. Are you hungry?"

"Yes, and thirsty," he croaked, his face heating.

"I will get you some water."

He grabbed his coat after she left and went outside to use the necessary.

Returning, he hung his coat on the back of a chair. Jenny brought a cup of water and a steaming stoneware mug of coffee to the table.

Exhausted from the effort after days of inaction, he leaned against the table. "Where is the rest of your family?"

"They are tending to the animals. Boyd should be back soon. Sit down. You still seem a mite wobbly." Jenny placed a plate with eggs, a biscuit, and ham before him. She had the same engaging countenance as Boyd, but as Boyd said, she was a far sight prettier.

His friend came through the door, all smiles. "Welcome back, old friend. Good to see you are up. Doin any better?"

"I believe so. I appreciate you and your family taking care of me. I had no intention of arriving ill." He shoveled a spoonful of eggs into his mouth. *Delicious.*

Boyd poured himself coffee and sat beside him. "Not your fault. How is your family and ... your friends?"

Jenny worked at the table nearby. *Please don't bring Mary up— at least not now.* "They are well and relieved to see me home from the war. Cannot believe how much my brothers have grown. 'Tis the biggest difference." He ate a bite of ham. "I have been giving thought to settling in the valley and possibly apprentice in a printshop. Might you know any printers around here?"

Boyd pursed his lips a moment before nodding. "Thad Bryant in Lexington has a small printshop, and it might be the right time. His only boy died at Guilford Courthouse." Boyd finished his coffee. "I'm going to town soon, and I will speak with him. If he seems interested, and you are feelin up to it, I can take you by to meet him."

Donald leaned back in the chair and breathed in without coughing. *A flicker of hope, finally.* He ate the biscuit. "This tastes mighty good."

Jenny came over and sat next to Boyd. "We are glad you came back. I hope the meeting with Mr. Bryant goes well for you."

Dressing and eating had exhausted him. "Still feeling peaked. Might rest." He rose and wobbled a minute before taking his plate to the basin at the work table.

Boyd followed him to the small room. "This may not the best time, but I wondered about your plans with Mary. Did all go as you hoped?"

Donald lay on the pallet and looked at the beamed ceiling. "No, not at all as I wanted." Boyd would understand about his failures in Alexandria, but he lacked the stamina or desire to address them now. "I think we saw the wisdom in going our separate ways."

Boyd leaned against the closed door watching him, his brows furrowed. "Not sure what to say. I expect 'tis good to realize that, as long as neither of you got hurt by that decision." Boyd studied him.

"Right." He winced.

"Why am I thinkin that one or both of you have been hurt? Want to talk about it?"

"Not sure, but not now."

"Rest. I need to get back out to the barn. Ma will be delighted you are doin better." Boyd put his hat on and opened the door.

Donald pushed himself into a seated position, his back against the wall. "I hope you do not mind my just showing up."

"Not at all. If you remember, we invited you to come back. Could be part of God's plan."

Might expect Boyd would say something like that. Who knew? It could even be true. Did God look out for folks who fumbled as much as he had lately?

CHAPTER 24

Mary huddled with the assembled neighbors in the churchyard amongst the headstones. It was a cold December day, and another sad one for the Whitcomb family—or what remained of it. The service for George Whitcomb had ended a few minutes ago, but everyone remained speaking softly amongst themselves. Soon they would go into the schoolhouse for a shared meal.

She took Martha's gloved hand and squeezed it. "Come inside with me and get warm. What can I do to help you?"

Martha's ashen face was a striking contrast against her black bonnet. "Your family and the Gordons have already done so much already. Your presence and your ma and Miss Polly's meals while Pa was failing have been a gift I will not soon forget. All of you coming alongside Teddy and me made it easier. We felt less alone."

Mary drew Martha close and hugged her. She could not imagine what losing both parents was like. "'Twas a blessing and a privilege. You would have done the same for us."

Martha walked with her to the schoolhouse. "'Tis been a difficult time, but it has given you and me more time together since spring. Each time I asked you over or I would come to the Green, you seemed unsociable or secretive." Martha removed her cloak and gloves. "I mean no unkindness. I know you have been grieving since coming back from Alexandria."

Mary swallowed hard. Martha's bluntness stung. In the past six months, she had withdrawn from family and friends, focused on her own pain and disappointments—and what had she gained from it? Nothing. Her own needs had dominated her thoughts and actions too long. She would make spending more time with

Martha a priority.

Removing her cloak and gloves, she placed an arm around her grieving friend. "I'm sorry I have neglected our friendship. You have been kind and understanding about my distress over Donald." She took their cloaks and hung them on hooks. It was most than just Donald, but she couldn't explain about the events in Charlottesville, a nightmare that still turned her stomach.

Philip approached them. "Martha, may I get you something to eat? There is plenty of good food over there."

Martha gave him a shy nod. "I would like that."

Philip tipped his head and left in the direction of the food tables.

She led Martha to a bench that had been moved to the wall. "Philip is a compassionate soul."

"He has always been sensitive to other's moods and needs." Martha's eyes followed him as he placed ham, beans, and potatoes on a trencher. "Philip understood how we felt after Tobias died. When he completed his chores at the Green, he came over and helped Pa. He is a kind and godly man." Martha lowered her eyes and blushed.

Martha and Philip. There was more going on here than admiring Philip's generous nature. Philip might be just the blessing Martha needed after so much loss. And she would be good for Philip too. They had a good chance of making each other very happy someday.

Unlike she and Donald, who would never have the chance.

Donald collapsed onto a chair and stared out the window of the Bryant Printshop. It was late December, the snow had begun to fall. It didn't seem like he'd been in the valley for three weeks already.

He had set the galleys under the platen and pulled for hours, which left his upper body muscles aching. But each day over the past fortnight, he grew more confident in learning the skills he needed. He was in the right place and learning a worthy trade.

And he preferred this physical exhaustion to the mental weariness those first few days brought trying to learn the many facets of the business.

Thad Bryant brought a tankard of water and set it on the table beside him. "See, I told you we needed a younger man."

Donald grinned. He'd initially found Thad Bryant's brusque nature formidable, but he got used to the man's gruffness over time.

Amos tried to stifle a laugh while hanging the printed papers over the ropes suspended from the ceiling. "You are doin a good job, son. Been Thad's journeyman nigh these many years, and I can tell you it took me a lot longer to learn it."

Donald wiped his brow. Nice gents who genuinely appreciated his efforts. "You warned me 'twas a time-consuming and a physically demanding task."

The lamplight made the large bald area on the top of Thad's head shine like a waxed table. "Amos is right. You are getting the routine. It takes time to estimate the exact amount of dampness the paper needs for the ink to adhere, but not tear." He lit his pipe. "Amos, go on home. You need to see to Trudy."

"She was doin poorly this morning when I left. She will be glad to see me come through the door." Amos put on his coat. "See you in the mornin."

Donald finished the water. "I best clean up back there." He went toward the back of the shop.

"Duncan."

Mr. Bryant's voice made him stop and turn. "Yes, sir?"

"Last week, you said you got a room at the tavern. I have an extra room where you can stay. With my wife and boy gone, 'tis only me. I understand if you prefer your privacy, but thought I would offer. Hard enough for a young fellow to save any money for the future without havin to pay rent too."

Donald strolled back and sat across from Thad. A lonely and kindly man resided under his crusty exterior.

"That is generous of you, sir. The Alexanders were gracious, but I did not want to impose on them any longer, so I got a room at the tavern. 'Tis a place to sleep and have a meal, but it can be lonely and noisy." He shook his employer's hand. "I appreciate your kind offer, sir. Perhaps I can be of help. I'm not much of a cook, but I can chop wood, hunt, and fish."

Mr. Bryant's eyes dulled. "You remind me of Fraser—my son. He died at Guilford Courthouse."

Donald stood. Todd Gordon's face came to mind. "I will never forget Guilford Courthouse. We lost many good men there—and at too many other places. But it sounds like the war may be ending soon."

"Let's pray it does. Bring your gear with you tomorrow, and you can get settled in."

Donald glanced at the man as he stowed letters and sticks. Interesting how everything seemed to be falling into place in ways he had not expected. If only it would ease the pain of losing Mary.

Mary stitched the hem on Sara's gown in the common room. The cold January weather had been confining, but the past few days had been milder. Walking would settle her nerves. She should probably go soon since she needed to return in plenty of time to help with any potential guests or supper. The front door opening and closing made her stiffen. Boarders or family?

Papa came through and placed the post items on the table beside her before taking a seat.

Might there be a post from Jean or the Duncans? Mary set the gown down and rummaged through them while Papa stood silently. His eyes remained fixed on her.

She sighed. Nothing. It had been six weeks. Surely Donald would have written home by now.

Papa leaned against the wall studying her.

"'Tis obvious you have something on your mind, Papa."

"I'm worried about you, lass. Since early summer, you have been easily provoked and withdrawn. 'Tis not like you to be so temperamental. I asked you months ago about what troubled you, and you said 'twas nothing. You are a grown woman, and I have tried to respect your privacy. But you have changed."

She went back to hemming Sara's dress. Looking into his face could easily bring on tears. As close as they were, she had kept him at a distance half a year.

He rubbed his hand along the oak table. "I thought once Donald returned, your moodiness would disappear, but when you came back from Alexandria, you seemed more melancholy. You were vague when I asked you about your visit. Heather says you no longer anticipate a courtship with Donald."

"'Tis true. He left Alexandria—and we did not part on good terms. There is no marriage to plan." There, she had said it, despite the lump in her throat.

He tilted his head, and his penetrating dark eyes made it harder to remain silent. "The Mary I have known these past twenty years would have come to me and wanted to talk about it. At times, I wonder where she went. I shan't press you if you have no wish to speak of it."

She cleared her throat. "When Donald came home, he had changed, but so have I. We were initially awkward and stiff with one another, but when we finally began to relax and feel comfortable around each other, I responded poorly to him." She could not tell Papa any more because it would encourage more inquiries. "I misunderstood him. By the time I went to Oronoco Street to apologize, he had gone. He told his parents he was going west, but no one knows where."

Papa shook his head. "That does not sound like Donald."

"I'm sorry I've been distant and out of sorts, Papa. I'm trying to do better. Each time the post comes, I act like a squirrel searching for nuts. I keep hoping to receive a note from Jean or Maggie, hoping for news of him."

"We can pray for that." He cleared his throat. "You need to understand, Donald has seen a lot of action for several years. War changes men. Thankfully, he came home uninjured, but not all injuries are obvious. Being battle-weary can have consequences. We need to be patient with all those who have served in the war."

He straightened, put his hat back on, and placed his hand on her shoulder. "I'm glad you told me. I know better how to pray for you."

She rose and threw her arms around him. "You understand having endured so much yourself when you were injured and taken prisoner. I regret not being more forthright, Papa. You are the last person in the world I want to push away."

Papa hugged her and stepped back, his brows furrowed. "Why would you want to push anyone away? Hmm. I need to get back to the barn now. I will leave you to your sewing. You may be more comfortable sharing your concerns with Heather, but remember, I'm here if you need me."

He walked toward the kitchen. It would have been difficult enough telling Donald about the attack—if she ever got the chance. She could never tell Papa.

CHAPTER 25

Feeling fidgety, Mary put the sewing aside. Exercise and fresh air would help. Mama was working in the kitchen when Mary poked her head in. "I'm restless and thought I would go for a walk unless you need me now. When I return, I can help with supper.

"By all means, go. A guest arrived while you and Papa were chatting. A fellow from Fredericksburg. I'm planning ham and beans for supper. Enjoy your walk."

"I shan't be gone long." She wrapped the cloak around her and headed outside. The crisp air, sunshine, and lack of wind made it pleasant. A gaggle of geese circled above landing in unison on the pond with the grace of dancers. Another time, she would have stopped at the bench, but her agitated state was better served by exercise. A walk along the river might soothe her. The ever-changing flow of the Potomack was a familiar tonic.

A few minutes later, she stopped near the river and rested on a large rock. The flow of water as it rushed by blocked out most other sounds. The recent rains had nearly covered the small islands. It must have been this way when poor Tobias died. Life was precious. *I don't want to be like the river, rocks, and islands, my life rushing by while I do nothing.*

Leaves crackled nearby. Her heart skipped a beat. She rose and moved to the side, where she would have a clear path to escape if needed. A chill went through her. Not ten yards away, a tall man approached on the same path she'd used.

He removed his hat. "Pardon me, miss. I did not mean to startle you." The man had a nice smile, and his deep voice sounded convincing, but it might be a trap. "I assure you, I mean you no harm. I'm staying at the ordinary and seeking the location of the ferry I need to travel on tomorrow."

"Pike's Ferry is over there, sir ... right around that bend. Excuse me." She moved to avoid his passing too close.

He touched the brim of his hat before continuing toward the ferry.

She wasted no time returning home. Once inside, she hung her cloak up and washed her hands.

Mama came into the kitchen. "I'm glad you are back. Do you want to make biscuits?

"Certainly." She put on her apron and gathered the flour and starter. "I think I met our guest a few minutes ago. He came to the river—in search of the ferry."

"Aye. He said he needed to go across to Frederick. He is a friend of Andrew Macmillan. He seems nice enough and attractive."

She placed her hands on her hips. "Mama, really?"

Mama winked at her. "Just an observation. Sara asked if you could help her with her embroidery sampler? I got her started, but she wants your guidance."

"Of course. She only needs encouragement. I can assist her after supper."

The biscuits finished, Mary took a loaded tray to the common room to set the table. The guest had returned and sat near the hearth with a notebook.

He rose, smiled, and nodded. "Ahh, the river nymph."

She curtsied. "Not quite. When you said you were staying at the Green, I should have mentioned that I live here. You caught me by surprise. I had not expected to see anyone. Few people walk that area of the river."

"Allow me to introduce myself. Joshua Howard." The man had a gentlemanly countenance and a warm smile. He seemed far less threatening now. "You appeared to be deep in thought at the river. I'm sorry I intruded on your privacy."

"No need to apologize." She finished setting the table when

several loud thuds came from the center hall, followed by a howl. "Help!" Sara screamed.

Mary darted through the door that led to the hall. Sara lay at the foot of the stairs.

"I'm here, Sara." Mary fell on her knees.

Mama arrived right as Mr. Howard bent over Sara.

"I'm a physician. May I examine at the child?"

"Aye, please do."Mama kneeled and drew Sara into her arms, brushing the tears from her face.

Mary scooted out of the way. A physician? He looked too young to be a doctor. He gently checked Sara's arms, legs, ankles, neck, and prodded her back, all while calmly asking her questions about what hurt. He acted and sounded legitimate. No reason to distrust him.

He took Sara's hand. "I believe you only fell a few steps. Is that right, Miss Sara?"

Sara's cries had quieted to whimpers. She nodded, and her eyes traveled between Mama and the doctor.

He faced Mama. "May I carry her into the other room where the light is better? I would like to examine her eyes."

Mama rose. "Certainly. Is there anything I can do to help?"

Smiling, he lifted Sara. "I think she is going to be fine, more frightened than hurt." He set her on the settee by the hearth.

Mama brought a lantern close. The doctor studied Sara's eyes and head.

"How do you feel now?" He asked.

Her breathing had returned to normal. "Better."

"Good. I think you should rest here a while, and allow us to wait on you. Would you like a drink of water?"

"Uh-huh."

"I will bring it." Mama left for the kitchen.

The guest continued to watch Sara. His confidence and calm demeanor put Mary at ease.

She sat on the settee beside Sara and held her hand. "'Tis a blessing you were here, Doctor, when Sara fell."

His focus shifted from Sara to her. His medium-brown hair was near the shade of her own, but his dark brown eyes looked like Papa's. "I'm glad to have helped."

Within minutes, the family gathered in the common room. Mama made introductions and told them about Sara's fall.

Papa shook the doctor's hand. "Please join us at our table for supper, Doctor Howard, unless you prefer to eat alone?"

"You are most kind, I would enjoy supping with your family." He turned toward Sara. "Are you hungry, lass, or would you prefer a broth?"

"I can eat." She left the settee and walked slowly to her place at the table.

Mary sat beside Sara and across from Doctor Howard while they ate. Doctor Howard observed Sara occasionally while taking part in conversation ranging from the war to Fredericksburg.

The doctor took another helping of ham. "Andrew told me Stewarts' Green served superior food." He turned toward Papa. "I mentioned to your wife that Andrew Macmillan had recommended this ordinary. My uncle is a physician in Fredericksburg and a good friend of Andrew's. 'Twas my uncle who mentored me and whom I trained under."

Papa sat back and lit his pipe. "If your medical practice is in Fredericksburg, what takes you to Frederick, Maryland?"

"My father is recuperating from a recent illness. I need to make sure he has the assistance he needs."

Mama smiled. "Well, we are grateful you considered Andrew's recommendation and decided to stay with us. Right, Sara?"

"Yes." She grinned. Her cheerful disposition had returned.

'Twas fortunate Dr. Howard had been there to examine Sara and reassure the family of her well-being. He even engaged Mark and Douglas in conversation.

When the meal ended, Mary rose and placed the dishes on a tray. "Sara, after I help Mama with these, do you feel like working on your sampler?"

Sara's eyes grew wide as her smile. "Please. I get so mixed up with the stitches."

"I will be back in a few minutes."

Mary didn't look back, but she sensed the doctor watching her leave the room. It left her with a certain sadness. If she weren't still pining for Donald, she may have looked at the doctor in a different light. But she couldn't imagine ever overcoming Donald leaving her as he did.

At least, not for a long, long time.

Mary set the dish-laden tray on the kitchen worktable as Papa and Mark left with lanterns to see to the animals. There was hot water on the hearth, but Mark should have brought more water in from the well. She would have to go out in the cold and dark to get it herself. At least there was plenty of light from the full moon. Mark would hear about this later.

She clutched the full bucket at the top of the well when arms came around her with a low growl. She screamed, and the attacker released her. Her heart racing, she turned and yelled. "Are you insane, Mark? Why did you grab me like that?"

Mark glared at her. "Excuse me, Miss Cranky. I just now remembered to get the water. What is wrong with you? You cannot take a joke anymore."

Papa came from the barn. "What is going on out here?"

Mark backed off. "Nothing. 'Twas only a gag to tease Mary. She has become a real killjoy."

Papa lowered his voice. "I wish you two would remember we have a guest who does not need to be frightened by a banshee." He turned back to the barn.

Mark glowered and stomped off in the same direction.

Still trembling, Mary wrapped her arms tight around each other, watching them retreat. Frightening the guest? A glance toward the Green confirmed it. Mama stood at an upstairs window, peering out. Would she always react in terror when startled? *I must not let that horrible day continue to shape my future, or it will forever threaten my peace.*

She owed Mark an apology.

CHAPTER 26

The tavern's server brought Donald and Boyd large tankards of steaming cider and bowls of rich venison stew. Donald lifted a chunk of bread in a salute. "Glad you could join me. I knew you would prefer this to having me cook at Thad's place."

Boyd grinned. "The food is decent here and should warm our insides on a cold evenin."

"And I can avoid being mocked for my lack of cooking skills." Donald put the bread down. Boyd had folded his hands and stared at him. "Go ahead and bless the food." His stomach growled, and his mouth watered at the savory aroma, but a meal with Boyd wouldn't begin till the food was prayed over.

Boyd bowed his head. "Lord, we thank You for this wonderful meal, our time together, and Your provision in every area of our lives. Amen."

Donald took a spoonful. "This is far better than anything I can make."

Boyd's laugh carried. "You got that right. I seem to remember …"

"Never mind. I never claimed to be a good cook. And, if you remember, war rations and a small fire did not provide a wealth of options. How are you and your family?"

"They are well and extend an invitation for you to come for dinner Sunday after church." Boyd smiled and studied him. "Have not seen you at church since you moved out. The church is only a few blocks from Thad's place."

Donald pushed the rich and tasty stew around in his bowl. "I wondered how long it would take you to bring that up. I don't know many folks in town yet. 'Tis too easy to not go." Hard to ignore Boyd's raised eyebrows and the pricking at his conscience. "I know, I know, church is not for socializing but for worshipping."

"Do me a favor. Thad has not been to church much since Fraser passed. Maybe by livin there with him now, you could encourage him to come with you."

"Nothing subtle about you, Boyd. Think you can catch two backsliders with one plea?"

"Probably." There was no guile in Boyd's face. "Thad and Amos said you are learnin fast at the shop. What has it been, about five weeks now?"

"They have both been patient with me, even when I ruined paper or spilled ink." He took another big bite of the stew. "I even interviewed a couple of gents purchasing Leicester lambs for a small article in the paper. Thad must have some confidence in me."

"He does, and that is part of the trade too, I s'pose. What does your family think of your new profession?" Boyd brought a spoonful of stew to his mouth.

Donald studied his bowl and continued chewing. Eventually, he would have to swallow and answer the question. *Should have figured Boyd would quiz me on that subject.* "I have not heard back from them."

Boyd squinted.

"I wrote them a while back—the last time you prodded me. I told them about Lexington and the printshop. I'm sure to hear from them before long."

"Good. They care about you and will appreciate knowin you are gettin settled. Any more thoughts on the lass?"

Hardly an hour went by when thoughts of Mary did not creep in. He had been encouraged by her interest in his plans, and when he kissed her and she responded with equal ardor, but then he ruined it. "What are you getting at, Boyd? I told you any future plans with Mary ended."

"When you explained what happened with Mary, something

did not set right with me. I don't understand why you left town without sayin goodbye to her, or tellin her where you were headed."

Donald pushed his bowl away. "You did not see how she reacted or hear her words. She wants nothing to do with me, and I should have realized it sooner. From the time I returned, she seemed distant and kept me at arm's length. I confused her moments of geniality for something more."

Boyd broke off a piece of bread and rubbed it in the gravy. "Maybe you should write to Mary, to get your thoughts straight. It might save you from regrets later."

Regrets about Mary? Remorse filled him whenever she came to mind. He had handled so many things badly. Write to her? What could he convey in a letter that would help anything? But it had been impulsive to leave without even saying goodbye to her or his sister.

"Ma wants you to bring Thad with you for dinner Sunday. You can both come straight from church." Boyd took a bite, never taking his eyes off him.

Gosh, the man annoyed him—particularly when he was right.

❦

Mary tossed the feed on the ground while the chickens' high-pitched, staccato voices pierced the morning. For late February, 'twas milder than usual. Teasing spring?

A rider approached the Green. The post rider. If only he brought news from Jean or the Duncans. She set the feed basket down, strode toward him, and took the post-packet. "I will bring you hot biscuits if you have the time."

"I can surely spare a few minutes for that." He stretched in his saddle as she turned to go inside.

She took the rider two biscuits and gave him a coin.

"Very kind, miss." He turned his horse and left.

Mary headed back to the kitchen. She removed her cloak, hung it on a hook by the back door, and rifled through the posts. One from Jean. *Finally.* She opened the parchment on her way to the window seat in the common room. "It had been three months. Surely they would have news of him by now."

Dear Mary,

I am thrilled to tell you, Peter and I became parents early this February. Our sweet Neil is beautiful, and I cannot wait for you to meet him. He is small but so dear. As you might expect, my parents are pleased beyond measure to be grandparents.

Wonderful news.

At long last, we received news from Donald. He is well and living in the Shenandoah Valley and apprenticing with a printer in Lexington. He lives with the owner of the Bryant Printshop. It seems Mr. Bryant is a widower who lost his only son in the war. Donald must be good company for him. He wrote that they are pleased with his progress in learning the trade. My parents are relieved to learn he is hopeful about his prospects and likes the friends he has made there.

He is safe, far away, but well.

You were upset in November when Donald left unexpectedly, and I knew you would be eager to learn about his well-being and whereabouts. Regardless of your hesitancy in recent months, I still believe you love Donald. In time, I hope he returns for you both to have an opportunity to clear up any misunderstandings.

Please write and tell me you will come to Alexandria and meet our dear Neil this spring or early summer.

Affectionately,
Jean

Mary took a deep breath. Answers at last. *I should be content knowing Donald is well.* And Jean, now not only a wife but a mother. She rubbed the knot on the back of her neck. How their lives had grown apart.

Could she be satisfied knowing Donald was safe and pleased with his situation? That he had found the employment opportunity he hoped for and had made friends? If she wrote to him at the printshop, would he think she was pursuing him? If he still cared for her, why had he not written in the past three months?

Her stomach knotted. But why would he? She had behaved abominably when he threw her to the ground. Why would he want a future with her after she struck his face and screamed at him? She leaned her head against the cold glass pane.

"Mary, are you ill?" Mama stood inside the common room with a basket of laundry. "You are as pale as these sheets."

"I received a letter from Jean." She held up the vellum.

Mama's eyes grew wide. "Bad news?"

"No, not at all. 'Tis good news. Jean and Peter's babe was born earlier this month ... and they are all well. His name is Neil."

"Wonderful." Mama set the basket down and joined her at the window. "Why are you distressed?" She put her hand to her chest. "Donald. Have they heard from Donald?"

"Yes. And he is also well and working in the Shenandoah Valley." Mary took her hand. "Come, sit down and read it." She handed her the missive and watched as she read it.

"Neil, how fitting, both a Scottish and Irish name." Mama's eyes narrowed. "'Tis all good news. So why did you seem so uneasy when I came in?"

"Donald is safe, and he sounds pleased with his job and location. I'm relieved in that respect. But I still feel terrible about the way we parted—and I still love him."

"Could you write to him and explain the misunderstanding?"

"I can apologize, but I certainly cannot explain the reason for my reaction in a letter. He may think I'm trying to chase after him.

It appears he has put it all behind him, and his interests are now in the valley."

Mama tilted her head toward the center hall. "That sounds like a rider approaching, might be a boarder." She returned the letter. "Stay right here, I will be back."

She reread the letter and put it in her pocket at the sound of a man's voice in the center hall.

A few minutes later, Mama returned. "We have a guest. Doctor Howard."

"Oh. Sara will be delighted. She was quite taken with him."

Mama sat down. "He has an engaging and affable manner, good qualities in a doctor. We were talking about your contacting Donald." Mama squeezed her hand. "I understand your quandary, but will you have any peace about it if you don't write to him? You could word the letter carefully to free him from any sense of obligation."

She rubbed the knot in the back of her neck. She needed to apologize and to wish him well. How he received her missive was not her responsibility. "I cannot argue with your reasoning. I will compose something later—after I think how best to frame it."

"Pray first."

"I will. Perhaps the words will come to me while I sew. I'll use the large table in the common room to cut out the material for your gown."

Mama's eyes lit. "'Twas sweet of you to offer to make that for me."

"I enjoy dressmaking, and it has been too long since you have had anything new. You always defer to everyone else's needs. Besides, my best work is with fabric and threads."

"I'm off to the kitchen if you need me."

She took the pattern and sewing basket from the corner cabinet and set it on a small table. After unfolding the lightweight green wool and placing it on the large table, she pinned what pattern pieces she could fit. The rest she set aside. Jean's letter and her need to write to Donald kept cropping up in her thoughts. *I must apologize for my reckless and rude behavior. And wish him well in his new endeavor. But let him know I still care for him. It must be worded perfectly.* "Get your mind back on the dress—a pursuit less fraught with disaster."

"Disaster? Am I interrupting, or do you typically converse with yourself?"

Doctor Howard's voice made her jump. She turned, then curtsied. "I did not hear you enter."

"I fear I have once again startled you."

"You caught me thinking out loud."

"I understand. I'm guilty of addressing myself at times. A habit my housekeeper says is due to living alone."

She laughed. "I suppose 'tis one way to be good company for yourself."

"Ahh, but that is not always the case. At times, I argue with myself."

She relaxed. "That could be troublesome. And who determines the victor in those conversations?"

He approached the table and examined the fabric, then searched her eyes. "They are not contentious arguments. Usually, I'm evaluating various treatments for my patients. Speaking of patients, how is the charming Miss Sara?"

"She is fine, and currently next door at the Gordons'."

He glanced at the green wool. "This is quite fine fabric. Forgive me. I should let you return to your enterprise. If I promise not to interrupt you again, may I sit over there and read for a bit?" He pointed to a chair by the garden window.

"You will not disturb me. May I get you coffee or cider?"

"Coffee would be perfect. I slept little last night. I thought I'd rest here before heading to Fredericksburg tomorrow." Doctor Howard's cheerful countenance took on a sad aspect.

"I will return with it soon." He had mentioned visiting an ailing father during his previous visit. Perhaps this had been another trip to see him.

Mama was cutting potatoes when she entered. "Do we have any coffee made I can heat up for Doctor Howard? He is in the common room."

"Aye, take him those scones, also. I asked him if he had eaten when he arrived after dinner, but he said he needed nothing. Supper won't be for a while."

Mary carried a tray to the common room with the coffee, scones, and jam and set it on the table next to his seat.

"Now that is tempting." He picked up a scone. He still had a contemplative expression.

"Is your father still ill?" His reason for traveling this way was not her business, but his engaging nature invited conversation.

He groaned. "Yes. The nurse I hired last month now has other obligations. I want him to live with me in Fredericksburg so I could see to his needs. But he is an independent man, with his own ideas, and has difficulty accepting his limitations."

"That is a perplexing problem. And your mother?"

"She died twelve years ago in an Indian raid." He sniffed and sipped his coffee.

"How awful. I'm sorry." What a horror the man's family had endured.

"My father's choices since her death are why 'tis difficult to reason with him. He is bitter and reclusive." He closed his notebook. "My father allowed a calamity to keep him from moving forward in his life and finding joy."

A chill traveled up her spine. "I'm sure he has suffered greatly."

"Yes, but he bore no responsibility for my mother's death. The attack was completely outside his control, yet he has allowed that sad event to keep him from the people and activities he loves."

She froze. *Convicting words.* "I'm sure 'tis hard for him to forget about what happened."

"Dwelling on something one cannot change can be a deadly trap and needs to be addressed with compassion. I want to respect my father's wishes, but I have no siblings and feel responsible for his care." His eyes were expressive. "My father and I responded differently to the tragedy. I chose to let it refine me—not define me."

"An encouraging and noble attitude to embrace." She tensed. "But possibly difficult to practice."

He closed his eyes for a few seconds. "Forgive my candor. I'm still frustrated at leaving him and not knowing how best to assist him. Pardon me for troubling you with my family difficulties. What is that you are sewing?"

"No apology necessary. I'm glad you felt comfortable addressing it with me. 'Tis easy to allow problems to preoccupy our thoughts." His comment, *The attack was completely outside his control, yet he has allowed that sad event to keep him from the people and activities he loves.* nagged at her. "'Twill be a dress for my mother. Please let me know if I can bring you more coffee."

"My thanks."

She returned to the table and began cutting the material. *Chose to let it refine me—not define me.* Oh, that she could alter her inclinations for her distress. He read for about fifteen minutes before leaving the room. Just as well. Doctor Howard proved as much a distraction as the letter she tried to compose in her head.

That night in her room, she sharpened a quill and dipped it in ink.

Donald,

I received a letter from Jean announcing the arrival of their precious Neil. She sounds happy to be a mother, and I'm certain your parents are equally delighted to be grandparents. Congratulations on becoming an uncle.

I understand you are apprenticing in a printshop in Lexington and enjoy your new surroundings. How wonderful you were able to obtain the work you hoped to find. I'm sure you will do well and find many friends as you continue to become established in your new community.

She set the quill in the glass inkpot and leaned back for a moment. How should she word this to take responsibility? Not to explain why, but to show contrition without making him feel beholden. She bit her lip and picked up the quill, tapping it on the side of the jar.

> *My primary purpose in writing to you is to apologize for my behavior that last afternoon while we were on our walk. I intended to speak with you about something important that occurred before you returned from the war, and I felt apprehensive and uncertain about how to address it. When the gun fired, you were chivalrous and tried to protect me from a perceived danger. I was nervous and reacted shamefully—but explaining why is not possible in a letter. I am asking for your forgiveness.*
>
> *While we once entertained plans for a future together, it seems that the years of separation have taken a toll, and for that, I'm very sorry. You will always remain precious, a man I care for and respect. I deeply regret the way we parted.*
>
> *Mary*

She leaned back in the chair and stared at the flickering flame shining through the etched glass hurricane on the candle holder. In the morning, she would read it again, then see what Mama thought. When it dried, she folded the parchment and brought it to her lips. The post rider would return on Friday unless there was another heavy snow. How would Donald receive this?

Maybe more to the point … would he respond?

CHAPTER 27

"What a body has to go through to get one of Fiona Alexander's tasty meals," Thad Bryant muttered.

Donald rolled his eyes at his employer. Sitting in the back of the meeting house during the service had been a good idea. There was less chance Thad's continual commentary would bother other churchgoers. Overcoming Thad's curmudgeonly excuses and convincing his crusty employer to come that morning had taxed his patience. What a pair of backsliders. "We might get something out of our Sunday morning sojourn," he whispered to Thad. "Could be we both need reforming,"

"Speak for yourself, chum. Don't need to hear a minister drone on about God's purpose in everything. Boyd has no shame, bribing us to come here with his ma's cooking."

Donald glanced up the aisle to where the Alexander family sat, and at the same moment, Jenny turned her head and smiled at them. A dark green bonnet and red curls framed her pretty face.

She quickly faced forward again.

"I see how 'tis," Thad snickered. "You have taken a fancy to the Alexander lass."

Donald scowled. "Hush, I'm trying to listen to the sermon."

"You needn't. I can boil it down for you later."

When the service ended, Donald and Thad went back to the cottage to get their horses for the ride to the Alexander farm. The early March wind blew the snow into drifts as they followed the trail.

Thad pointed to several downed branches on the path. "That is what heavy wet snow will do. Spring cannot come soon enough."

"Agreed. I'm eager for the trout fishing you told me about."

"South River is good for that. Personally, I'm hankering for Fiona's victuals. Been a while since I had one of her meals. Randall and Fiona were good to me after Priscilla died. They visited, brought meals, and had me out to the farm. I guess they figure now you are living with me we can fend for ourselves. What a joke." Thad's brows furrowed. "When you were staying with 'em, did you tell 'em you could cook?"

"No." He shook his head. "And Boyd would be the first to tell you that I'm a wretched cook. Could be they knew you were lonely, and now that I'm here, you have company."

"Humph. No way you can take Priscilla's place."

He sighed. "And I have no intention of trying." The man was daft.

Thad snapped his hat on his thigh to get the snow off. "The sun rose and set by that woman. None like her. Priscilla was the best thing that ever happened to me, and losing her made me the angriest I have ever been with God, especially after losing Fraser."

"I'm sorry, Thad. It sounds like you had a good life and a wonderful family. 'Tis a loss to understand why things happen the way they do, and I'm sure 'tis easy to grow bitter. Boyd challenged me when my attitudes were headed in the wrong direction. Maybe that is why I like being around him."

"You are not such a bad fellow yourself, other than waking me up at all hours of the night with your screaming."

His chest tightened. "Sorry about that. Believe me, I want the nightmares gone even more than you do."

"Are you sweet on Jenny Alexander?" Thad gave him a smug grin. "She seems to have you in her sights."

He swallowed hard to rid himself of the lump in his throat. "No." He had no intention of leading the lass on. Jenny was sweet and pretty, but Mary still filled his heart and mind.

Mary sat in the Whitcombs' main room, watching Martha pour their coffee. Martha had invited her over to sew, but she had been unusually quiet. "How have you and Teddy been? We missed seeing you at services on Sunday."

At Martha's sheepish expression, Mary set aside the pins and Mark's breeches and went to her. She put her arms around her friend's shoulders. "What is troubling you?"

"Would you mind carrying the cups? I will get the ginger biscuits."

"Certainly." What else could happen in the Whitcomb family? They had lost a mother, two brothers, and a father. "Sit down and tell me what has you this unhappy."

"Teddy and I were not at church on Sunday because we had an argument. I know that sounds awful. Better to have attended services than fight with each other."

"You both have been through so much, losing Tobias and then your father. May I ask what you and Teddy squabbled about?" She placed the cups on the table and sat next to her friend.

Martha clutched her hands together. "You remember our aunt and uncle in Williamsburg? The ones I visited a couple of times over the years?"

"Yes, of course. I remember when you visited them in Williamsburg while James attended William & Mary."

Martha nodded. "You may have forgotten, a couple of years ago, Teddy spent a few weeks with them."

"He enjoyed his time there as much as you had. Why does this have you upset?"

"He is seventeen now and wants to attend the college. Our aunt and uncle have encouraged it."

"But that leaves you here alone. How can you manage the farm by yourself?"

Martha took a sip of the steamy brew. "They have asked me to come to live with them also." She looked up briefly but then averted her eyes.

There was more to this than Martha shared. "You loved Williamsburg. I'm surprised you are not thrilled at the generous invitation."

"I … I am not that eager to leave here."

The fire crackling in the hearth made the only sound. Martha ran her fingers over her apron.

"Might the reason you are not packing your trunk have anything to do with Philip Gordon?"

Martha's blush answered that question. "Philip has been helpful here since Pa passed." Martha fidgeted. "Even before that, when Tobias died, he was understanding and kind. It had not been that long since he lost Todd."

"Martha, you don't need to tell me about Philip's sweet and generous nature. We all love him. I have suspected his attachment to you for a while. Does he know of your feelings?"

"Yes." Martha folded her hands and looked directly at her. "Teddy told him yesterday morning about our uncle and aunt's offer. It troubled Philip. That afternoon he told me he did not want me to go to Williamsburg. He asked me to marry him and said he would come here and work the farm with me." Martha's brow furrowed.

Mary put her hand to her lips. Joy filled her heart, something sorely lacking of late. "That is wonderful. So why are you troubled?"

Martha focused on the braided rug before facing her again. "I know Philip is … slow. He is … not intelligent by the world's standards, but he senses things and understands people's needs. And he loves me. 'Tis just … I'm uncertain of what others will think if we marry."

"People around here know Philip. They would not knowingly be unkind." The thought that someone might belittle Philip was outrageous. "Does what others think matter if you both love each other?"

Martha sniffled. "'Twould be hurtful if folks made fun of us. Does wondering what others think of such a match make me shallow?"

"No one wants to be mocked for their choices. I'm happy for you both. Do his parents know he asked you to marry him? Does Teddy?"

"Teddy is fond of Philip but cannot understand why I would choose to stay on the farm and not move to Williamsburg. The money from a sale would help us both."

"Teddy is seventeen and not in love."

"Philip has not told his parents yet."

Mary laughed. "I bet they suspect more than you think. *Nothing* gets by Polly."

"Then you think I should say yes?"

"You mean you gave him no answer? That might confuse Philip. Don't make him wonder and wait."

"I know I should. And you understand more than most the pain in hesitating."

Mary picked up her sewing, pricking herself with the needle. "What do you mean by that?"

"Wasn't your confusion and reluctance to commit the reason Donald left?"

She glared at Martha. But how could she fault her friend, when she had not been forthright with her? Martha was partially right. She had admitted to being confused and unsure about marriage. And Martha knew nothing about what happened in Charlottesville or about the events in Alexandria with Donald.

Mary rubbed the blood spot from her thumb. "Donald's and my situation is different. I have many regrets. But this is about you and Philip. The two of you have found a special bond." Mary took Martha's hands in hers. "Do not let what others might think deter you from what you believe is right. 'Tis obvious you love Philip, or you would have jumped at the opportunity to leave all this and move to Williamsburg."

"I cannot disagree with you. I'm sorry if I misunderstood or offended you about Donald. Besides, perhaps your interests have moved to another gentleman."

Martha could be vexing at times. "What are you talking about?"

"Philip told me about your guest, an attentive doctor." She grinned. "He said the man could not take his eyes off of you during supper."

"Philip made a mistake. The man is a friend of Mr. Macmillan. He was cordial to all of us, so don't let your imagination run wild." Philip had not been completely wrong. Joshua Howard had shown an interest in her, engaging her in conversation during and after dinner.

Her stomach knotted as she returned to sewing the breeches. It had been three weeks since she'd posted Donald's letter. And still no word from him. How long might she have to wait for an acknowledgment?

What if he chose not to respond?

CHAPTER 28

Donald and Boyd cast their lines into the South River. The budding trees teased an end to what had been a harsh winter for Virginia. April held promise. "The sunshine feels good, and 'tis great to have time away from the printshop. Don't get me wrong, I'm grateful to be working there and learning more all the time."

Boyd pulled his line in. "As things turned out, linkin you with Thad worked out well for both of you. He is amazed at how proficient you have become. And Amos seems more relaxed and relieved to have more time to care for Trudy."

"Amos still comes by the shop. I think he likes Thad's company."

Boyd cast his line again. "When Fraser died, and then Priscilla took sick and passed, Amos came alongside Thad. Seemed to become his mission to help him in the shop even more."

Donald cast his line again. "Thad still grieves the loss of his wife."

"He is lonely. Priscilla was sweet-tempered and friendly." Boyd laughed. "But she took no nonsense from him. When she worked at the shop, she almost always deferred to him. She had a subtle way of winnin him over to her way of thinkin when he wrote news articles. Your apprenticin at the shop and livin in his cottage seems to have renewed his spirit."

"I don't know about that. He can be mighty surly and gripes about my cooking."

"Well, on that, we can agree. Heard anythin from your folks?"

"Yes. They are all well. Enthusiastic because the war is winding down, and peace seems more possible. They were pleased I was working at a profession. I'm an uncle now. My sister and her husband had a boy in February."

"What about Mary? Did they write about her?"

"No. Though I'm sure Jean would have let her know they heard from me, where I am, and what I'm doing. Those two are like peas in a pod." Did Mary even think of him, or was she grateful to put her relationship with him behind her?

"You never wrote to Mary?"

"No. Thought about it but saw no point in adding to any embarrassment or irritation she may have felt. Why do you keep bringing Mary up?" The way they parted continued to invade his thoughts, and Boyd bringing her up regularly did not help.

"I'm not so certain the end of that story has been written yet. And, to be honest, I'm concerned about my own sister." Boyd's sideglance left no questions.

"Jenny? She has been kind and gracious. I assure you I have no designs on her and have done nothing to lead her on."

"I know that. Been watchin you. But she cares for you and thinks you are unattached. If there is even a small chance that you have a future with Mary, I don't want her growin anymore smitten with you." Boyd's lips pressed in a straight line. A protective brother if there ever was one.

"I will be mindful of that." Donald cast his line again and chuckled. "But then, who wouldn't be smitten with me?"

Boyd splashed him with cold water, which incited retaliation on his part. The fishing had ended for the day.

Life had taken on a normal routine with work. And Boyd, Thad, and Amos offered friendship. So why was Donald so restless? If only he could stop thinking about Mary—and wondering. Yet she came to mind every day. Many times every day.

Was Boyd right? Should he write to her?

Mary cut the fabric for Martha's wedding dress at the large table in the common room.

Philip ran into the room, breathless. "Come to the Whitcombs'. Martha is sick."

She put the scissors down and went to his side. "What is wrong?"

"Martha was on the kitchen floor when I arrived to start planting their south field. Said she got sick and fainted."

Mary ran behind him to the Whitcombs'.

"Should I go for Doctor Edwards?" he panted.

"Let me check on her first. It may not be that serious. Was Martha lucid?"

Philip's brows squeezed together. "She wasn't stiff, but I wouldn't say she was loose when I helped her to the bed."

"No, I meant, did she make sense when she spoke?"

"She was embarrassed and sweating. Maybe she has a fever."

"'Tis possible. Yesterday at services, Mrs. Turner said there has been some influenza in the area."

"Oh no! People can die of that. Hurry faster, Mary." Philip took hold of her arm.

At the cottage, Mary entered Martha's room. Philip knelt on the floor by the bed, rubbing Martha's cheek. Her face was damp, and her cheeks had a rosy pallor.

Mary pointed to the washstand near the door. "Philip, please go get some fresh water for that basin ... and bring a cup."

He sprinted out of the room.

Martha's cheeks were hot. Her eyes opened. "Mary."

A chill went up her spine. Mama would know what to do, but she was with Polly at Amelia Turner's. "Martha, what happened?"

"Started feeling bad yesterday." She coughed. "Sick to my stomach in the night and again this morning." Martha moaned and closed her eyes.

"We will get Doctor Edwards. He will know how we can help you."

Philip returned, carrying a bucket and splashed water into the basin. "What should I do?" Beads of sweat had formed on his forehead, and the veins on his neck throbbed. He was making her anxious. No telling how it affected Martha.

"Fill that glass with water and bring it to me." She kept her voice as calm as possible. No need to have Philip more alarmed than he already was. "I'm going to try to cool her off, but as a precaution, your suggestion to go for Doctor Edwards was a good one."

Philip dampened the cloth hanging on the washstand rail, filled the glass from the bucket, and brought them to her. He got on his knees and leaned close to Martha. "I'm going for the doctor and will be back as soon as I can, dear one. I love you, and want to marry you, so you must get well."

Mary lowered her head and brought her fingertips to her lips. His tenderness was sweet. *Don't cry, 'twill only upset him more.* She swallowed. "Don't fret. She will surely be fine in a day … or so."

Fear etched his face. "I'll take the horse to save time."

She nodded.

When he left, she wiped off Martha's face with the damp cloth. "Let me loosen your stays and help you to get comfortable. You sound congested. I'm going to fix you an herb tea."

"Philip," Martha rasped. "I didn't mean to frighten him."

"I know. Don't worry about Philip. He needs to feel useful and will be more at peace once Doctor Edwards gets here." So would she.

Mary chewed her lip. Martha was weak and coughed as she helped her out of her gown and into bed. *Martha had finally found peace and joy—now this illness? Please, Lord, let this be nothing serious so she can recover and marry Philip. These two deserve happiness.*

Mama came through the Whitcombs' door later that afternoon while Mary heated chicken broth. "I came as soon as we got back from Amelia's. Philip said Martha is ill and that Doctor Edwards was here. Is it true that he fears it might be influenza?"

Mary nodded. "'Tis possible, or a bad cold. Martha is feverish and sleeping right now." Mama brought a measure of calm. "Martha got sick last night and hasn't been able to keep anything down but small sips of water. The doctor left a poultice and this syrup. He said she needed light foods and rest. I thought I would give her some broth when she wakes. Hopefully, she can keep it down."

"Would you like me to stay?" Mama asked.

"No. You have the family and Green to attend. I want to stay here and care for her. Philip will, no doubt, return. Would you mind packing a satchel for me and have him bring it?"

"Of course. Philip is very anxious."

"I know. Doctor Edwards tried to reassure him that Martha just needed rest and time to heal. It might be best if you or his parents had something to keep him occupied."

Mama patted her arm. "Aye. Otherwise, he will hover and worry."

Hours later, Mary fetched fresh water to bathe Martha. Worrying was pointless. Bringing down the fever was her mission, but so far, she felt like a failure. At least the syrup had subdued the cough somewhat.

Back inside, she held Martha's head and brought the cup of water to her dry lips. "Do you feel like some more broth?"

"I'm so parched," Martha whispered.

"Just take sips of the water." Martha's skin was still too warm. She wrapped a damp cloth around her neck.

"I'm so thankful you are here," Martha whispered.

"I wouldn't be anywhere else." Caring for Martha had been stressful, but, in an odd way, rewarding. Mary felt needed and useful for the first time in … she couldn't remember how long it had been. It had taken her mind off her own troubles.

◉❧⚙☙◎

Mary took the bread she had made from Martha's hearth. She had spent the past two hours preparing food so Martha could

178

concentrate on recovering.

Philip approached, his wistful pleading expression brought a lump to her throat. "I finished the planting. How is Martha? May I see her?" For the past two days, every time he completed his chores at the Green or the planting at Martha's, he had been a recurring visitor.

Mary smiled, "She has been more alert and kept down an egg this morning. Let me go check on her and see if she is awake."

Martha, wearing only her chemise, stood in her room, holding on to the chest of drawers with both hands. "I needed to get up. There are chores to do. Is that soup I smell on the hearth?"

Mary put an arm around Martha and led her to a chair. "'Tis cock-a-leekie. Philip and I have taken care of all the chores. Your only job is to get well and be his radiant bride in slightly over a fortnight."

"I cannot thank you enough for all your ministrations and support."

Mary clasped her hands together. "The doctor's remedies and everyone's prayers seemed to have been the biggest help." Martha's improvement in the last four days had brought everyone relief. "Philip is outside and eager to see you."

Martha's eyes lit up as she sat on the settee.

Mary tucked a shawl and coverlet around her. "You must bundle up so as not to catch a chill." She smoothed Martha's hair. "I will fetch Philip."

Mary sighed. Fear for Martha's health had provided perspective on herself. Her unkind words and foolish behavior that ended her relationship with Donald would always be a regret. But she was healthy and survived an attack that could have ended quite differently. She mustn't let her foolish past actions destroy whatever might be ahead.

She was finally ready to discover or plan where the future would take her.

Mary sat on the floor at the Whitcombs' pinning the hem of Martha's wedding dress. "The periwinkle suits you. Your iris should still be in bloom and be the perfect accent."

Martha shifted on the stool. "I'm so thankful for all you did for me when I was ill, and for all your hours of work on the dress. The embroidery around the neckline and stomacher is stunning."

Martha's restored health and appreciation filled Mary with joy. "You will be a lovely bride. Let me get the mirror so you can judge."

Martha moved a distance from the glass. "'Tis beautiful. Philip tells me that you made him new breeches and a fine linen waistcoat."

"His parents furnished the material the same as you did. My labor is my wedding gift to my dear friends." She smiled. The task had also nurtured her recent plans of taking in work as a seamstress.

"Your generosity and support have been the biggest gift. Will you have any trouble finishing it by next week?"

"None at all. Now, let me help you take it off without getting stuck. There are other places 'tis pinned."

She followed Martha into what had once been Mr. and Mrs. Whitcombs' bedroom. The quilt Mama, Amelia, and Polly made covered the bed. The dark blue and green patches reminded her of the Gordon plaid she had seen in Thomas and Polly's home. New linen curtains framed the window. "This room has a whole new look. You have made it your own now." She helped Martha remove the gown. "I will take this back home and complete it, and I shan't let Philip see it."

Martha smoothed her hair. "Amelia Turner said she and the twins are organizing the food for the wedding dinner."

"Mark will be grateful Emily and Ellen will be busy coordinating the meal, giving them less time to shadow him." Martha laughed with her.

Martha pulled the dress she had worn earlier over her head. "You wait. One day Mark is likely to marry one of them."

Mary helped with the ties. "Those girls are adorable but inseparable. Mark would have to marry both of them, and that would never do."

"Don't worry about the twins." Teddy's voice came from the main room.

They walked out of the bedroom and stared at him as he opened the kitchen door to leave.

"One day, Mark and I are each going to marry one of the twins. Thing is, we have not decided who is going to marry whom yet."

Mary gathered the dress and her sewing basket. "I will bring it back in a couple of days."

"I can hardly wait." Martha tilted her head. "Have you ever given any more thought to hiring out as a seamstress?"

"Yes, I have been pondering just that quite a bit lately. Sewing and needlework have always been a source of joy. Planning on how to go about it has given me a sense of renewed purpose. I just need to put together a plan and discuss it with my family."

"I'm so pleased for you. You deserve to find something that gives you pleasure."

Anticipation and hope lightened her spirit for the first time in a long time. "I think you are right."

CHAPTER 29

Donald wiped the sweat from his brow and continued gathering type and arranging them in composing sticks. He rubbed his eyes. Were they watering because his head ached so bad? No wonder with as little sleep as he had gotten last night. Blast those nightmares. With more hours of sleep, he could see the tiny type easier. Across the room, Thad talked with a neighbor when he could be helping him put the sticks into the galleys. The clock on the sideboard confirmed he was running late. His stomach churned, and his throat parched. As he turned for the cup of water, two of the composing sticks tipped over, scattering type on the floor. The sound drew Thad's scowl and the neighbor's attention.

"What is wrong with you, Duncan?" Thad bellowed, and his face turned an angry red.

Donald's chest tightened. Rage bubbled up from deep inside, and the pounding in his ears increased. He struck the type case with his fist, tipping it over and sending type flying everywhere. He ignored Thad's harsh retort as he stomped out the door. The bright sunlight only aggravated his throbbing head.

Donald ran to the woods, stopping only when he approached the river. Propped against a tree to catch his breath, he bent over and retched until he felt drained. Exhausted, he trod down the slope to the river, fell on his knees and scooped up water to wash his face. *Why, why, God, do I act like this when I get frustrated? Impulsive and destructive. I never used to be hot-headed. I don't want to live this way. First Brady's Mercantile and now Thad's shop.* He respected these men. They had offered him opportunities. He rose from the muddy bank, leaned his back against a nearby oak tree, then slowly slid down it and sat. What if he lashed out at someone? He deserved Mary's fear and rejection. Blood spattered his breeches and the sleeve of his shirt. Must have been from the type case. Sure enough, his arm was cut. He needed to get back to the shop to try to make amends—even if Thad fired him. Perhaps the headache would pass if he closed his eyes for a couple of minutes.

Leaning against the tree, his thoughts turned to Todd, John, and so many others who had perished in the war. He was alive, had a job and friends. Continuing to act rashly could cost him everything that mattered—as it had with Mary. But how could he let it go? A gentle breeze ruffled his hair. *I can do all things through Christ which strengtheneth me.* He could almost hear Boyd's voice in the words.

Philip and Martha's wedding at the Green had been a first. Mary grinned when Papa hugged her. "Your idea to have the wedding and festivities here in the common room was perfect, lass."

"It seemed only right for Philip and Martha to exchange their vows in the place they had met and grown to know each other."

Mama came alongside Mary. "We need to refill the tables. The scones and pasties have disappeared."

In the kitchen, Amelia Turner filled plates. "This has been such fun from planning to completion."

"Everyone seems to be having a fine time," Mary said. Martha and Philip looked so happy. She loaded the plates onto the tray.

Mama picked up a couple of cider jugs. "My side hurt last night from all the laughter."

Mary nodded. "Between the two of you and Polly, I could hardly keep up with all the humorous cooking quips."

Mama hugged her. "When you have spent as many hours in the kitchen as the three of us have, you will have comical anecdotes of your own."

Mary giggled. "The three of you have provided me with a whole arsenal of tales to tease you about for years to come." She took the tray to distribute the food to the tables along the edges of the common room. The decorations she and Martha had done the previous day gave it a festive atmosphere. Spring flowers from all their gardens were on the tables with ivy and other vines braided and placed over the windows.

As the fiddle music started, Martha and Philip, along with several others, gathered to dance the reel. Papa approached her and held his hand out. "I believe this is our dance."

As he led her to where the dancers stood in their lines, Mary laughed and pointed to Mark and Teddy leading Emily and Emma to the floor. "Those fellows will never be free of the twins after this."

"True," Papa had a sly grin. "But I suspect their constant grumbling about the twins shadowing them is becoming more an affectation than an annoyance."

"Hmm. An interesting thought to ponder. I'm gathering more ammunition to torment my family and friends."

Partners faced each other in two lines, and a violin accompanied the fiddler's calls while the dancers executed the figures and sets. The dancing continued for the next hour with other couples joining in the revelry.

Mary danced with Cole Turner following the reel with Papa. Out of breath, she sat on a bench against the wall observing the newly married couple. Philip hid nothing of his devotion to Martha. *How sweet.* Would anyone ever look at her the way Philip beamed at his bride? Doubtful. Most people were more discreet about their feelings. Not Philip, but that was part of his charm.

Papa approached with cups of cider and took a seat beside her. "You look lovely today."

"Thank you, Papa. 'Tis my wedding gown."

"What? Have you an announcement."

"No, not at all. 'Tis the gown grandmother got for me during my visit to Philadelphia six years ago. I wore it to Jean's and now Martha's weddings. That was all I meant."

He took her hand. "One day we shall have a wedding celebration for you, poppet. You will be a beautiful bride."

She tilted her head and smiled at him. "You have not called me poppet in years, not since Sara's birth."

"I suppose 'tis more an endearment for a little lass."

"I may never be a bride, Papa. I hope you and Mama will not be disappointed if I never marry. Perhaps I will be occupied in other endeavors."

"You are but twenty-one, much too young to abandon the idea of finding a partner to share your life. None of us know what the future holds. You may be surprised."

She sighed. "I love you, Papa. You have always been such an encourager. I promise I shan't close any doors to a possible match someday, but when all the wedding festivities are behind us, there is something I wanted to address with you and Mama."

His eyebrows rose in question, but she smiled and walked away. She wouldn't bring up the idea of being a seamstress until after the Green returned to its normal activities. Excitement filled her just thinking about telling her parents about her plans.

CHAPTER 30

Donald took a deep breath before entering the Bryant Printshop. He walked past the water vat to where Thad sat on a stool spreading the lampblack over the galleys. Type still lay scattered all over the floor.

He held his hat in front of him, "Thad, I'm sorry. I don't know why I blew up the way I did. I never used to lose my temper—but lately—. There is no excuse, and I know I don't deserve your forgiveness."

"How bout pickin up the type?" Thad's voice was low, not gruff.

Donald kneeled down and began gathering the type into his hat. What else could he say? How long would it take for Thad to tell him his services were no longer wanted?

Thad finished with the lampblack and stared at him. "Have you had any supper?"

"No. I wasn't feeling well. Got sick. I'm not hungry."

"Pulling the lever takes strength. You need victuals for that. If you think yer stomach can take it, there are ham and beans on the hearth."

Thad's calm manner unnerved him. *Yell at me. Tell me how disappointed you are with me.* Donald served the food on plates and brought it to where Thad gazed out the front window.

"Sit down and eat."

"Yes, sir." It smelled good, but he had no appetite.

Thad took a bite and continued staring at him.

He took another bite but had a hard time swallowing it. If only Thad would complain and accuse him of being undependable, he might feel better.

Thad focused on the wall beyond where he sat. "Had a brother. Willy was young but older than me by a couple of years. He had grand ideas of going west, but went to Alexandria in '55 and got mixed up with the war. Came home in late '57 after the Siege of Fort William Henry up north. When he came home, he was never the same. The war changed him. He got angry all the time. Finally, got in a fight and was shot." Thad shook his head and looked him in the eyes. "Our pa had no understanding, which only made it worse for Willy."

"I'm sorry." The lump in his throat made eating impossible. Thad had lost so many close to him.

"After you exploded and left this afternoon, I wondered … if my Fraser had come home, would he be struggling like you? I sure wouldn't want him to have ended up like Willy."

Donald closed his eyes and lowered his head. "Too many men have died, but I survived, and it wrenches my gut." How many times over these years had he wondered why he survived?

"Feeling guilty for living is foolishness." Thad wiped his mouth on his sleeve. "I figure the best way I can help you is to put the past behind us and give you a chance for a better future."

This man, with all his losses, had extended him mercy. "I will do all I can to prove your trust, sir."

A baby's cry startled Mary awake. It took a minute or two to remember she was not at home but in Alexandria with Jean. She rubbed her eyes. Jean and she had stayed up too late last night, sharing news. The clock on the dresser showed it was now well after seven.

Peter greeted her on the stair landing when she left the bedroom. "I am off to the shop. Jean is feeding Neil in the nursery."

"I apologize for arriving so late last night, but no one expected the wagon to suffer wheel problems."

"'Twas no trouble. We are simply pleased you came. As you see, we are up at all hours. Jean is grateful for your company and help." He touched the brim of his hat. "I will see you later at dinner."

In the nursery, Jean held Neil while yawning. "The hardest part of motherhood is how little sleep one gets. Here, take the stool."

Mary drew it near and sat. "I should have been more sensitive last night and insisted we continue our chat this morning."

"Don't be silly. The time got away from us. Please help yourself to whatever you can find in the kitchen."

"May I bring you something, coffee, perhaps? Or do you plan to nap after Neil is finished?"

"I might nap after dinner. Bring water, and maybe a scone." She smiled through half-open eyes.

Twenty minutes later, with Neil changed and returned to his cradle, they descended to the main floor.

Jean put another scone on her plate. "I thought about what you said last night about your letter to Donald. 'Tis unlike him not to respond."

She had told Jean only part of the story of that day on the quay and Donald's efforts to protect her. "Perhaps he is angry or hurt. My response that day was harsh. Or, 'tis possible he has developed other interests since he has been in Lexington." She tensed. There, she had given voice to her fear.

Jean's eyebrows lifted. "Donald did not mention any young ladies other than his friend's sister, and his comment did not suggest he has taken a fancy to her. Even if he had, that would not stop him from acknowledging your apology. Something else is afoot. He has always been fair-minded and would never hold a grudge, certainly not with you."

"Nevertheless, 'tis over three months, and I must give thought to another future for myself."

Jean bit into her scone. "I applaud your plans to become a seamstress. I'm tied to the house, but please feel free to go to Mrs.

Parker's this morning if you wish. She might be the best person to answer your questions about what dressmakers charge for their work. Neil will nap until shortly before dinner."

"Perhaps, I will." Mary stiffened her back. 'Twas time to seek a useful vocation and not simply wait for what could not be. It had been a year since the attack in Charlottesville. She must focus on the future and not allow the past to cripple her.

☙❦❧

Donald and Boyd rode their mares beside the Alexanders' wagon after church. Jenny sat between her parents.

"Thad regrets not being here today, Mrs. Alexander. He was disappointed to miss your dinner."

"We will look forward to Thad joinin us another time."

Jenny smiled his way, and Boyd's eyebrow quirked in Donald's direction.

"We are glad yer joinin us." Randall Alexander's deep voice was easy to hear over the rumble of the wagon wheels. "'Tis a shame Thad missed the sermon this mornin. Would have done him a world of good."

Donald nodded. "I agree." The pastor's talk on persevering through life's trials and losses had been powerful and heartfelt. "Thad looked pretty rugged this morning. Said he felt poorly and wanted to go back to bed." The man was cantankerous more often than not, but Thad was wise and had a tender heart. He had benefited by Thad's generosity in overlooking his earlier display of temper. He sighed. Fortunately, there had not been another outburst. If only he could escape the horrors that plagued him at night and unexpectedly during the day.

Donald followed Boyd inside. Savory smells filled the room. "I'm much obliged for your invitation. Whatever you have on your hearth reminds me of my ma's beef stout stew."

Mrs. Alexander grinned. "Ye has a keen sense of smell, lad. 'Tis exactly that. Do you think ye could carry a bit home with ye for Thad if I put it in a crock?"

"I certainly will. 'Tis mighty kind of you and will certainly cheer him."

Boyd took down a jug from the kitchen shelf. "Pa, after services, Bailey said something about a robbery."

Mr. Alexander nodded. "Remember a few months back when the post rider came through here? Said he was carryin the post and was robbed of his mail pouch. Well, Bailey said they think they found the pouch near Captain Kennedy's mill."

Boyd poured the cider into cups and passed them around the table. "Were the posts still inside?"

Mr. Alexander shook his head. "Cannot tell. Everythin in the pouch was mush."

After Boyd offered the blessing, Mrs. Alexander and Jenny served the stew and rounds of bread. Jenny's coy smiles were endearing but also required a measured response.

Boyd tore off a piece of bread from the round and passed it. "Did they ever catch the thief?"

Mr. Alexander took a piece of bread and passed it to his wife. "Nay. But it made me wonder whether the post I was waitin fer from my brother was in there."

Mrs. Alexander placed her hand on her husband's sleeve. "Ye think the lost mail came from as far away as Culpeper?"

Boyd poured more cider into his cup. "No way of knowin, Ma. The post riders travel between many towns. They might have posts they pick up from Culpeper and take to Charlottesville and others they would deliver to other locations. And everywhere they stop, they might be pickin up other pieces to be delivered elsewhere. Everyone pays for the service."

Jenny's forehead wrinkled. "Do ye think the dispatches might have anythin to do with the war, Boyd? That could be dangerous."

"'Tis doubtful. Those are transported by military couriers."

Donald nodded. "I served as a courier several times, but there have also been plenty of civilians who have been transporters."

Jenny ladled more stew into their bowls. "I did not know post riders needed to fear bein robbed."

Donald took another bite of the stew. It tasted exactly like Ma's. Had any of his or his family's letter's been amongst the ill-fated posts?

⁂

With the gardening finished, Mary gazed toward the pond but didn't linger, even though a sunny day made going back to the kitchen less appealing. *All work and no play ...*

Mama looked up from rolling out pie dough when she came through the door. "Were the three baskets of produce the girls brought in all there was?"

"Yes, do you need help, or is there time for me to go for a walk?"

Mama tilted her head. "Is something troubling you?"

"I'm just restless and wanted to think."

Mama wiped her hands on her apron and headed to the common room only to be back seconds later. "The clock on the hutch said noon. You can get your walk and do me a favor at the same time. You can take a basket of berries to Mr. Pike. When the Simpsons came over on the ferry yesterday, they mentioned they were staying at the Green. Mr. Pike raved about our berries. Care to walk as far as the crossing? The next crossing is at one. You should be there in plenty of time not to miss him."

She spotted a bowl of berries by the window. "Certainly, I can do that."

"Those are for the pies. Mr. Pike's berries are in that basket on the hutch."

Minutes later, Mary walked past the pond, hardly disturbing the resting geese and preening ducks. The gentle breeze made the July heat far more pleasant. She dipped her hand into the basket.

Mr. Pike would not miss two, or three, or four of the delicious berries.

Her visit to Alexandria last month had been exactly the encouragement she needed. Mrs. Parker had advised her on prices for specific sewing jobs as well as making suggestions on ways to advertise her services. Mama, with all her years of selling fabrics and notions, would provide invaluable information, but speaking with Mrs. Parker first had been intentional. Sounding informed and confident when she approached the subject of starting a dressmaking business with Mama and Papa was essential.

Her time with the Duncans and O'Brians had been both a bruising and a balm. *I love the family, but memories of Alexandria with Donald and learning more of his life in Lexington feels like a scab being peeled off too soon.* Seeing the Cameron Street Tavern and the quay had been painful reminders of their last day together. A day so hopeful at the onset yet had ended so miserably.

She leaned over and pulled wildflowers. Life had not turned out as she had hoped. Certainly not like her friends. Jean, married and a mother, and Martha married. Even learning of Patrick O'Brian's recent nuptials only poured salt on her wounds. Papa was right. She was only twenty-one, hardly a spinster—yet.

Why had Donald not written, even if only to acknowledge her letter? Had he not accepted her apology and forgiven her? Mama's words came back. She had not written to Donald to get a response but to apologize—and she had done that.

She must put aside her disappointment and focus on her future. One without Donald.

CHAPTER 31

D onald placed the type in the composing sticks. *Concentrate on the task at hand. You can do nothing about Jean's letter now.* He should have waited to open it, but Jean's script had caught his attention. If there had been an emergency at home, he could not wait.

Thad opened the windows. "The hot weather will make the paper dry quicker. You are becoming a fine printer, Mr. Duncan."

"At least I'm getting a bit faster at setting the type." Thad's approval meant everything. "Fixing the carriage yesterday buoyed my confidence."

"As you have discovered, keeping the machinery running is essential. Now, all we need to do is to get you to stop the thrashing and screaming in the night."

"You will get no argument from me on that subject." The sweats, nightmares, and floundering left him exhausted.

Thad took off his apron. "The varnish and lampblack are on the galleys. I'm off to get us pasties from the tavern. I won't be gone long."

Thad walked out the door and by the front window. The print job needed completing, but the letter in his pocket invaded his thoughts. Setting the composing stick down, he pulled it out to reread.

Donald ~

I hope all is well with you and that by now, you are gaining proficiency as a printer. Perhaps you will come home for a visit and bring a sample of your work.

We are eager for you to meet Neil. Your nephew is five months now and quite the charmer. Peter has received several new commissions for work. He continues to make lovely pieces of furniture.

Our parents are well and keep busy, Papa with business and working for the new Mayor. In addition to all Mama does, she spends time at a house not far from here, giving aid to wounded soldiers. Cameron and Will vex our parents even more than you did. Perhaps they collaborate and think there is safety in numbers. Cameron is now a fit horseman and has been invited to ride more than once with the gentry.

Brother, I have a bone to pick with you. Last month, Mary spent a few days with us. 'Twas good to see her again if only for a brief visit. She was grieved, and I was disappointed to learn that you never responded to her letter. She specifically wrote you to apologize for a misunderstanding you two had on your last day here. First, you leave us suddenly without announcement, and now this silly grudge you seem to harbor against her. 'Tis not at all like you to treat a friend this way, much less Mary, whom we all believed you intended to marry. I'm certain she will recover from the affront and find favor with another who appreciates her fine qualities. Is your neglect in responding to her due to an overriding interest you have developed in your new locale?

Nevertheless, we all wish you every happiness and hope that you will explain your reasons and even return for a visit.

Jean

He folded and stuffed the fine vellum into his pocket. *What letter from Mary?* He never received any communication from her. And an apology. What had she written? Jean said he had grieved Mary. *What must she be thinking?* He picked up another composing stick. Thad would be back soon.

After work, the two men walked to Thad's cottage. He only half-listened to Thad rambling on about an advertisement they needed to add to the next issue. Mary must still care for him, or she would not be upset by his silence. What should he do? Let her know he never received her letter? Go to Stewarts' Green and attempt to heal any injury he may have caused her? But how? He lived several days away.

"Where are you, lad?" Thad stopped in front of his stone dwelling and stared at him. "You have not listened to a word I said."

"I'm sorry, sir. I received a post from home that distracted me."

"Bad news? Come inside."

"No. My family is well. I'm at odds as to how to clear up misunderstandings."

"'Tis bout Mary?"

"What do you know about Mary?" Boyd must have told him. Seemed unlike him to—

"You call Mary's name out often enough at night, I feel like she is living here with us. More than a bit eerie." Thad lit the lamp before twilight. "Want to talk about what troubles you?"

Not hardly. He took a deep breath and studied the man. Perhaps he might have insight. Thad treated him more like a son than an employee.

"You want cider or ale?" Thad grabbed the jug of ale. "If 'tis about a woman, better have the ale."

He put his hand up. "Cider. I want to keep my wits about me." A half hour later, after giving an abbreviated retelling of his and Mary's relationship and the day's missive from his sister, he leaned back on the worn settee.

"Sounds like you need to write to her."

"I should, but if her post failed to arrive ..."

"'Twas that the misunderstanding that led you to leave Alexandria and come here?"

"It probably hastened my departure, but I already planned to pursue a printing apprenticeship."

"Let me ask you something." Thad handed him a pasty. "If you fail to clear up the misunderstanding, will you have any peace?"

Thad was right. The last thing he needed was something else to haunt him. He would write to her.

That night, Donald gathered paper and sharpened a quill. He would write to Jean and Mary and post them different days as a safeguard against possible loss.

> *Dear Jean,*
>
> *I was both pleased and perplexed by your recent letter. 'Tis good to hear all is well with you, Peter, Neil, and our family and to be brought up to date on their activities. However, I'm surprised to learn about the letter you referred to from Mary. I never received any such correspondence from her since arriving in Lexington. Had I received a letter, I can assure you, I would have responded. I have formed no attachment. Mary owes me no apology. If you see her or correspond with her, please let her know I did not receive a letter, and no apology is needed. I would never want her distressed in any way. I will write to her also but wished you to be aware in case another post is lost.*
>
> *I'm fortunate to work for Mr. Bryant. Each day I learn a new facet of the printing business. He has taught me much and has been a patient mentor and friend.*
>
> > *My love to all.*
> > *Donald*

He read it over, set it aside to dry, and dipped the quill back into the ink bottle.

> *Dear Mary,*
>
> *I received a letter today from my sister full of news but also a rebuke. She indicated you had written and apologized for a*

misunderstanding on our last day together. I never received any letter from you. 'Twould seem that the post was lost. Let me assure you, no apology is needed. When the gun fired that day, I frightened you when I wanted to protect you. Fortunately, you were only in danger from my clumsy efforts at chivalry. 'Twas not the first time I caused you to fall and landed on top of you. I recall our game of blind man's bluff years ago ended in a similar fashion. I would never want to cause you distress. You have always held a special place in my heart.

Jean seems quite taken with motherhood and their new son. No doubt, you found that to be the case during your recent visit to Alexandria.

I found work in Lexington as an apprentice to Mr. Thad Bryant in his printing shop. He has been patient and helpful while I have been learning the business. He is a recent widower living alone and invited me to board in his cottage. I help with the chores and occasionally get lucky hunting and fishing. My cooking skills are minimal, but we are not going hungry. My friend, Boyd Alexander, lives near here. Many Sundays after church, we go to his family's home for our one decent meal of the week. The Alexanders are also Scots, so their food reminds me of home.

If I can get away, I may try to return for a visit before winter. It would be good to spend time with family and friends even if only for a few days. I hope you and your family are well.

My warmest regards.
Donald

He reread the letter. Hopefully, this would clear up any confusion and put Mary at ease. His abrupt departure from Alexandria had been impulsive, a foolish response to being hurt by Mary's indignation. Would it open any doors? That would certainly be his desire.

At the slightest sign of encouragement, he would do everything in his power to win her back.

CHAPTER 32

Mary walked along the path from the Whitcombs' farm. The warm September afternoon, free of humidity, tempted her to keep walking, but she needed to help Polly and Mama with the preserving.

Mama was standing at the worktable, slicing onions, when she entered the kitchen. "How is Martha? Is she feeling better?"

"Yes, the sickness seems to have passed, and she is excited about becoming a mother. And Philip … he had us both laughing. He is like a mother hen. He left the harvest and returned to the cottage to make sure Martha was not overtaxing herself."

Polly carried a large pail of peppers and green tomatoes to the table. "What were the two of you doing that that would tax her?"

Mary tied her apron strings. "We went through a box of old clothing and fabrics to set aside pieces for the quilt I will make. Hardly a strenuous activity."

Mama's and Polly's eyes met, and they laughed. Polly shook her head. "I best talk with Philip. He will never get the harvest finished if he checks on her several times a day, particularly now that Teddy is gone."

Mama piled the onions into a large porcelain bowl. "The men sent Mark over to help him. I wonder how Teddy is adjusting to school? Mark misses his company."

Mary set several green tomatoes aside to slice. "I'm sure he is relishing his new life there."

Mama handed Mary a knife. "I don't remember Teddy being fond of his studies under Mr. Martin, but perhaps now that he is older, he will find them more to his liking. Did you tell Martha about the order for Miss Russell's gown?"

"I did." Mary added the tomatoes to the onions. "If the garments I sew please Mrs. Russell and her daughter, it might foster additional opportunities for me amongst other families. I'm eager to start on that rose silk for Miss Russell's gown."

"'Twas nice of Amelia to recommend you to them," Mama said. "If you need any assistance with the gown, I have worked with silk before."

Mama and Polly had both given her such encouragement in her new venture.

Mary folded her hands as if in prayer. "I hoped you would. I worried about my inexperience with silk when I agreed to the job. I shall thank Mrs. Turner when I see her."

"Please take the men their meals. That way, they won't need to stop working and come back here."

Thirty minutes later, walking back to the Green, Mary picked wildflowers growing along the path. A rider approached on the lane. The post rider—perhaps with further instructions or requests from Mrs. Russell? She met him, took the packet he handed her, and fished in her pocket for a coin. When she entered the kitchen, she set the basket down.

"I will put those in water." Mama poured water into a jar.

"They were pretty, I could not pass them by." She went through the packet, mumbling. "These are for Papa." Her heart skipped a beat. One had Donald's script.

Mama stopped and put the flowers down. "What is it, Mary?"

"A letter from Donald." She waved it in front of her.

"Go ahead. Go and read it." Mama winked at Polly.

She raced to the common room and perched in the window seat. Her hands shook as she cracked the seal, opened it, devouring each line.

He never received my letter. Of course, I was disappointed you did not answer. Oh Donald, I never told you why I was frightened, why I yelled at you, and then ran away. She laughed. That game of blind man's

199

bluff they played when life had been much simpler. His tripping and falling on her was no accident, but another opportunity to tease her.

I would never want to cause you distress.

Her hand went to her chest. *You have always held a special place in my heart.*

Did he still love her? Donald sounded pleased with his work and living situation. She held her hand against her mouth. He might try to return before winter for a visit to spend time with family and friends. Surely he would not tell her that if he did not want to see her. *My warmest regards* sounded hopeful.

She took a deep breath. *God, You answered my prayer. He wrote to me.* Perhaps there was reason to hope.

Donald handed Thad his jacket. "I finished straightening the shop. We still have some of that supper left from last night."

Thad's eyes widened. "Any other choices?"

The door opened, and Amos came in. "I told Trudy I would be at the tavern for the celebration. You two want to join me?" Amos picked up the paper on top of the stack set on the table.

Thad stood and put on his jacket. "What celebration?"

Amos perused the paper. "Avery said he would give a pint of ale to the first fifteen gents arriving after six, celebrating the first anniversary since Cornwallis surrendered at Yorktown."

Donald shook his head. "Avery is always finding an excuse to celebrate at the tavern."

Thad raised an eyebrow. "'Tis a tavern."

Amos folded the paper and put it in his vest pocket. "Said Lydia is serving shepherd's pie."

"Sure, we can come," said Thad.

"Sounds good to me," Donald agreed. "Thad can avoid my cooking another night."

After entering the dimly lit taproom, Donald followed Thad and Amos to a table by the window. Nine other men were seated at tables nearby. His mouth watered at the savory smell of the pie and cornbread when Avery's wife brought it to the table. She made several more deliveries to the surrounding tables.

Avery shouted out, "A toast to General George Washington, our glorious Commander and the victory at Yorktown."

"Huzzahs" were heralded throughout the room.

Donald served the three of them large portions of the steaming pie from the crock.

Amos took some cornbread. "You still want my help for a couple of weeks, Thad?"

Thad nodded and glanced at Donald. "I asked Amos to help at the shop for a bit if you wanted time away. 'Tis been near a year, and I figured you might want time to head north and see your folks before winter and travel gets rough."

Donald stared at the two men. How could he ever repay them? For days he had wanted to broach that subject with Thad, but he hated leaving him with all the responsibility of the shop.

"Yes. I would be grateful to go back and see my family." *And Mary.*

Thad sipped at his ale. "Well then, October is a good time to do that."

"Aye, Trudy is doing well right now and can spare me," Amos added.

"We can discharge you for a bit." Thad put his jug down. "But be sure and come back. I have grown to depend on you."

"My thanks to you both." He could be gone for a time and not feel like he left Thad without help. He would stop at Stewarts' Green on the way home.

Thad nodded. "Sure, lad. Please bring back a few of your ma's recipes and cooking tips." The two men broke out in laughter.

The generosity of his friends moved him, even as they teased him. He'd not soon forget the grace and kindness Thad had extended. His willingness to teach Donald the trade he'd wished most to learn. Indeed. He owed the older man much.

It was time to go back home. Time to tell Mary of his outbursts and nightmares. He would do all he could to secure her heart and be the husband she deserved.

CHAPTER 33

Donald paced himself throughout the days of riding with the crisp weather with the leaves in all their yellow, orange, and red glory energizing him.

If he arrived at Stewarts' Green early in the afternoon, he would have a better chance of getting a room—as if the Stewarts would turn him away. *Please, Mary, be home and not traveling.* Had she gotten his letter? How would she receive him?

His heart pounded as he entered the lane that approached the Green. An axe rang out. Mark chopped wood by the barn, but he set the axe down and came to meet Donald.

"We heard you were in the Shenandoah Valley."

Donald dismounted and shook Mark's hand. "I have been, but had time off to spend a few days with the family. Thought I would stop here for a visit, stay the night if you have room. I will continue home tomorrow."

"There's always room for a Duncan. You know that."

"Is Mary here?" *Please say yes.*

"Inside, I think. I'll take your horse, go find her."

Donald forced himself to walk to the door, even though his feet wanted to race as much as his heart was.

Mary set the rags and broom outside the last of the rooms she had cleaned. She needed to close all the windows now that the fresh air had cleared the odor from last night's guests and their two infants. Voices drifted from below. Who was Mark speaking with? Her heart skipped a beat.

Donald. Could it be?

Her pulse skittered as she leaned out the window at Donald's chestnut mare. *He is here. He said he would come.* Her fingers struggled to untie the apron as she ran to her bedroom. Peering in the mirror, she tucked loose strands of hair back into her cap, then splashed lavender water on her neck. At the top of the stairs, she stopped. *Calm down.* She grabbed the banister with an unsteady hand and descended to the center hall.

The front door opened, and Donald entered. He removed his hat, dipped his head, and grinned.

Joy bubbled from deep inside. Could he sense how fast her heart beat? "What a pleasant surprise."

"I'm on my way to Alexandria for a few days with my folks, and thought I would stop here and spend the evening—if you have space."

"We have plenty of room." His sea-green eyes bore into her. Her mouth went dry.

Sara ran into the hall, yelling. "Mama, Donald Duncan is here."

He bent down on one knee to greet her. "Good day, Sara."

Mary took Sara's hand. "Come to the common room and get warm by the fire. You must tell us about Lexington and your work."

Mama entered the large room from the kitchen with arms open and pulled Donald into an embrace. "You are just in time for dinner. You must be hungry after your travels."

He winked at Mary as he hugged Mama. "I timed my arrival perfectly. A home-cooked meal is always appreciated."

Mary took a step toward the kitchen. "We have hot cider on the hearth. I will be right back with a cup to warm you."

"Nay, lass," Mama said. "Stay here with Donald. Sara and I can do that."

Donald faced her, a tentative smile formed. *We never used to be awkward around each other, but so much has happened. Could they bridge this divide?* She motioned him to sit on the chair nearest the hearth and sat on the settee directly across from him.

He leaned forward. "Did you receive my letter? The one I wrote in August?"

"Yes. Yes, I did."

"Might we take a walk after dinner? I want to spend time with your family, but I think we need to talk."

"Yes. We can walk to the pond if you like."

Mama and Sara returned. "Take a seat at the table, Sara and I will bring in the dinner. We can ask the Gordons to join us later this evening. They will want to see you, too."

Papa, Douglas, and Mark entered. Papa shook Donald's hand and thumped him on the back. "What a pleasant surprise. Come and sit down. It smells like dinner is ready. You must tell us all about your new home and work."

Papa offered the blessing. He passed the platter of chicken to Donald. "We understand you are a printer's apprentice in the Shenandoah Valley."

"Yes, sir. I arrived in Lexington at an opportune time. The owner of the printshop, Thad Bryant, needed help. He already had an assistant, but the man needed to care for his ailing wife."

"Sounds like perfect timing," Papa said.

"Mr. Bryant, a widower, invited me to live with him. I think he was lonely."

Mama passed the beans. "Does he not have family nearby?"

"He lost his only son at Guilford Courthouse."

Everyone was silent as they glanced around the table at each other.

"What is wrong?" Sara asked.

"'Tis where Todd died," Douglas said.

Sara grimaced and lowered her head. "I forgot which battle."

Donald set down his fork. "I would not expect you to recall that."

Mary patted Sara's back. "I'm sure you are an able assistant and companion for Mr. Bryant."

Donald laughed. "I've tested the man's patience more than once when I have slowed the printing process down, and my cooking leaves much to be desired."

They all laughed, breaking the tension.

Papa winked at Mama. "God often works in mysterious ways. He places people in our paths at exactly the right time. 'Tis a reminder of His provision and presence."

Mary rearranged the food on her plate while the others ate and chatted. On their walk, she would tell him of the attack in Charlottesville. *I cannot do this by myself, Lord. I need the right words, and to not fear the outcome. Help me.*

Papa leaned close. "Mary, are you well?" he whispered.

"I'm fine."

Donald cleared his throat. "Sir, may I take Mary for a walk?"

Papa glanced at her, then nodded. "Certainly. One could not ask for a nicer fall day. Mark, Douglas, we have work to do."

"Sara, please help me clear the table," Mama said.

"I will get my shawl and be right with you." Mary carried the platter to the kitchen, set it on the table, and picked up her cream knit shawl.

Mama approached and hugged her. "I will be praying for you."

"Please pray I will have the right words." So much depended on it.

Mary did her best to appear unruffled as Donald held the front door open for her. A gust of wind blew countless leaves from the trees as he took her arm. *Calm yourself. 'Tis the right thing to do.*

"You are trembling. Are you warm enough?" His concern was touching.

"Yes." She continued walking across to the path that led to the pond. Her tremors had nothing to do with the weather. She wrapped the shawl tighter. "You sound pleased with Lexington and your position."

"I'm grateful for the job, and Thad Bryant has been a mentor as well as an employer. Boyd Alexander has been a good friend. He made the last two years of the war bearable and introduced me to Thad. Boyd said 'twas providential I came to the valley when I did, and I'm inclined to believe him." He looked directly at her. "But I wouldn't say everything worked out the way I hoped. That day on our walk along the quay, I planned to ask for your hand."

"Oh, Donald." She put her hand to her throat. "I'm sorry I hit you and said the things I did—and for running away. I was terrified, but please, believe me, I was not afraid of you."

His questioning eyes searched hers.

I must do this. "That day … I was already anxious when we walked along the river because there was something I needed to tell you. And I was afraid. Then the gun fired. When you pushed me to the ground, I panicked because it reminded me …" She swallowed. "I ran back to the O'Brians' home. I wanted to apologize by the time I got there. But 'twas too dark so I waited until early the next morning. When I arrived at your home to explain, your mother said you had gone."

He took her elbow. "Do you want to keep walking, or shall we go sit at the pond?"

Her legs shook. "I would like to sit."

He brushed the leaves off the bench and sat facing her. "I should never have left Alexandria, without saying goodbye to you or Jean. My pride and my own problems overruled any wisdom."

She took a deep breath.

He held her hand. "When the gun fired, it triggered memories of battles, fear, and death. I panicked and frightened you. I'm sorry."

"No, Donald! You have nothing to apologize for. You only meant to keep me safe." She pressed her lips together and took a deep breath. "I need to explain why I responded the way I did." His hand caressed hers. She peered into his eyes. "I don't understand the evil acts people commit."

He nodded. "We can agree on that."

She clutched her hands together. "Last June, when I accompanied Jean and Peter to Charlottesville, we stayed at an inn on the outskirts of the town. Peter needed to make a delivery to his client. Jean took ill and, hoping to help her, I went out in search of the apothecary the inn recommended. When I approached the street where the shop was located, it looked empty. The previous evening, we heard Governor Jefferson and the Assembly were meeting locally. Later, we learned British troops had been dispatched there in hopes of capturing the legislators."

His brow furrowed. He took her hands and held them. "I heard about that. You all were in incredible peril. Thank God you were not hurt."

Her lips trembled.

"What is it?"

She pulled from deep inside for all the courage she could muster. "I *was* hurt."

His eyes grew wide. "What?"

"When I drew near the apothecary shop, a British soldier approached me smelling of strong drink" She rocked back and forth. "He dragged me inside a vacant shop. and attacked me … in the worst way."

She couldn't look at him, couldn't risk seeing the disgust on his face. His silence was deafening.

⚜

Her words took his breath away. He opened his mouth, only to snap it shut again, unable to find the words. No—too angry to find them. His jaw tightened, and his hands clenched hers as a picture formed in his mind. A horrible, evil picture. Rage burned through him hotter than when he'd broken the crockery, much hotter than when he'd scattered the type.

Then the sun glinted off the tears on her face.

She needed soothing, not his fury. Would she let him hold her? Gently, so as not to startle her, he slid his arms around her and drew her close. She stiffened for an instant but then sagged against him, her silent sobs wracking her body. His anger drained, washed away by her tears … by her needs. What was done was done, and he couldn't change that, but he could reassure her.

"I'm so sorry you were violated," he whispered in her ear and caressing her back. When her sobs subsided, he pulled back and placed his hand on her cheek. With his thumb, he wiped her tears. "What happened to you was awful—unconscionable. I wish I could …" He pulled in a deep breath. "You survived, and I will thank God every day for that."

She lowered her head. "I felt filthy—ashamed."

His throat tightened. Her suffering made him ache. He took her hands in his. "You have nothing to be ashamed of. You were completely innocent. You were helping my sister."

"If only I had waited—waited for someone to go with me. The surroundings were unfamiliar." She turned her head away.

He took her cheek and brought her face back so she would see him. "'Twas completely outside of your control." How could he convince her?

"I wonder. Over the years, my parents admonished me of the risks of venturing off on my own." Her voice wavered, and she kept her eyes lowered. "But I never heeded their warnings. Walking helps me to organize my thoughts and settle down when I'm anxious."

"There is nothing wrong with taking walks. You must not blame yourself. I thank God you escaped." *I'm beginning to sound like Boyd.*

"I did not escape. He left me in the deserted building. I gathered my wits and made my way back to the inn, then attempted to act as though nothing happened."

He raised her chin to see her face. "You never told Jean?"

"No. She knew I had a problem, but I feigned ill health, and since she had been sick, she and Peter believed me."

"Did you tell anyone—your mother?"

"Eventually, I had to. Mama knew something was terribly wrong with me. At times, my temper, and the way I avoided or treated people was insufferable." Her eyes, full of pain, met his. "Precisely like I treated you that day by the river. Even the sight of a man in a green jacket makes me ill."

He dropped her hand and leaned back. "The soldier wore a green jacket?"

"Yes, and a helmet with a plume." Her eyes squinted. "Why?"

"Sounds like the uniform worn by Banastre Tarleton's Dragoons. It makes sense. I recall now. They were involved with the raid on Charlottesville." His chest tightened. "Tarleton and his men were ruthless and merciless at Waxhaws. Thank God your life was spared." He lowered his head a moment, trying to push the image of her attack from his mind. He took her hand again, and they sat in silence for a time.

Mary sniffled. "I wish I could forget what happened, but thoughts of it still plague me—night and day."

"I understand, dearest. My memories haunt me also. There is a great deal we both must learn to put behind us."

"How do we do that?" Skepticism etched her face.

"I'm not sure. One day at a time. Perhaps we can help each other."

⊙⚜⊙

Strength returned to Mary's limbs, like life flowing back into her as the burden of her secret was lifted. She had been right to tell him, no matter the consequences. He needed to know that her words and actions that day in Alexandria had nothing to do with him. Donald had been kind—and sympathetic—but would the attack always be a barrier between them?

Donald drew her hands to his chest. "I don't understand the evil

210

acts people commit any more than you do. What I've witnessed, and have been part of, still haunt me day and night. It has changed me. I have acted out in anger for no explicable reason. I have no advice to offer you." He placed his hands on her cheeks. "One thing I am sure of is that my feelings for you have never changed. I love you, Mary Stewart. And what happened to you does not alter my feelings in any way."

"You cannot know how I have longed to hear that. I love you also."

He caressed her cheeks and kissed her lips gently, then with more intensity. She backed off. Would she be able to forget that monster, and freely be the loving wife she wanted to be, and he deserved?

"You were hurt … and I will do all I can to help you heal. Would your love for me have changed if I returned home injured?"

"No, of course not."

He took her hands, rubbing the backs of them with his thumbs. "I can be patient—and will do everything in my power to make you feel safe. I asked your father years ago if I might court you, and he agreed. Now, I'm asking you, will you be my wife?"

She must trust again. She wanted to trust again. But even more than that, she wanted to be his wife. "Yes, Donald. I will."

He encircled her with his arms and kissed her again, not as before but with an ardor that stirred her. She returned his kiss, surprised by her own desire. This time he pulled back.

"More of those, and I may forget I need to speak with your father. And soon."

CHAPTER 34

Mary hung her cloak on the kitchen wall and walked to the hearth to warm her hands. Sara and Mama's voices came from the common room. She could wait no longer and headed in that direction.

With embroidery threads and scissors between them, Mama and Sara worked at the table. A loosely woven sampler held taut in an embroidery ring rested on Sara's lap. Mama glanced at Mary. "Come near the hearth and warm yourself. You left your gloves on the shelf by the door."

And my heart in the barn.

"Yes, I forgot them—again." A glance over her shoulder confirmed it. Mama studied her like a cat eyeing a mouse. Mary turned her backside to the warmth and smiled, trying not to show the excitement bubbling inside her. "Donald is in the barn with Papa, but I expect he will join us soon. Shall I heat up cider?"

"Keep working, Sara, I will be back in a few minutes." Mama followed her into the kitchen. "I shall help you, lass."

"Please bring me some cider, too," Sara called after them.

"Well?" Mama asked as soon as they entered the kitchen.

"I told Donald everything. He was compassionate and assured me of his love."

Mama hugged her. "I knew he would. And you? How are you feeling?"

"I love him, and I told him so."

"Thank you, Lord."

Mary placed tankards on a tray while Mama heated the cider. "Donald is hurting in his own way. I think he has been impacted by the war more than I thought. We have both changed, but we now have hope for a shared future." She could not keep the wide smile back. "He asked me to marry him—and I agreed. That's why he is in the barn now with Papa."

Mama beamed. "I have always believed you and Donald would work this out. I think you will be a balm to each other, and aid in each other's healing."

"That is my hope."

"Lass, we will need to plan a wedding."

Nothing had ever sounded so good to Mary.

Donald entered the dark barn. "Mr. Stewart?"

"Over here. Tending to my horse." Mary's Her father leaned his elbows on the side of a stall. "What can do I for you?"

Despite the chilly weather, Donald was sweating. "Sir, 'tis been years since you gave me your permission to court Mary. I wanted to tell you I have asked her for her hand, and she has agreed. We would like your blessing."

Matthew came out of the stall, grinned, and shook his hand. "You most certainly have my blessing. I could not be more pleased for both of you. Shall we go inside and see the ladies?"

That went well. Why had he worried?

He followed Matthew Stewart through the door into the kitchen and its aroma of spiced cider. Mary and her mother turned toward them.

"Well, Papa, what do you think?" Mary asked with that familiar coy tilt to her head.

Mr. Stewart winked at his wife then gathered Mary in his arms. "'Tis good to see that smile on your face. I believe you two will find happiness. Shall we go to the other room and discuss plans?"

Mrs. Stewart gave Donald a hug. "We could not be happier. You have always been like family, but now I will be proud to call you son."

He choked. "I ... I am grateful and humbled. You have always made me feel welcome. The union of our families seems meant to be."

He took Mary's hand, and they followed her parents into the common room. Would they think him irresponsible or impulsive for not having any plans in place?

Mary had a sheepish look. "We have made no specific arrangements yet."

Mrs. Stewart whispered something to Sara. "Where are Douglas and Mark? We have to have them here for the party, too." Sara chirped.

"They are on the other side of the barn loading wood to bring inside," Matthew said. "Go tell them there's hot cider."

Mary's father picked up a tankard. "Sit down, Donald. I know your folks will be glad to have you home. After talking with them, you will have a better idea when you want the wedding. Please stop here on your way back to Lexington."

"Yes, sir. Mary and I will begin to make plans. I need to obtain a place for us to live and find a time that will accommodate my employer."

"Of course."

The boys and Sara came through the door. Mark walked up to him and slapped him on the shoulder. "Sara told me the good news. Took you long enough to get my sister off our hands."

"Mark!" Mary said. The laughter and merriment continued through supper.

Donald and Mary shared their news with the Gordons' and then walked back hand in hand to the Green. Before going inside, he drew her close, breathing in the lavender fragrance of her hair. His eager lips found hers. Mary's response was timid, yet still fed his desire for her. *Go slowly, remember what she's endured.* Stepping back, he caressed her cheek. "I love you, Mary. I am so thankful you agreed to be my wife."

"I'm looking forward to that day and hope it won't be long."

"No longer than it must." He touched her cheek again. "We will no doubt have trials ahead of us, but if we are patient and forbearing with each other, I believe we can be truly happy."

CHAPTER 35

Mary watched Donald ride down the lane the next morning. When he was out of sight, she went to the henhouse to gather the eggs. Much had happened in his short time there, and last night had gone by too quickly. How would Donald's family react to their tentatively planned spring wedding? With surprise, but also joy. 'Twould have been fun to see their faces when he told them. She could hardly believe the joy that filled her. They were going to be married. Donald had been kind and sympathetic about the attack. How could she have been so fearful of telling him? After all these years, they could finally be together—far from the war and all its consequences.

She almost knocked Sara over when she opened the henhouse door. "What are you doing out here? 'Tis chilly. Come back inside with me."

"Mama told me you were getting the eggs." Sara had an odd expression on her face.

"What troubles you?"

"Why do you have to live so far away when you and Donald marry? I will miss you."

Mary put her arm around Sara's shoulder. "I know, poppet. I will miss you, too." They returned to the kitchen, and she set the basket on the table. "Donald lives and works in Lexington now." She kneeled and wrapped her arms around Sara. "I wish we were not to be far from each other, but it happens when people marry. They leave home and make a new life somewhere else."

"Martha did not have to leave home. Philip only had to go up the hill to the Whitcomb farm. Jean lives in Alexandria, where she can see her family anytime she wishes."

She rubbed Sara's back. "At times, it works out that way. But Mama came all the way across the Atlantic from Scotland and married Papa. She is far from her family and may never see them again."

"I fear I won't see you again. Sometimes people go away and don't come back."

"You need not fear, poppet." She smoothed the furrows on Sara's brow, then hugged her. "We will see each other as often as we can, and I will send letters. Perhaps you can write to me also. Sometimes, we imagine a situation to be so much worse than it is."

Sara sighed. "Will your wedding be like Jean and Peter's in Alexandria? Or will it be like Martha and Philip's here?"

"I expect we will be married here at the Green, perhaps in the spring. You can help us with it."

Sara's eyes lit up. "Well then, we should sit down with Mama and start planning."

She laughed and hugged her sister. "Not yet, but at the right time, I know we will want your ideas."

Sara scampered off, and Mary wrapped her arms around her middle. She would miss her family, the Gordons, and the Green. But in her heart, Mary knew this was what she wanted. What she'd always wanted.

Donald rode to the printshop. Odd, to find it closed. It had to be about four, judging by the sun. Thad and Amos had left early. He peered in the tavern, but he saw no one he knew.

He entered Thad's cottage. Silence but for the clock ticking on the stone mantel. *Four fifteen, but no Thad.* In the kitchen, a small beige dog curled up in front of the hearth raised his head.

"Who are you ... and what are you doing here?"

The dog approached and sniffed him, then followed him as he

searched the cottage bedrooms. *Empty.*

Thad was not in the barn when he saw to the mare. He returned to the cottage and put his gear away, then ate a piece of bread and cheese. Thad must have gone to Amos and Trudy's. He would walk the three blocks and see.

When he reached the Porters' road, something seemed amiss. Two couples stood outside. Thomas Harvey, the owner of the dry goods shop, looked solemn. Donald's stomach knotted. This was not a festive gathering.

"Mr. Harvey, I just got back to town. Is Thad here?"

"Glad you are home. He is inside with Amos. They will be pleased to see you."

Donald walked through the door to a room full of people. He groaned. Thad and Amos stood at the far end by the hearth. Both looked weary and wore black mourning bands.

Thad spotted him and came near. "'Tis a sad event you have come back to. Trudy passed day before yesterday. Buried her today."

"I thought she was better, or I would not have left when I did." He extended his hand to Amos. "I'm so sorry for your loss."

Amos clasped his hand. "Don't fret for leaving. None of us knew Trudy was so near the end. Even the doctor thought she had rallied. But she took a real turn for the worse three days ago."

Thad took him aside. "Hope your visit went well. I stayed here last night, and I think I will again tonight."

"I will see to the shop. Please tell me what I can do to help."

"Open the shop tomorrow. I will get there in the morning to get the *Journal* out."

"Anything we can do to help Amos? He said they had no children. Any other family around?"

Thad shook his head. "No, but he has friends. Boyd and his family were here and left a short time ago. He suggested that if you returned by the end of the week, we might bring Amos to their house for dinner after church."

That sounded like Boyd. Always trying to get them to church.

"Good idea."

Thad glanced at Amos, then pointed to the table. "Get yourself food to eat. Folks brought more than we can finish, and we don't want it to go to waste."

He served himself a bowl of stew and took an oat and barley cake. The local ladies had provided quite a spread. "By the way, I noticed you took in a new tenant at the cottage—a dog."

"Scruffy. A real mess when he showed up a week ago. Looks better now since he had a bath and some food. He is good company." Thad plopped part of an oatcake into his mouth.

The man was as soft on the inside as he was gruff on the outside. "I will feed the horses. I suppose you want me to feed Scruffy, too.

"Indeed," said Thad before he rejoined the others comforting Amos.

Life was fragile. The war had taught Donald that first hand. Each day and each relationship should be treasured. He wouldn't waste time securing a place for himself and Mary to live. He had already squandered enough opportunities in making her his bride.

Mary knocked, and Martha opened the front door, "Come in, come in." Her friend had a glow about her and had grown thicker around her middle.

Mary stepped inside the warm room. "Are you feeling up for a visit?"

"I am much better. There is chocolate warming in the kettle and coffee I made earlier for Philip if you prefer that."

"Chocolate sounds wonderful."

Martha walked to the hearth. "And is there sewing in that basket you have?

"Yes." She set it down and followed Martha. "I need to finish Miss Russell's stomacher. The rest of her garments are almost completed. Mama and I plan to take them to the Russells' by the end of next week. I have enjoyed working with such nice fabrics for her garments."

Martha handed her a steaming cup and sat at the table by the back window that faced a small garden and the barn. "Philip is in the barn sharpening tools, but he frequently comes to check on me." She laughed and placed her hand on her chest.

"I think 'tis sweet that he is attentive, and always wants to make sure you are well."

"Yes, the man is very protective." Martha tapped her fingers on the table. "Well, are you going to tell me any more about your plans with Donald? Once you finish with Miss Russell's garments, you will need to start on a gown for yourself for your wedding."

"We have no specific plans yet. Donald needs to learn when he will be able to get away as well as find us a place to live. I plan to make a dress for the wedding with the deep coral fabric we got a while ago."

"You have not heard from him since he got back to Lexington?"

"He has only been gone for ten days. I'm sure he is busy now that he is back in the valley." Mary kneaded the knot on the back of her neck. "He will write when he can." Perhaps this week, she would get a post from him. 'Twas no different than when Donald was gone to war, she still impatiently waited for the post courier to come.

Martha rubbed her middle. "'Twas not that long ago the two of us had few hopes of marriage, and you planned on becoming a seamstress. Now, look at us. I'm married and soon to be a mother, and you will be getting married before long.

"Our lives have indeed changed." She set out her threads, needles, and embroidery scissors. "I still have hope of taking on sewing jobs. Donald and I spoke about it when he returned to the Green. I don't know if there is a need for a seamstress in Lexington. But if I can add to our income, 'twould allow us to save for a home of our own. Initially, we will lease a dwelling."

I will miss you, Mary." Martha had a wistful look.

"And I, you. But I'm certain we will return for visits to see our families." In the past few days, she had begun to realize that one could be excited and happy about marriage and a new home while pining the parting with loved ones. "How is Teddy? What do you hear from the student?"

"He has made several friends and is quite taken with the school and town. He will return over Yuletide, but I fear he is losing interest in the farm."

A half hour later, Philip came through the door. "Good day, Mary, glad you came by." He washed his hands and sat at the table next to Martha. "I was sorry I missed seeing Donald. Martha told me you two plan to marry. I'm happy for you."

"That is very kind. He was disappointed not to have seen you, too."

"Will Donald move back and start a printshop here?"

"No. He is happy working at the printshop in Lexington, so I will move there." She gathered her sewing notions. "I must get back home now. I have enjoyed our visit."

Philip put an arm around Martha. "Come back soon, Mary. Martha loves your visits. I hope you and Donald will be as happy as we are."

"That is my hope, too." She hugged Martha.

CHAPTER 36

Donald held his coat closed, shivering as he walked to the printshop. The penetrating cold made it feel more like January than late November. The ten days he had been back in Lexington had been busy at the printshop. Amos had come by most days and helped them put out the *Journal*, but mostly he sought their company. Poor man. He seemed bereft since Trudy's death, and an unspoken sadness permeated the shop.

Donald unlocked the door and went inside. After getting the fire going in the hearth, he gathered the type and arranged them in the composing sticks.

Less than an hour later, Thad entered the shop. "Got the wagon wheel fixed." He took off his coat and walked toward the galley. "Good, you got things started. We have plenty of ink in the jugs, but we are low on paper. It will take you a day there and back, but you need to get to the warehouse tomorrow to purchase more. The wagon should be fine now for the trip. Remember to take the tarpaulin in the event of rain or snow."

"Yes, sir. I will stay at Oak Tavern. They have a barn where I can secure the wagon overnight." He needed to post a letter to Mary to let her know he arrived home and that Thad said he could go whenever he needed time away to get married. He was waiting to tell her he had found a proper dwelling for them, but that might take a bit more time. Tonight, he would write to her.

Amos arrived about an hour later, far more cheerful than in recent days. "I smell coffee, the perfect tonic to take the chill off a man."

Once the paper was on the drying racks, they stopped for dinner.

The three of them sat on the benches near the hearth, eating the tavern's venison pasties.

Donald bit into his and eyed Amos and Thad. They looked like they had something to say. Some error he had made? "What is on your mind?"

Thad poured them each more coffee and sat back down. "You made any more plans when you want to marry and where you are going to live?"

"No. I checked on a rental at the edge of town, but it resembled a shack. I'm still looking."

Thad set his cup down. "Well, we have been talking and have a plan. We wondered what you would think about moving your bride into my place."

Thad's cottage? Donald cleared his throat. How could he decline without offending him and sounding ungrateful? "That is a very kind offer. You have been generous letting me stay in your home all this time, but it might be a bit crowded for the three of us."

"You dunderhead. The last thing I want to do is hover over two lovebirds." Thad's face turned beet red. "Amos asked me if I wanted to live with him at his place. Said he wanted the company."

"Well, you could have mentioned that first." So that was what these chaps had been up to. A lump formed in his throat. They were a treasure.

"The place is furnished, but I will take your pallet to sleep on, a few linens, and my chair. I won't need much else."

Donald cleared his throat. "That is more than I could have hoped for. We need to discuss the cost."

Thad smiled. "The cost will be that you will care for the horses, and if your Mary gardens, some produce occasionally."

"Scruffy comes with Thad," Amos added.

Could Thad really ask for so little? "Sounds like you have it all figured out, but that hardly seems fair to you."

Amos grinned. "I'm grateful for the company. Seems like the

best plan for all of us. Besides, Thad says I'm a better cook than you are."

Donald's chest swelled. "I can't begin to express my gratitude, and I'm sure Mary will feel likewise." He would get a post off to Mary with the good news. They would be able to marry soon.

◉❀❀❀◉

Mary washed her hands in the kitchen after chores. "Are we still planning on going to the Turners this morning?"

"Aye, in a few minutes," Mama said. "Mark is going to check on Sara till we get back. Amelia said Aaron finished the cradle. If we complete the quilt today, we can present them to Martha after church Sunday."

Mary spread honey on a biscuit. "Sara and Laura are excited about the little dollies they made for the baby."

"Aye. I'm glad we are giving the gifts Sunday because the girls are getting quite attached to those dolls. Polly and Laura will be here at nine, and we can leave then if you are ready. Papa is hitching the wagon for us."

She ate the biscuit and licked the honey from her fingers and lips. "I keep wondering why Donald has not written." Her stomach clenched. *Had he even gotten to Lexington? Suppose something happened to him?*

Mama caressed her cheek. "He has probably been busy. There may be a very good reason for the delay. Be patient, lass."

"You know I have not yet mastered that virtue."

The post rider came by after dinner. Mary's heart skipped a beat as she wiped dishes and watched through the window.

Mark took posts from the rider and handed him a coin. He came inside with an odd expression on his face. "Two posts for Papa."

She sighed and set the dish down. The rider would not come

again for days.

Mark strolled to the door that led into the common room. He pulled out a post from his coat and waved it above him. "Anyone here know a Donald Duncan?" He ran through the door.

She growled and took off after him. "Give that to me!"

Laughing, he continually dodged her. "That will cost you another piece of mince pie."

"You can finish the pie for all I care. Give me the letter now!"

He handed her the missive. "It used to be more entertaining to annoy you."

She grabbed the letter and held it close. "You will get your just deserts, Mark Stewart."

"I shall be satisfied with a piece of the pie." He wandered back toward the kitchen.

She broke the seal, opened it, and sat in the window seat.

Dearest Mary,

Forgive me for not writing sooner. I waited to have more definite information to share. It has been busy at the printshop ever since I returned.

I have sad news to pass on. Amos Porter, the gentleman I mentioned who worked with Thad Bryant, lost his wife while I was gone. She had been ill for a time. Thad and Amos are close friends, and the sadness with Trudy's passing is palpable. Thad is a comfort to his friend since he knows well the loss of a beloved wife.

"Oh, how sad, indeed."

After I returned from my visit north, I told Thad and Amos about our plans to marry. They both extend their best wishes for us. Boyd and his family also are pleased to learn of our upcoming union. Everyone is eager to meet you.

"'Tis encouraging."

Thad informed me that I could take the time away from the shop whenever we established a date for our marriage. They know of my search for a proper place for us to live.

Today, Amos is in far better spirits. Apparently, he invited Thad to live with him. Thad has offered us the use of his cottage. The only payment he wants is for me to care for the animals. 'Tis a quaint, fully furnished stone cottage with two bedrooms. There is a garden in back and a vacant hen house. I'm sure you will want to fill it so we can enjoy the eggs and chickens.

Both gents are lonely and seem happy at the prospect of living together. The next thing for us to do is set a date. I'm eager for us to be married. Perusing this year's Virginia Almanack, March 1 and 8 are Saturdays. I suggest the first of March. However, I defer to you and your family if you have another preference. I will wait until I hear back from you to write to my family about a date.

I promise to correspond soon. I long to see you and hold you in my arms again, dear Mary.

Your Donald

She pressed the letter to her chest. *He is safe and well—and eager to marry.* Since they could not marry during Lent, early March would be her wish rather than waiting until late April. An eternity. *A little less than three months away.* She stood and twirled around. Mama appeared in the doorway. "What do you think of a wedding on the first of March?"

Mama hugged her tight. "I'm so pleased you heard from him. All is well."

"Yes. 'Tis wonderful news." She shared Donald's letter. "Do you see any reason why I should not let Donald know the first of March is our choice also?"

"I think we should talk to your father first." Mama's lifted brow spoke louder than her words.

"Of course." *Patience, Mary.* When would she learn to temper her eagerness?

Donald pulled the wagon out of the Oak Tavern barn and hitched the horse to it. The waxed tarpaulin was tied in several places over the paper reams to keep them dry. He wrapped the scarf over his head and around his neck. That and his heavy coat and gloves should protect him from the cold. He put on his hat, ready for the trip home.

The owner of the tavern walked toward him on his way to the barn. "Hope the other gent didna keep ye from sleeping last night."

Donald rolled his eyes. "His coughing at dinner was bad enough, but 'twas a rough night with his room right next to mine."

The tavern keeper grunted. "Sure didna figure on snow. Be careful."

Donald steered the horse away from town and onto the route home. If the snow kept up, the three-hour ride back to Lexington would take much longer. He would have headed home yesterday but for the darkness.

The sick fellow had said the snow followed him from the west, so staying at the tavern an extra day was not an option. Thad needed the paper at the shop, and waiting might put him days behind.

For a while, the mare kept up a good pace. The snow-covered branches on the surrounding trees were beautiful, and the area silent but for the horse's muffled hoofbeats and the wheels tracking through it. The intensity of the snow increased and continued to blow. In places, it made the trail hard to distinguish. His throat was beginning to ache. He should have gone last night. Traveling in the dark would have been better than this.

CHAPTER 37

Mary placed the holly stems in a basket and headed inside the Green. The greenery on the tables in the common room gave it a festive appearance. The Gordons would join their family for dinner and celebrate the arrival of the new year.

In the kitchen, the savory smell of pork roast with neeps and tatties made her mouth water. She switched her cloak for her apron. Mama carried the large platter from the pantry. "Oh, there you are. The wee ones have had such fun arranging the pine branches you brought in. And the fragrance has wafted throughout the Green. When you finish with the holly, I could use your help here."

"I will be back shortly as I suspect the girls will want to place the holly also."

Laura and Sara stood side by side, and equal in height, in the common room admiring their work. Mark and Douglas came through, resupplying wood for all the rooms. Preparations for the evening were in full swing.

Sara approached and tugged at her skirt. "What do you think of the pine stems on the window sills and the tables?"

"They smell wonderful.

"May we arrange the holly, too?"

"I will leave the basket with you. Enjoy yourselves."

Laura took the basket. "Ma said that Philip and Martha will come around four."

"Good. Do you know if they are staying with us tonight instead of traveling home in the dark?"

Laura put her hands on her hips. "You know my brother. He will want to get home."

"Ah, yes. He would not rest well without checking on the animals tonight."

Sara's eyes lit up. "We got the games out to play, draughts, and fox and geese."

Mary laughed. "You finish arranging the holly while I go to the kitchen to help."

Mama gave the bread dough a final pat. "Polly will be here later with the pies."

Mary sighed. Tomorrow would be the beginning of a new year, one full of promise and many changes. Two months and she would be a bride. "I wonder what Donald is doing right now? Do you suppose he will celebrate the new year in Lexington with Mr. Bryant or his friend Boyd?"

Mama grinned. "If he is with Boyd's family, they most likely will have a fete. Scots make quite a thing of bringing in the new year and Hogmanay. The "first foot," a tall, dark-haired man to cross the threshold of a friend or neighbor at the beginning of the new year, is believed to bring luck."

"I forgot about that." She laughed. "'Twill not be Donald with his red hair. I wonder what 1783 will bring?"

"Peace, I hope, and good health for all." Mama placed the loaves by the hearth. "I thought we might get started on your dress tomorrow."

"Oh yes, what a wonderful way to start the new year."

❦⚜❦

"Feeling any better, lad?" Thad's voice sounded far away.

Donald coughed. "No. Head hurts something fierce—chest feels tight." He continued coughing.

"I put a poultice on your chest as the doctor said." Thad's hand was cold on his head. "You still have a fever."

"Thirsty." Donald licked his dry lips and swallowed as best he could against the pain.

❦ 229 ❧

Thad lifted his head and put a cup to his mouth. "I should never have told you to rush to get that paper back here. Never thought we would get hit with such a bad storm."

The water soothed his throat. Too much effort to tell Thad not to blame himself.

"Fiona Alexander brought soup by again. Said she and Boyd will be back tomorrow after church."

"Uh-huh."

Thad placed a cold damp rag on his head. "You gotta get well, lad. This has been going on for too long."

His coughing returned, and his head throbbed. *Will this kill me?* He couldn't allow it to, not when he was preparing to wed Mary at last.

Mary leaned over the table in the common room, cutting the salmon-colored muslin while Mama folded and placed the pieces already cut in piles.

"Mama, look in the wooden box where I keep my ribbons and notions. Mrs. Russell had two blue cards left of lovely Brussels lace I did not use on the gowns I made for her daughter. I asked her for them in payment for my work."

"'Twas farsighted of you, lass. Now we will have it for your neckline and sleeve ruffles."

"It had more value to me than any payment. Mrs. Russell seemed pleased with the bargain because she could tell her husband the gowns only cost what she spent on the fabric for them and my labor."

"The lace will be a striking contrast against the salmon."

"I plan to soak it in weak coffee to give it a creamier color."

"Aye, 'twould be lovely." Mama glanced up. "Sounds like your father is back from the Turners'."

Papa entered the common room, followed by Doctor Howard.

"Look who I saw coming up from the river. He said Pike's ferry is running, even in this cold."

Mama went right to him. "How nice to see you again. You are officially our first foot."

He bowed. "I'm what?"

"'Tis Hogmanay, and in a Scot's home 'tis said that the first tall, dark-haired gentleman to cross the threshold is a sign of good fortune."

"I'm honored to be the bearer of a blessing then." Doctor Howard removed his hat.

Papa raised his hand. "I will see to the horses. I have more to do before I come back inside."

Mama took the doctor's outer coat. "I will bring you hot cider to warm you." She walked toward the kitchen.

He took a seat before the fire. The black armband he wore tore at Mary's heart.

"I see you are in mourning, sir. Am I to assume 'twas your father?"

He nodded. "Yes. I have returned from his funeral. Your father indicated you had a room available for me to stay the night."

"Yes, you are our only guest so far." She took a seat near him. "I'm sorry about your father. I know how concerned you were for his welfare."

"I appreciate that. I'm grateful we had time together toward the end of his life. When I arrived in Maryland, I noticed a change in him. He seemed to have mellowed in his unhealthy attitudes."

"Will your travels to Frederick now come to an end?"

He started to answer when Mama entered carrying a tray of steaming cups. "You wear a mourning band. Your father?"

Doctor Howard told Mama about his father's illness and passing. He appeared more resigned than melancholy. Several times he seemed to be studying her. The man had shared his wisdom with her. She must remember to thank him.

"I hope that my father is finally at peace. The bitterness he harbored for many years had disappeared by this last visit. He spoke of longing for heaven and once again being with my mother."

Mama's sympathetic smile brightened. "I pray that this year will be a better one for you."

"You are too kind, ma'am. My concern about his care will no longer be a worry."

He smiled at Mary. "To answer your earlier question, Miss Stewart, I have settled my father's estate and lack a reason to come this way again—currently."

His expression suggested he might want a reason.

"You are always most welcome here," Mama said. "I am off to the kitchen. May I get you anything else?"

"No, I'm fine. I may sit and enjoy the fire." He faced Mary when they were alone. "'Tis nice to see you again. I enjoyed our last conversation."

"I did also."

"I'm pleased to know that." He came to the table. "It would appear I have once again interrupted your sewing. Another dress for your mother?"

Her stomach knotted. He might be disappointed to learn of her upcoming marriage. Or was that simply vanity on her part? "No, this dress is for me—for my wedding."

"Oh." His brows lifted as he took a step back. "I see." He cleared his throat. "Andrew had not mentioned you were engaged. I offer you and your intended my best wishes."

"Our engagement is recent, and we have not yet informed Mr. Macmillan."

"I see."

"Doctor Howard." Mary straightened and folded her hands at her waist. "Your comment about not allowing past trials to determine one's future helped me more than you can know. I thank you for those words. They made all the difference."

He tilted his head slightly. "I'm happy to have been of service, Miss Stewart, however unintentionally."

Mary relaxed and gestured to the hearth. "Please feel free to enjoy the fire, doctor. I will return to my work." Timing and circumstances had the power to alter lives and raise a myriad of what-ifs. If Doctor Howard hadn't stopped at the Green those months past, would she have had the courage to face what had happened to her? Or ever share it with Donald?

CHAPTER 38

Scruffy licked Donald's hand, brushing away the last cobwebs of sleep. Rays of sunlight streamed through the windows. He shifted on the pallet. The sweat-dampened blanket smelled as bad as he did. Breathing took effort and left him spent. How long had he been there? The room grew dark as sleep returned.

A door closing roused him the next time. Boyd stood in the doorway, grinning. He pulled up a stool and sat beside Donald. "Good to see you awake—at last." Boyd steadied Donald's head and lifted it. "Drink some water." Boyd pressed a cup to his cracked lips. "I'm heating some of Ma's cock-a-leekie. You need to get meat on those bones, or your Mary won't recognize you." Boyd rose and pulled a mattress into the room. "Brought this from home. You need something fresh."

The water relieved his parched throat and thirst. "How long have I been here?" His voice cracked like a dropped egg.

"Quite a while. 'Tis the middle of January."

"That long? I'm soaked."

"I know. I'm here under orders to clean you up, get you on your feet, and fill you with food." I will switch the mattress with this one after we get you cleaned up."

"Shabby assignment."

"Aye. But I lost the game of draughts with Thad at the shop, so I got the job." Boyd brought over a basin of water. "Got warm water from the kettle." Boyd lifted him off the smelly mattress and helped him to sit up.

Donald coughed until he thought he would pass out. The room moved around him. Dizziness made him lean to the side until

Boyd propped him back up. "I'm weak as a kitten." He gasped and shivered as Boyd stripped him of his shirt.

Boyd washed him with a damp rag from the basin, continually rinsing him with warm water. "You will feel much better when we get the stink off and get food in you."

After dressing him, Boyd switched the clean straw mattress for his soiled one and helped him back on to the pallet. A relief to recline again. "Took all my strength—grateful for your help."

Boyd nodded. "I know you are. No one asks to take ill. You scared us all with that fever, but the doc said you have made progress and will improve. 'Twill take time. Now, to get that soup in you." Boyd returned a couple of minutes later with a steaming bowl.

"Thad and Amos and the shop?" He coughed. "Left them in the lurch."

Boyd sat on the stool. "They are doing fine. Keeping busy has been the best thing for Amos. No need to feel sorry for them." He set the bowl down beside him. "Come on, let me get you propped up again."

Donald ate a little of the cock-a-leekie, then waved the rest away. "Tasty, but tired."

Boyd gave him a clean blanket. "Sleep will restore you."

"Not always." He remembered waking up thrashing in the last day or so with Thad leaning over him.

Boyd turned somber. "Thad mentioned you are still plagued with night fits."

Donald rubbed his throbbing temples. "Reliving battles, sounds of cannons and guns, of men crying out, and the smells." The sight of men's vitals and damaged appendages were still so vivid. "My chest pounds, head hurts, and fear overwhelms me." He coughed. "Am I a coward? Have I gone mad?"

"You are no coward. I can attest to that. Nor are you mad, only human and moved by suffering and the cost of war. I still fight the same things, but not as much."

"Might be a burden to Mary when we wed."

"Mary loves you. None of us are free from adversity. The Lord experienced trials and even told his followers we would face them. But He also said He would be with us in them. When the events of these past years trouble me, I remind myself I cannot change what happened. But I can live each day thankful for life and all its blessings. I decide for that day to do the best I can."

Never any judgment from Boyd, only compassion and wisdom. "At times, 'tis dark, and I wonder if I will ever escape this suffocating hole."

"I know," Boyd stood. "Christ says that He will be a lamp unto our feet and a light unto our path. Hold onto that thought when it gets dark." Boyd put his hat on and took the bowl. "I have an errand to run, but I'm leaving the kettle here. When I come back, we are going to get more soup in you." Scruffy curled up by the pallet and closed his eyes when Boyd scratched him. "I'm also going to get you off that pallet and walking."

He nodded. "Yes, preacher."

"Been called worse."

"I'm indebted to you—for all your help—and your encouragement. You've made me reflect on a faith I haven't been feeding lately." A faith he planned to feed and grow with Mary and their future children.

Mary passed the paper to Laura and Sara, sitting at the table by the garden window. "Now, I want you to write the names of the months."

Laura inked her quill and wrote February. "This is the first day of February."

"Correct. I should have been more clear. Please write the months in order, from the beginning of the year to the end."

Mary wrung her hands while both girls set about their task.

The frost had long since melted, and the sunlight made the ground glitter. Still nothing from Donald. Had something happened to him? Surely his friends would have sent word were there a problem. Did he have second thoughts about their marriage? She twisted the strands of hair that had escaped her cap. Their wedding was a month from today. Had another post been lost?

"Why do we need to learn to write the months?" Laura scooted her paper across the table.

She scanned Laura's paper. "Your letters are much improved. The ability to write is important, not only to correspond with others but also to write instructions and make lists."

Sara passed her paper. "How do my letters look?"

The girls studied each other's work. Competition was clearly at play here. "Sara, I think you have gotten better at forming your letters."

Mama entered the room, waving a post and smiling. "For you."

"You see, I received a post from a person who could write their letters." Her heart raced. *Finally.*

Mama set down the basket she carried. "'Tis from Jean."

"Oh." Perhaps Jean had news of Donald. "This is why 'tis important to learn to write. If Jean did not know how to write, she would not be able to send me a letter."

Mama added. "And I'm writing down all my recipes for Mary to have when she moves to Lexington."

The girls looked at each other, and then Laura nodded. "I suppose you are right."

"I want you to practice writing the simple words I listed here while I read Jean's letter. Later, when you improve, I have a fun game to play."

Mama pulled the strips of lace from the basket. "The lace is dry, and I thought you would want to see it. 'Tis a lovely creamy color."

She examined it. "Exactly what I hoped for. I will get back to work on the dress this afternoon." She opened the vellum missive and began reading.

Dear Mary,

I'm sure this finds you preparing for your upcoming nuptials. I remember how busy I was sewing garments as well as finding needed household items for our home. I expect Donald will find a wagon to transport everything.

Finding a wagon was not what kept her awake at night.

We will celebrate Neil's first birthday when Patrick and Emily visit us next week. He has grown so much and is such fun. They stay only a week, which is perfect since we intend to arrive at the Green on the twenty-seventh. Please inform your parents to plan on us for a room starting then. We will return to Alexandria on March third. I believe my family will spend the same dates, though perhaps you have already heard from them.

'Tis odd that we have not heard anything from Donald in several weeks. He did indicate in his last letter that his employer offered him his home for the two of you. Perhaps he has been preparing your new home or is busy at the printshop.

Her stomach tightened. She was not the only one who felt slighted. Why had he been remiss in corresponding with everyone?

Knowing you, I'm sure much of your time has been spent sewing, embroidering, and planning all you need to pack. I'm certain whatever you have been creating is beautiful, and I am eager to see it. March will be here soon, my friend—and almost my sister.

We all send our love,
Jean

Apprehension seared her thoughts. Donald would not slight her or his family. Something must be wrong. Surely if something had happened to him, one of his friends would notify them. Wouldn't they? She must write to him at the printshop. Perhaps it was only more trouble with the posts getting lost, but she must know.

CHAPTER 39

Amos was already at the printshop, mixing the lampblack and other ingredients needed for the ink, when Donald arrived. "I know, I'm late. I was helping Thad collect his things to load on the wagon later. He will be here soon." Donald sat in a chair to catch his breath.

"You look spent."

"Gathering Thad's gear at the cottage and placing it near the door to load it left me winded."

Amos grabbed the beaters. "I suggested he move to my place now to give you time to spruce up that cottage for your bride."

"That was both gracious and wise," Donald muttered as he rose. Cleaning that place was going to take time and effort. "The composing sticks are calling me."

"Getting your strength back?"

"I still tire easily, and except for a lingering cough, I feel better each day. The doctor says my chest is clearing."

Thad arrived an hour later. "Good thing we got started on getting my things ready to go. I had no idea how much needed to be moved or gotten rid of."

Donald set the type onto the galley. "Boyd and I will load it on the wagon in the morning and take it to Amos's place."

"Grateful for your help. We got to get you stronger and fatten you up in the next week before you head north to get your bride." Thad held the handles of the two leather-covered ink balls and beat the ink onto the type. "Did you let her know you were sick? Women fret something fierce when they don't know what is going on."

Donald looked up from arranging the composing sticks. "I wrote when I got stronger and could tell her I was on the road to health. Why fill her with worry?"

Amos and Thad exchanged glances before returning to their work.

"What?" Donald asked.

"You will figure it out once you are married." Thad snickered.

Mary had meant well going to Martha's to assist with laundry and heavier housekeeping tasks. Now, she wished she had stayed home. No correspondence from Donald gave her enough anxiety. Her friend's annoying questions had not helped.

Papa shouted from the sheep-pen. "Is Martha well? You said the baby was not expected until late March."

"Martha is fine." She continued on the path to the Green.

Inside the kitchen, Mama lit up like a lantern. "The post came, and there is a letter from Donald. 'Tis on the hutch."

"At last." She picked up the parchment and went to the common room and plopped on the window seat, not even removing her cloak. She broke the seal and opened it.

Dearest Mary,

Please forgive me for not corresponding with you sooner. Weeks ago, I went to our paper supplier in another village. The drive back to Lexington was long and complicated by a snowstorm. All of this resulted in my being beset with a bad ague.

Her hand went to her pounding chest. "Oh no."

I have been ill for weeks, sometimes barely conscious. The doctor and friends provided me with good care, and I am forever indebted to them. These past few days, I have been up and walking, and each day I grow stronger. I did not want to worry you.

Worry me. How could I not be—with no news from you?

I did not write or let anyone here inform you. Knowing how strongwilled you are, I feared you would insist someone bring you here.

Me strongwilled? She sighed. *Well—perhaps a mite.* She would have gone. Still, he should have informed her.

I'm eager to see you again and at long last marry. All is progressing well here. Amos suggested Thad move his belongings over to his cottage soon to allow me time to ready this home for us. My plan is to arrive at the Green around the twenty-seventh. Thad offered the use of his wagon, so there will be plenty of room for your luggage. The cottage is furnished, and I will see that it is clean before I depart.

I hope you are as excited about this new venture as I am. I love you and am counting the days until we are together again.

My regards to your family and my eternal love to you.

Your Donald

She reread the letter. The heaviness of the past weeks lifted. She must tell Mama. 'Twas tempting to run back to Martha's to answer those pesky questions that had belabored her this morning.

Mama entered the room. "Well?"

"He has been very ill." Mary handed her the letter.

"This certainly explains why you heard nothing from him. What a relief that his health has improved and that he will arrive as expected. Our prayers are answered."

They had. Very fervent prayers at that.

Mama pinned the hem of Mary's wedding dress with Sara and Laura nearby, their eyes wide.

"Turn again," Mama said.

Mary swiveled slightly on the crate as Mama continued pinning. *Only two more days until Donald arrives.* "Thank you for your help. If you had not made the apron and adorned my bonnet, I would be further behind than I am."

"I'm pleased to do whatever I can." Mama glanced at the girls. "You two were such a help yesterday in the garden and out front clearing all the refuse away."

Laura picked up the pincushion. "Ma said she is going to let us help decorate in here with ribbons and dried flowers."

Mary smiled at Mama. Their strategy was in play. Let the girls take part in decorating to keep them from getting underfoot.

Papa and Mark each carried a bucket of wood into the room. Mark had a silly smirk on his face. "What are you all dressed up for—going to a party?"

She sighed. "How will I ever get along without your constant quips, dear brother?"

"Such a pity, you will have no one to keep you humble."

Papa set his pail by the hearth. "You look lovely, lass." He turned to Mark. "Go ahead and take that upstairs. We have a few more trips to fill all the rooms. We still need to clear space in the barn for Donald's wagon." He chuckled. "Hope 'tis a big wagon."

"So do I." She should probably mention all the rest of her personal items and household goods already crated in her bedroom and ready for the journey south. But then again, they'd know soon enough and complain loudly as they loaded the wagon. She controlled the grin she shared with Mama before stepping off the crate.

Donald loaded the crates into the back of the wagon, spread a tarpaulin over them, and tied it down. Then he double-checked the wheels and hitch. The cottage was clean and in order, and the wagon was ready to roll.

He studied the sky, grateful for what promised to be a beautiful day. He shuddered, remembering the snow and cold the last time he took the wagon out.

Thad and Amos strolled down the path in front of the cottage and neared the wagon.

"Nice of you two to come by to see me off. I'm indebted to you for the loan of the wagon and the horse. My mare alone could not manage the anticipated load. And you are all settled in now with Amos, right?"

"Sure, sure." Thad handed him a bag of food to eat the first day of his travels. "I appreciate you taking those things to Priscilla's sister. Don't know why I waited this long after her passing to give her clothes and possessions away."

Amos said, "Nothing like moving to motivate a soul to part with what they don't need."

"Since you are going through Culpeper, it made sense, and Prudence will be glad to have it. I sent her a post, so she will be expecting you."

"The next time you see me, gents, I will be a married man."

Thad laughed. "Your life will *never* be the same."

"'Tis a good thing," Donald replied.

Amos nodded. "You will learn things about yourself you never suspected before."

"True, true," Thad said. "She will keep you on the straight and narrow."

Donald laughed. "You don't even know Mary yet. She is beautiful, lively, and a pleasure to be around."

"Lively, huh?" Thad's eyes held a warning. "Watch she don't wear you out. And, let her know right from the start who is boss."

"I agree. Let her know from day one," said Amos.

"Humph. Is that how it was for you two?" Donald asked. No missing the side glances Thad and Amos gave one another. "Exactly what I thought. Wish me luck. I'm on my way."

The journey to Stewarts' Green couldn't go fast enough, but he'd not race there and take any undue risks. He planned to arrive in one piece to claim his bride.

The return trip to Lexington would be far nicer with Mary at his side.

⊙⊱✦⊰⊙

Donald had fought the urge to hasten the horses the last few miles. The pounding in his chest and the longing to see Mary increased as he turned into the lane to the Green. In minutes, he'd hold her in his arms. He'd barely stopped the horses and set the brake before his feet hit the ground.

Mary opened the door, beaming and beautiful. "At last. I have been up since before six wondering when you would arrive."

"You, up before six? I'm flattered." He wrapped his arms around her, pulling her close, breathing in the clean scent that was uniquely her. When his lips met hers, there was nothing timid in her eager response. He ended the kiss reluctantly.

"This is nice, but I doubt we can stand here like this for long," he whispered in her ear.

She stepped back and tucked her arm in his. "We should go inside."

"One more kiss, for I suspect we will be surrounded by family and friends the rest of the day." He drew her close again and tasted her lips. "I look forward to more of those," he whispered. "Inside, woman, before we are found out."

Sara ran up to him when they entered the common room. "Do you really have to leave in a few days?"

Mrs. Stewart laughed. "'Tis a fine thing to say, lass. Donald just arrived." She patted Sara, then hugged him. "We are delighted to see you and grateful for your safe arrival. Mark will care for your horses and take the wagon into the barn."

Mary took his hand. "We should get your things. I will show you to your room." She led the way back outside. "Your family is due here later today."

"I would have arrived yesterday were it not that I needed to make a delivery and get the services of a wheelwright in Culpeper." He grabbed his haversack. "But I'm here now and ready to marry tomorrow."

Yet as much as he relished the idea, as much as he desperately wanted Mary for his wife, longer for her to be by his side the rest of his life, even now, the lingering fears of his nightmares intruded.

Mary scanned the common room, her heart brimming with joy. There were the O'Brians, Duncans, Gordons, and Stewarts, the people she loved most in all the world. *'Twill be difficult to leave them in a couple of days.*

Donald, seated next to her on the settee, squeezed her hand.

Mama and Polly eyed each other with mischievous grins. "We have a wedding gift for you." Maggie followed them into the center hall. The three women returned a couple of moments later. Mama carried a large bundle. Smiling, they unfolded a quilt and held it out for all to see.

Mary rose and examined it. "Oh my, 'tis beautiful." They had sewn a cream-colored quilt with squares around the edges of the Duncan and Stewart tartans. a large green-and-blue Duncan plaid square adorned the center. "Wherever did you get the tartans?"

"Maggie deserves the credit," Mama said. "She had the Duncan tartan. She got the word out—and got responses. She made the medallion and sent it as well as the fabric with a guest we had at the Green a few weeks ago."

"I located each of the tartans in town," Maggie said. "Alexandria was settled by Scots, so 'twas not difficult."

Mama folded it. "'Tis from the three of us." She placed it on a table.

Donald leaned close and whispered, "Tis stunning and will go nicely on our bed."

Adam Duncan packed his pipe by the hearth. "Talk in town suggests peace is nigh. 'Tis said we signed an Armistice at Versailles, France, last month. This war is finally ended."

"Heaven be praised," Maggie said.

"I have sad news for you, Matt," Adam Duncan said. "Wasn't William Alexander, Lord Stirling, a relative of yours?"

Papa nodded. "Yes."

Donald's brothers perked up, and Cameron elbowed Mark. "You have a British Lord in your family?"

"William Alexander is a relative on my Scottish mother's side," Papa said. "What news do you have of him?"

"He died last month."

Papa leaned back in the settee. "I'm sorry to hear that."

Adam tapped his pipe. "Do not be fooled by his title, lads. He was heir to the title Earl of Stirling, but he was also a Patriot general who served well in many battles. General Alexander fought off British forces long enough for General Washington's Continentals to escape at the Battle of Long Island. The British took him captive during a retreat, but later freed him in a prisoner exchange."

Papa placed his arm behind Mama. "I was incarcerated on Manhattan Island at the time. 'Twas after that battle in late September of seventy-six. The raging fire on the island caused such panic that I and other prisoners were able to escape."

Donald's grip on her hand tightened, and his eyes glazed. "Please, no more talk of the war. If you will excuse me."

Papa raised his hand when Donald left through the door to the kitchen. "I agree, best to speak of weddings and not war."

Mary bit her lip. Was Donald still ill?

When he did not return, she went in search of him.

CHAPTER 40

Mary held the lantern high and scanned the area. He had been lighthearted until the subject of the war came up. "Donald?" Someone moved near the fence by the barn. She tensed for a moment, then recognized his profile and approached. She set the lantern down. "What is wrong?"

"I needed fresh air." He focused straight ahead.

She wrapped her shawl tight against the cool evening air and put her arm through his. "Tell me what is bothering you."

Weariness etched his face. glistening in perspiration. "I hate talk of the war."

"I know. I'm sorry the conversation went there. What can I do to help?" She reached in her pocket and handed him her handkerchief.

"Nothing." He turned back toward the pasture and wiped his face. "I'm sorry. Sometimes I break out in sweats."

She swallowed hard. "I understand. When I think about … my heart races, and I sweat." She rubbed his arm. "People are bound to talk of the war—and the prospect of peace. It cannot be avoided."

"I know." He faced her, his face distorted in pain. "I don't fault anyone for that. 'Tis a struggle I must overcome. Every day in gathering and printing the news, the subject of the war comes up."

She leaned her head on his shoulder, her tears dampening his waistcoat. His arms went around her.

His voice cracked. "Some days are more difficult than others— and the nights. They are the worst."

"How do we solve that?" Even holding her, he seemed distant. "The war is over. We must focus on the future and our life together."

"The memories linger." He stepped back and took her hands in his. "You need to know, I still have nightmares … at times I yell in the night. I don't want to frighten you." He shook his head. "I fear life with me will be a burden."

She shuddered and drew her shawl tighter. "I understand more than you think. I also have terrifying memories, fear, anger, and fitful sleep."

He stroked her cheek. "My sweet Mary."

"They have all been my unwelcome and recurring companions." The heat under her shawl rose to her face. *Tell him.* "Sometimes, I get anxious when I think about—marriage. Will my memories and fear return—when we are intimate?"

His shoulders sagged, and he sighed. "I love you and will do all I can to make you forget about what happened."

Tears filled her eyes. "'Tis just it, you cannot rid me of my memories any more than I can rid you of yours."

He took her in his arms and kissed her damp cheek. "We must each try to ease the other's anxieties and be patient with one another. 'Tis good we voiced our concerns."

She took his hand. "We should go inside before they think something is amiss." Mama was right. She had reminded her to be honest and practice patience with one another.

⚜

"Get up. Get up. 'Tis your wedding day."

Mary's eyes flew open. "You startled me, poppet."

Sara tugged her arm. "'Tis half-past six. Mama is in the kitchen preparing breakfast."

"I'm awake. I will be down as soon as I dress."

Sara climbed off the bed. "Laura said the bride and groom were not supposed to see each other before the wedding. Shall I ask Donald to hide?"

"No, silly. 'Tis an old superstition. And I'm not keeping to my room until the wedding. There is too much to do."

"Mama told me to gather the eggs, but I wanted to make sure you were awake first."

"You are sweet for checking on me, now off to do your chores while I dress."

After Sara left, Mary opened the nearly empty wardrobe. There hung the sheer pale green nightgown Mama had barely finished in time. Mary's pulse raced as she hugged herself. Was it anticipating tonight's passion or nerves? Likely both. But when Donald had kissed her yesterday, she'd felt none of the fear, not a bit of the horror of the attack had intruded on their moment. Surely, that boded well for ... later.

She set aside the blue linen dress she would wear until later today and as a traveling dress tomorrow. Placing the deep coral gown beside it, she sighed, then giggled. Her pleasure in wearing it for her wedding would surpass her many hours of delight in creating it. The day had finally arrived, and she was as jubilant as the birds singing outside her window.

❦

Donald and Mark stared at the trunks and crates that were to be packed onto the wagon.

Donald shook his head. "I had no idea your sister had so much to take with us."

"The pile grew bigger daily for the last week. 'Tis a good thing you are leaving tomorrow or there most likely would be more." Mark flexed his muscles. "I'm here to offer my services."

"We best breakfast and get started. With the younger boys to help, it should go quickly."

Donald followed Mark to the common room table where their mothers had set platters of eggs, ham, and biscuits. Pa and Mr. Stewart were deep in a discussion about the Confederation Congress. The younger boys were listening. No sign of Mary yet. He took a seat and served himself, then passed the platters to Mark.

"I brought two tarps and plenty of rope to tie it all down in the wagon." He pursed his lips. The trip back to Lexington would take longer than anticipated to not overwork the horses.

There would be enough opportunities while they traveled to discuss where they would stay along the way, including in Charlottesville. Boyd had reminded him that part of the healing process was in facing one's fears. He was struggling to do just that. If Mary could experience Charlottesville with him, and feel safe, perhaps it would lay to rest some of her fears.

Cheerful conversations wafted into the center hall from the common room as Mary reached the top of the stairs. Papa and Mama beamed up at her.

Papa extended his arm as she descended. "You are stunning, my dear."

Mama wiped a tear away. "So bonny, lass. Everyone is here."

They entered the room to the smiles of her family, the Duncans, and O'Brians. The Gordon families and Turners stood near the garden window. Donald stood with the pastor in front of the common room's hearth. Mama's sniffles and the muscle ticking in Papa's cheek made her throat tighten. Was that Papa's arm shaking or hers?

Then Donald took her hand. His warmth filled her, strengthened her. The trembling ceased, and her breathing relaxed. Donald caressed the back of her hand with his thumb. Everything felt so ... right. Surrounded by those she loved most in the world, the pastor repeated the familiar scripture from the Book of Common Prayer. Her joy was complete as they exchanged their vows. Then Donald leaned toward her, sealing the vows with a kiss she didn't wish to end. A kiss that promised so many more.

The ceremony she had waited years to celebrate had only taken a few minutes but had forever changed her life. She was—at last—

Mrs. Donald Duncan.

Donald's sea-green eyes held her captive. "We are man and wife. Time to greet our guests and enjoy what smells like a fine dinner." He placed a hand at her back, and they walked through the room, receiving hugs and well wishes from all.

After the dinner, Mama cornered them. "Your father and I have a gift for you. Would you come into the parlor for a couple of minutes?"

She and Donald exchanged a smile. "Of course." They had already packed the quilt into the wagon. What could it be?

Papa motioned for them to sit. "Your mother and I wondered what we might give you that would be helpful—and have lasting value. I thought about writing it out on a scroll, but Heather suggested she wanted to embroider it." Papa stood beside the chair where Mama sat, his hand on her shoulder.

Mama looked at Papa with the expression that always embarrassed their children—like they were the only two people in the room. Mama picked up a canvas-wrapped, thin, rectangular-shaped package and handed it to them. "'Tis something to remember on good days and difficult ones."

Donald unfolded the canvas. Inside, a rough-hewn frame surrounded a sampler, not unlike the ones she made when Mama taught her how to embroider. They read the words stitched in dark blue threads.

Charity suffereth long, and is kind; charity envieth not;
charity vaunteth not itself, is not puffed up,
Doth not behave itself unseemly, seeketh not her own,
is not easily provoked, thinketh no evil;
Rejoiceth not in iniquity, but rejoiceth in the truth;
Beareth all things, believeth all things,

hopeth all things, endureth all things.
1 Corinthians 13:4–7

Mary drew in a deep breath. "You could not have given us anything more meaningful. How perfect. I love you both more than I can say."

Donald lifted the oak frame. "I can assure you this is most appreciated and will always hang in a special place in our home."

Papa took Mama's hand. "We need to return to our guests. By the way, I saw the wagon. Very impressive, Donald, how you fit it all in."

Donald's brows raised as he laughed. "It surprised me too, sir."

Mama hugged Donald. "Please call us Matthew and Heather or Mother and Father … whatever makes you comfortable. No more Mr. and Mrs. Stewart."

"Yes, ma'am."

Alone in the room, Mary held the framed sampler. Donald stood behind her with his arms around her, nuzzling her neck. "Do you suppose they know how much we need this?"

"I suspect they do. They have had their own challenges." *Mama knows my struggles—and Papa undoubtedly understands Donald's.*

<hr/>

The dancing done and her feet aching, Mary and Donald enjoyed the group gathered in the common room, visiting, and telling stories. When Mary went to the kitchen to replace the empty cider jugs, Jean and Martha followed her.

Martha rubbed her lower back. "I think we will likely go home soon. Philip worries because I tire easily."

Mary hugged her. "We certainly want to keep you and that baby healthy—and Philip less anxious."

"He is a doting soul," Martha said. "'Tis been a delightful day, full of joy and fun."

Jean rocked little Neil. "I agree, and I finally got the sister I always wanted. That deep coral color is stunning. What you do with a needle and thread always amazes me."

"The cream lace around your sleeves and neckline accents it beautifully." Martha picked up extra cups. "Did you know she made it detachable?"

"No." Jean's eyes grew wide. "Show me."

Mary blushed. "You are both quite generous." She set her jug down. "Only the lace around the sleeves, not the neckline. The dress could be less formal at times." She spent the next few minutes showing Jean and Martha how by lacing ribbons through bound holes in the hem of the fabric and in the lace, she devised a way to easily remove the lace ruffles. "Come, ladies, we need to get the cider out to the others."

The Turners and Philip and Martha left around seven. Mary hugged each one as they prepared to depart. Goodbyes were difficult, not knowing when they would see each other again.

At nine, Donald held his hand out to her. "We should excuse ourselves. We have an early start and a long ride ahead of us."

Mark chuckled. "Mary—an early start? That I would like to see."

"Oh, hush! You will miss having me to constantly taunt," Mary said.

Mama and Papa stood to the side, smiling at her and holding on to one another. Their obvious emotions were paradoxical—joy for her and Donald's new life together, and loss for the distance and time that would separate them.

But Mama's nod of encouragement, so slight she'd have missed it if she hadn't been watching, gave Mary a tiny boost of courage. It was time to face her greatest fear—with the man she loved beyond everything.

While Donald saw to details downstairs, Mary studied each area of her bedroom, her sanctuary for so many years. The safe harbor she had escaped to after losing her mother and where she had fled in frustration after Papa remarried. She ran her fingers along the window sill. Heather, her nemesis, had become her dearest friend. And still, the room had been Mary's haven where she had dreamed about her future, her respite where she'd healed from trauma, and finally her retreat where she waited for Donald's return. Few possessions remained except what she would need in the morning. The room had already taken on a different and detached aura. Her life had transitioned. The fragrance of dried lavender and yarrow filled the air. Bless Mama for placing it on the table near her bed.

Their bed.

Sudden panic made her tense. *No! Forget what happened. I cannot let that brute's actions destroy our joy in being together. Donald deserves more than that.* She took a deep, shuddering breath. *I deserve more than that.*

Donald entered the room, put the lantern down, and drew near, her back against his chest. She stiffened when he wrapped his arms around her. Breathing out, she turned toward him and put her arms on his shoulders. "I'm sorry I …."

"Don't fret." He caressed her chin. "Twill take us time to adjust to married life. I will be more mindful not to surprise you. I want you to feel safe, loved, and cared for."

She melted into him. "I love you and want to please you in every way." How could she feel such peace while her heart seemed aflutter?

"I have no doubt you will. Now tell me or show me, how do I help you out of this very handsome gown?"

He loves me and would never hurt me. I love him—and this is right. She turned her back and moved her hair out of the way of the gown's lacing.

CHAPTER 41

Clutching a flickering lamp, Mary walked up the rickety stairs to the room the tavern keeper had given them. Donald followed with what they needed to get them through the night. She wiped the dust off the washstand in the dark and musty room. They would be off early in the morning, so they did not need a palace, but truly the place was disappointing. Nothing like the Green. Donald was surveying the floor. "Please tell me you are not looking for rats."

He chuckled and set his sack and her satchel down. "I will return as soon as I take the wagon to the barn." He took her in his arms and kissed her. "Four days married, lass. How are you enjoying our adventure?"

She rubbed the back of his neck. "Other than our accommodations, everything is perfect."

He scanned the dingy room. "It leaves much to be desired, but 'tis a place to get a meal and sleep. The inn last night near Culpeper was nicer."

She put her arm through his. "You are a kind, generous, and loving husband, and we have been blessed with good weather. What more could I ask for?"

"Exactly. We are making good time."

She kissed his neck. "I appreciate your understanding of why I did not want to stay in Charlottesville."

"'Twas not the same inn you stayed at with Jean and Peter. I intended to provide you with a positive memory of the village and some healing. I want you to be content … not anxious. Now, I'm off to see to the horse and wagon, but first, a kiss." One kiss led to another and another. "You are too alluring. I promise to be right back for more of that."

She disrobed and put her nightgown on, sat on the bed, and jumped when it creaked. She groaned. This could be a long night.

When Donald returned, she smiled and threw back the cover on his side of the bed.

He grinned. "This room is beginning to look more appealing." He disrobed and climbed under the coverlet.

Hours later, she awoke, her heart racing. Donald thrashed and yelled. She put her arm over him. Sweat poured from his face. "Wake up, sweetheart."

He flung his arm around and hit her.

She cried out.

He reached for her. "Oh Mary, I hurt you. I'm so sorry."

She bit her lip and steadied her breathing. "You had a bad dream. You are safe."

He held her close, pain in his voice. "Please forgive me."

"Of course, dearest. 'Twas unintentional." She remained in his arms until he finally fell back asleep. Donald's suffering was as real as hers. She well understood his embarrassment and regret for hitting her. She must find some way to help him.

⬥

Donald said little the next day as they continued their travels. Looking at Mary was difficult. His stomach turned just eyeing the bruise on her arm that morning. "I'm guessing 'tis about two. Are you comfortable?" If she had pain from where he struck her, she probably wouldn't say.

She smiled. "A bit stiff and sore from the ride, but I'm fine. The food we got from the tavern keeper sufficed, but 'twill be good to rest at Teasville."

"Yes." He had apologized again this morning, and she had been understanding, but his shame and embarrassment lingered. He had hurt her—what he feared most had come about, and only a few days into their marriage.

The rhythmic stomping of hoofbeats made him drowsy. He usually had no trouble falling back to sleep, but last night was different. What if he hurt or frightened her again?

She put her arm through his. "You have been rather silent today. Are you tired or troubled?"

"I'm a bit weary."

She squeezed his arm. "Months ago … after the attack," she sighed. "Without warning, Sara grabbed me for a hug, and I reacted without thinking. I hit her. I love my sister and felt horrible for hurting her. The shock and fear in her eyes tore me apart. I couldn't tell her why I responded that way. And I was awake when it happened. You were asleep when terror came. I know you did not mean to hit me."

The tender look in her eyes warmed his heart. He took her hand and brought it to his lips. "I love you, Mary Duncan."

Mary fidgeted on the wagon seat as they entered Lexington. "I'm so glad we got here while it is still light." Small cottages and shops lined the dusty road in an inviting array.

Donald squeezed her hand. "'Twas my intent. I wanted you to see the town for the first time before dark."

"How much further?" Her heart raced as she leaned forward.

Donald patted her skirt and laughed. "Down that lane." He turned the horse, and within a few minutes, he pulled up to a small stone cottage. "This is it." He got down, came around, and helped her off the wagon. "We can take a few things in now, I can get the rest later. I should also let Thad and Amos know we are here."

They entered together, hands clasped. She reached up and caressed his cheek. "This is our first home, Donald." A large stone hearth that served as the source of heat, as well as for cooking, covered most of one side of the room. "This is charming," she said. "We will need to get a fire started." A settee, chair, and small table were on her left. On the other side, doors to what must be the bedrooms. A table and chairs stood in the center of the room. Donald pulled back dark drapes and opened windows, bringing light and fresh air into the place. She removed her shawl and bonnet. "'Tis cleaner than I expected of a home for two bachelors."

Donald's eyebrows raised. "We can thank Thad's late wife for the charm. But it took more than a bit of elbow grease to tackle the grime. Come see the bedrooms." He took her hand and led her into a room with a draped window with a chest of drawers in front of it. A bed, a wardrobe, and a rocking chair were the only other pieces of furniture in the room.

"Home at last," she said. "I will unpack the marked crates first. They have the essentials and bed linens. I cannot wait to put our new quilt on the bed."

He drew her close. "I'm glad you are eager to make up the bed." His mouth found hers, and for a time, she forgot the mental list she'd been making. His eager lips and gentle hands on the back of her neck stirred a passion so new.

He pulled back and chuckled. "There is a horse that needs tending, a wagon to unload, and an employer I need to report to."

She drew in close for another kiss. "And I have a home to ready."

When Donald was out the door, she studied the room. A few dishes were set on the shelves. Their household goods would fill in the gaps. There was much work ahead unpacking and finding a place for everything, but she had never looked so forward to a task before. Soon, it would truly be their home.

Donald tended to the horses and then carried the crates into the cottage. "Tell me where you want each crate."

She pointed to the bedroom. "The ones with the blue mark in the bedroom, the black mark in the kitchen and the rest can go in the other bedroom. I can unpack those later."

"I had no idea you were so efficient, Mrs. Duncan."

"I cannot take credit. 'Twas Mama's suggestion."

He placed the last crate inside. Mary was placing fresh linens on the bed in their bedroom. Her smiling face and slightly disheveled hair warmed his heart.

"The quilt looks lovely."

He wiped his brow. "'Tis grand."

She pointed to the window. "I will make lighter curtains for the window to let more light in."

He took her hand. "Come with me. I want to show you the back." In the back of the cottage, he guided her to a garden plot. "We can plant herbs and vegetables and that over there is the henhouse. Thad said we would have no trouble getting a brood of chicks to raise."

Voices came from the front of the cottage. They retraced their steps. Boyd, Thad, and Amos greeted them.

"I'm so glad you came by. I want you to meet Mary." He made the introductions. "Come inside."

Once in the cottage, Boyd set a basket on the table. "I rode by a while ago, heading to town and saw the wagon. Didn't take much convincing to get these two fellows to join me in welcoming you both home."

Donald pulled a couple of chairs out for them to sit. "This saves me a trip to the shop to let you know of our arrival." He glanced at Mary. "We have not even gotten any fresh water from the well yet to offer you."

"Don't need a thing." Thad set his hat on the table. "Stopped at the tavern to get a few of Avery's wife's pasties for you since we figured you would be short on food."

Mary drew back the cloth covering and peeked in the basket. "How thoughtful of you."

Donald's stomach rumbled. "Lydia's pasties are wonderful. You will love these, Mary. 'Twas good of you to think of us."

Mary sat on the settee. "They smell wonderful, and offering your home, Thad, for our use is incredibly generous."

"Seemed only right," Thad answered. "There are staples on the shelves, but you will need to get to the mercantile for more supplies."

"Ma wanted me to extend an invitation to dinner when you got home," Boyd said. "Does tomorrow at two work? Thad and Amos can part with you for a couple of hours, right? Especially if they are also invited."

"Of course." Thad's eyes lit up. "No passing up one of Fiona's meals."

Mary smiled. "Please thank your mother. We appreciate the invitation. I'm eager to meet your family."

Thad and Amos rose. "You two need to get settled."

Donald took Mary's hand as they walked the men to the door. "Our thanks, again. I will be in the shop early tomorrow."

He put his arm around Mary as they stood in the open doorway, watching their friends depart. "Thad can be gruff, but he is a caring person, and Amos is a kind and generous man."

"They seem very nice, and 'tis obvious they are fond of you."

"You will enjoy Boyd and his family. Fine people, and they will love you. Jenny is probably about your age. You will likely find much you have in common, and you can ask Mrs. Alexander about your seamstress plans."

"I was thinking just that." She tugged at his sleeve. "I can help you unload the wagon."

Pride filled him at her eagerness to work by his side. "Not needed, my love. You can start on the unpacking. You will have a far better idea of where everything should go that I."

He couldn't resist the playful tap on her bottom as he left her in the doorway. Her answering gasp had him grinning into the night.

CHAPTER 42

Mary rolled out the dough for pasties. They'd never had such a thing at the Green, but she liked them and so did Donald, so she would learn to make them if it was the last thing she did. This was her third attempt, and they never seemed as light as the tavern keeper's wife's. After the last failure, she had approached Lydia to ask if she could observe her making them. Lydia had been flattered and graciously invited her to come to the tavern and watch yesterday morning. She had been in Lexington a week and had more disappointments than successes in the kitchen. Today would be different.

The root vegetables and meat were diced and ready. The dough had chilled in the root cellar. She used a bowl to shape the pastry rounds needed. The bake oven at the hearth had heated. Scooping the mixture on to half of the circle, she folded the other half over, crimped the edges, and brushed the top with egg before placing the pan into the oven. "Don't fail me!"

"Why do you think I might fail you?" Donald asked from the doorway with a quizzical expression on his face.

"Not you … the pasties."

He put his arms around her. "I'm sure they will be fine. But then I'm not one to throw stones at anyone preparing a meal. Besides, I did not marry you for your cooking skills."

"Obviously." She cocked her head. "Well, why did you marry me?" She put her fingers through his rusty-colored hair before kissing his freckled cheek.

"You are baiting the hook, woman." His smile always made her concerns seem a trifle. "You have other skills that serve us quite well. Let me see, I wed you because—you are kind, beautiful, smart, amusing, and—because you understand me, and yet still love me."

"Is that all?" She poked him in his chest.

"'Tis a start." He washed his hands and sat at the table. "Did you nap after I left this morning? I regret waking you again last night."

Her heart ached for his nightly struggles. "I managed to sleep a bit more."

He cocked his head as he studied her.

"Quite a bit more." She took the chair beside him. "Please don't fret about disturbing me when you have bad dreams. I woke you when I suffered one the other night. I truly believe, with God's help, both of us will recover in time. Please promise me you won't withdraw from me. That you will be honest with me when you are troubled. I know too well the temptation to hide and keep everything inside. We need to be open, patient, and forbearing with one another."

His fingers wrapped through hers. "I promise. There is much to be thankful for. We've survived perils many others have not." He kissed her fingers. "We have loving families and friends."

She rose, sat on his lap, and placed an arm around his shoulders. "We have good health, you have work you enjoy, and we have a place to live."

"We have love." He stroked her cheek and pointed to the embroidered sampler hanging on the wall. *"Beareth all things, believeth all things, hopeth all things, endureth all things."* He kissed her forehead and then her lips. "And we have each other."